WARRIORS of DRAGONSROD

BY
ROBERT UMBER

PUBLISHED BY
ROBERT UMBER

Dragonsrod Chronicles: Book One, Warriors of Dragonsrod:
Paperback Second Edition

WARRIORS of DRAGONSROD

Written by Robert Umber

Paperback Edition 2013

Copyright 2013 Robert Umber

All rights reserved. No part of this book may be reprinted in any manner whatsoever without prior written permission from the author/publisher.

All characters, events and locations depicted in this book are from the imagination of the author. Any resemblance to characters, names, locations, events and/or other creations have no relation to any other individuals and places, either known, or unknown to the author and is purely coincidental.

ISBN 9781482798678

Contents

ONE
Goldeye

TWO
The Dragonsrod Council

THREE
Handoe and Sandstorm

FOUR
Maxum

FIVE
The Seer and the Egg

SIX
Zare

SEVEN
The Lucky Gambler Inn

EIGHT
Into the Shadows

NINE
Burying the Hatchet

TEN
Cranch Hollow

ELEVEN
Moira

TWELVE
The Clouds of War Approach

THIRTEEN
Prophecies of the Mystics

FOURTEEN
A Change in Plan

FIFTEEN
The Resistance Fighter

SIXTEEN
A House Divided

SEVENTEEN
Where To Now?

EIGHTEEN
From Bad To Worse

NINETEEN
Elmshir

TWENTY
The Things That Aren't As They Seem

TWENTY-ONE
The Travels of General Zmoge

TWENTY-TWO
Goldeye The Suspicious

TWENTY-THREE
Handoe's Crest

TWENTY-FOUR
The Night Escape

TWENTY-FIVE
Betrayal

TWENTY-SIX
Handoe's Trial

TWENTY-SEVEN
The Abyssins

TWENTY-EIGHT
Goldeye's Proof

TWENTY-NINE
The Hatching

THIRTY
Duel At Dusk

THIRTY-ONE
Myters

THIRTY-TWO
Dragonsrod Dissolved

THIRTY-THREE
The Vordral Attack

THIRTY-FOUR
Moira's Moment

THIRTY-FIVE
Battle At the Border

THIRTY-SIX
The Dash For Freedom
THIRTY-SEVEN
Aftermath

MAP OF DRAGONSROD

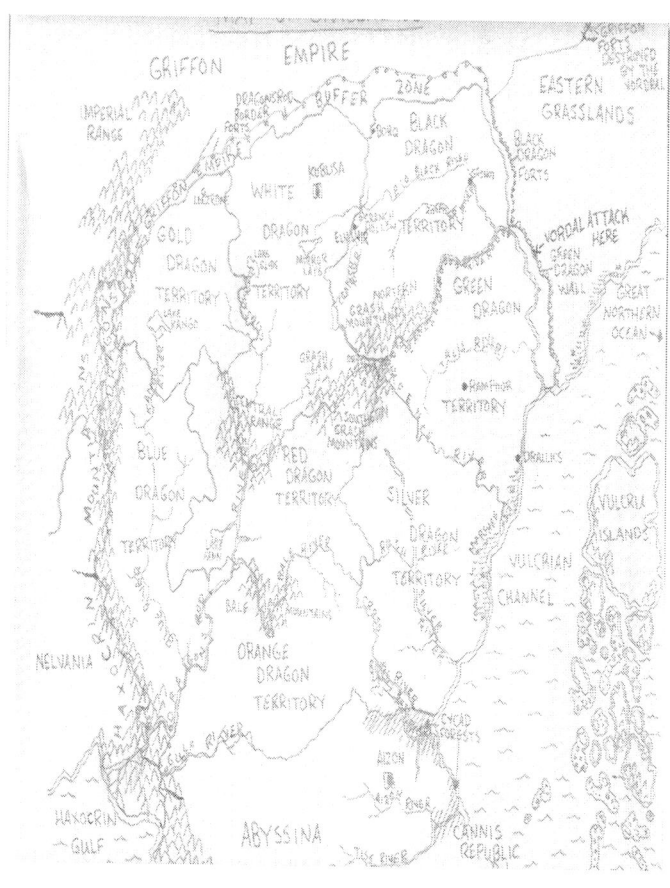

I dedicate this, my first published book, to:

My parents, thank you for your love and support.

My writing group, Ken, Mike, Lisa and my beautiful wife, Cathy. The reading and brainstorming sessions were a tremendous help.

The many other people over the years who have contributed in one way or another in the progress of my writing.

You, the reader, thank you for reading this book, I hope you enjoy it.

CHAPTER ONE
-GOLDEYE-

Grand Council-Leader's mansion; Kublisa, Dragonsrod.

Goldeye was an old dragon. He had seen the horrors of war and he had seen the beauties of peace in his many years. He was leader of his White Dragon Clan and also was the Grand Council-Leader of the Dragonsrod Republic. This was a country made up of eight provinces and "united" under one governing body, the Dragonsrod Grand Council. He had no shortage of things to worry about. Internally, the Red dragons and the Blue dragons, living in the central and western provinces in the country, were dealing with a bad drought. These two regions produced over one-third of the country's food supply. Crops had been lost and livestock were starving. They were looking to Kublisa (The capital city and the seat-of-government in Dragonsrod) for help. This issue had not been, and would not be ignored. In fact, it was top priority.

Then there were the issues between the Black dragons and the Green dragons, living in the provinces to the east and south of the dragon capital city. They have been at odds with each other over their border. The fertile Sandrega River Valley runs the entire length of their provincial boundary Black Dragon Territory to the North and Green Dragon Territory to the South with the river itself as the boundary. Neither recognized this and claimed all of the valley as theirs. They cannot even agree to work together on a defensive wall that was being built on their eastern borders with the wastelands. Since there was no threat from the East, he viewed this particular issue to be trivial.

I'll let them handle this one themselves, he thought.

He felt as though his mind were being picked and prodded and stretched and pulled in a thousand different directions. He was restless with a kind of nervous energy. He walked out from his darkened bedroom and onto a large, open balcony overlooking the colorful domes and spires of the capital city. These lit buildings, coupled with the cool, predawn air were a comfort to him. Like a tonic, it seemed to numb the effects of a constantly running brain. Tonight, however, it didn't appear to be working.

Griffons! There was an unwelcome burden he could easily do without. These powerful creatures have created a large empire by conquering most of the land to the North and west of Dragonsrod. They were a direct threat to the dragon territories. Worse still, Dragonsrod and the Griffon Empire were not on friendly terms. In fact, they had recently finished fighting a bloody war, which resulted in the creation of the Buffer-Zone, a hilly, scrub-land in the North that stretched to the nearly impassable, mountainous border to the West.

The old dragon cringed as he ran a four-clawed hand through a long, white beard that hung from his crocodile-like face. His mismatched eyes (the right emerald green and the left, a deep set gold, hence his name) narrowed as he gazed at the skyline of the city. He was an active participant in the war versus the griffons and had many memories, most of them bad. Time was slow to heal all wounds and he was no exception. That bloody, horrible conflict had been over for the last five years and the two sides have not spoken to each other since. Until now. The griffons were paying a visit, or at least an ambassador was.

"Seven years," Goldeye whispered. "It should never have lasted that long… *never!*"

"Can't sleep again?" came a gentle female voice from behind him.

Goldeye craned his scaly neck over his shoulder to see his wife, Moira, approach him, carrying a blanket in her clawed hands.

"Too much on my mind," he confided as she lovingly wrapped the blanket over his shoulders. "One of the many burdens of my job. Though I try, I just can't leave it at the office."

He was several years older than Moira and was about a head-and-shoulders taller. On average, male white dragons were bigger, physically, their snouts and ears were longer and their brows were heavier. Females had

Warriors of Dragonsrod

eyes, slender, more graceful bodies and longer hand claws. Both sexes had upright postures with long, muscular arms and legs and were counter-balanced by strong, efficient tails.

Moira placed her left arm around her husband and leaned into him.

"You need to get some sleep," she said.

He didn't reply. They stood in silence for a few moments and watched the skychanging from inky indigo to a lighter shades of blue against the brightly lit city skyline.

"How's our clutch?" he asked, casting her an affectionate gaze.

"It's fine," she returned. "The two guards are still at the nursery entrance and the nursemaids are still watching over the eggs."

"Hmm," he grunted.

This was his first clutch. Goldeye had been wed before, during the Griffon war. However, while he was on campaign in the then griffon-occupied Gold Dragon Territory,he learned that his wife had died from a respiratory disease called *Jymaxia*. The devastated White Clan leader vented his fury at the hated griffons. Many of them would fall under the sharp blade of his sword. After the war, Goldeye would focus on rebuilding the war-torn northern provinces of Dragonsrod, including his own White Dragon Territory. He had no time for anything else. That is until a couple of years ago, when his eyes fell on Moira for the first time. The attraction was instant and surprisingly (to him anyway) mutual. She was like a shot in the arm to him. She rejuvenated him, made him feel young again. He felt even younger still after finding out he was going to be a father.

They were a good match. Moira had a knack for reading his facial expressions. She was not a mind reader, but it seemed she could guess correctly what he was thinking.

"Only a week until the griffon ambassador arrives," she said.

"Hmph!" he grunted, his eyes glinted and narrowed. His body tensed and stiffened.

"Have you seen any griffons since the end of the war?" she asked.

He clenched his teeth and snarled. "No."

"The war is over," she said, her grayish-green eyes gazing deep into his mismatched ones. "It's time to move on. I think the griffons feel that way too."

"Maybe," he countered, the veins still bulging in his neck as he gripped the blanket a little tighter. "Time can't heal all wounds."

"They can heal the ones that matter, Golds," she replied calmly.

She called him Golds in an effort to calm him down. It always worked. Maybe it was her soothing voice, or the way she looked at him, or the way she touched him, only they seemed to know.

His facial muscles loosened and the twinkle returned to his eyes. "You're right. When the ambassador arrives, I'll be on my best behavior…"

Alarms boomed through the mansion like metal spoons banging against a cast-iron pan. Goldeye dropped the blanket and ran into the house toward the nursery.

A terrified look spread over Moira's face. "No, no, no," she muttered, clasping her hands over her mouth as she followed him.

Goldeye padded through the house and down a hallway leading to a metal door, which had been pried open. He briefly surveyed the bodies of the two guards, white dragons in full body armor, slumped on both sides of the doorway with crossbow bolts sticking out, just above the chest armor, piercing their necks. They were beyond help. He threw open the door, his eyes wide and his mouth agape at the horrifying scene that lay in front of him.

The two nursemaids, white dragon females in blue gowns and white pinafores, lay motionless on the floor. Behind them sat the nest with churned up blankets, one of the nursemaids' caps and crushed remnants of six eggs.

"NO!" he shrieked, with a horrified look on his face.

"Councilor," came a male voice from behind him. "What happened?"

Goldeye didn't answer. He pulled the coverings away from the destroyed nest. His eyes moved to the rear of the nest and saw one egg, coated in mucus and shell fragments... but intact otherwise.

"Sir?" the other dragon asked, peering over Goldeye's shoulder.

"Yes," Goldeye said, seeming to read what the other dragon was about to ask. "Yes, one survives, Gisko!"

"Blessed fortune, sir!" the dragon named Gisko responded, his green eyes fixed on the

Warriors of Dragonsrod

egg that Goldeye was covering up again.

The nursemaids gasped and moaned as they slowly got back up. Gisko turned to help them. Goldeye left the surviving egg where he had found it. He sat down in front of the devastated nest, folded his arms and glared out into space, deep in thought, his eyes narrowed. He forced his breathing into a slow and deliberate pace. The nursemaids straightened their uniforms and Gisko sent them to tend to Moira, whose wailing echoed through the house.

"What-what do you want me to do, sir?" Gisko asked with a shaky voice.

"Where are Handoe and Sandstorm?" Goldeye asked with an even tone to his voice.

"They've been in the northern Buffer Zone for the last seven weeks or so, sir."

Goldeye's brow furrowed. "What are they doing up there?"

"On assignment, sir," Gisko said, looking surprised at the stunned expression on Goldeye's face. "I thought you knew. Councilor Zare has them chasing a fugitive."

"Get them here," Goldeye ordered. "Contact them through the wires, carrier pigeon, smoke signals, I don't care! They are the best detectives in Dragonsrod and I want them here!"

"At once, sir."

Gisko quickly exited leaving Goldeye to himself once more.

How could this have happened? He knew he had enemies, but they were mostly political. He didn't think any of them would stoop to the level of doing something like this. Or would they? A rage was building inside him like a dying fire that had just been stoked. He had not felt this in quite some time. If anyone was to try and get to this last egg, they would have to go through him first.

CHAPTER TWO

-THE DRAGONSROD COUNCIL-

Dragonsrod Grand Council Building, Kublisa

The Dragonsrod Council Chamber had bore witness to countless debates over legislations, acts, resolutions, laws and bills and measures in its hundreds of years in existence. The building had been temporarily abandoned during the war with the griffons, as they drove on the city — the only time that has happened to date. Dragons, from every clan, have been named Grand Council-Leader in the country's long history. Some were strong and effective as leaders — some not so much. Some Grand Council Leaders served long tenures in office. Some only served one term and were gone.

Dragonsrod was a democratic country. Its ruling members were elected to a term of eight years. Each clan elected its own representatives and had no term limits. So many other creatures lived in this country that the laws had to be fair, unbiased and democratic. So democratic, in fact, that if a griffon wanted to live in Dragonsrod, it could not be discriminated against or harassed *period — end of story — that was the law!* Griffons did live in Dragonsrod. Their numbers were small and scattered and they kept mainly to themselves.

The presently empty council room was normally open to the public for touring. Banners representing the eight clans hung from the high ceiling over the amphitheater. A stone podium stood alone on the sandy floor in front of row after row of seats that stretched into a half circle and sloped up the further back it went. In a matter of minutes, this quiet room will explode with the echo of hundreds of voices from the clan leaders and their entourages as they fill the room to capacity. Those representing other animal species with larger populations attended the council meetings and of course, so did the press. When council was in session, however, it was closed to the general public.

The delegations splashed into the council chamber and took their places. The Green dragons sat down at the far right as they entered the chamber. Red dragons sat next to them. The White dragons and Gold dragons filled out the left half of the room. Across a row of concrete steps, the Blue dragons were stationed, followed by the Orange, Silver and Black dragons with the councilors sitting at the bottom step before the podium. The room was abuzz on the subject about the attack on Council-Leader Goldeye's family.

The atmosphere was tense and electric. Everyone was starving for news. The green dragon leader, Robsko stood up and approached the podium. He was second in rank next to Goldeye, who wasn't present, for understandable reasons. Robsko, was a muscular dragon with a short turtle-like head and face with a stunted crest standing up from of his nose. A small, inward curving horn sat on top of his head lined up perfectly over two short, triangular ears. (This description is average among green dragon males.) He reached down inside the lectern and picked up a stone gavel and pounded it once on the stand's top.

"This meeting will now come to order," he bellowed in a low, gravelly voice, his red, snake-like eyes coursed over the mammalian, reptilian and bird-like faces of the delegations looking back at him. "By now, all of you have heard that Council-Leader Goldeye's family was attacked last night. Regrettably, the attacker, or attackers, are still at large."

Whispers and hisses echoed through the hall.

"Silence!" Robsko ordered, pounding the gavel on the podium. "Since Council-Leader Goldeye cannot be with us today, his adjutant, Gisko, is filling in for him."

Gisko clearly looked nervous. Whatever color he had in his face seemed to have drained into his tunic as he approached the podium. He gave the appearance that he would rather be *anywhere* else but here.

Robsko turned to him. "Acting Councilor Gisko, the podium is now yours."

Every eye and ear in the chamber now bore down on the young white dragon.

"Good morning," Gisko said, clearing his throat before continuing. "I spoke to Council-Leader Goldeye before coming here… he wanted — in fact, he insisted — I tell you that one egg did survive the attack."

Many in the delegations broke into cheers and applause while others sat silent, their faces blank, not showing much emotion at all.

"Come to order!" Robsko called as the outburst slowly died away.

A large gold colored dragon with a short snout over a square jaw with horse-like ears, named Zhangi, stood up. His beady, black eyes settled on Gisko. "Why would he give out that information, knowing the attackers could come back and finish the job?"

"Unlikely!" barked the blue dragon leader, Jossic, standing and facing Zhangi. "It's a message to the attackers that their mission failed. In addition, security at his mansion is *drum-tight*, nobody gets in or out without us clearing it first."

"And where was this *drum-tight* security last night when it was needed the most?" came the raspy, high-pitched voice of the Black Dragon Leader, named Zare, now standing and facing

Jossic.

Blue and black dragons closely resembled the white dragons, physically. Both had alligator-like faces, straight postures, long arms and legs and sturdy tails. Physical features was about all they had in common. The two clans did not like each other that much due to some long standing animosities…

"Is the Black Council-Dragon suggesting that my security is not suited for the job?" Jossic asked, puffing up his chest and stepping on to the floor, his indigo eyes shooting daggers at Zare, who only flashed a crooked grin.

"In this case," Zare replied, also stepping on to the floor to stare down Jossic. "Yes!"

Robsko slammed the gavel so forcefully on the podium, the handle shattered, the head twirled end-over-end to the floor and hit with a soft thump.

Gisko shuffled away from the podium, his green eyes bulged and his mouth hung open.

"This behavior will not be tolerated," Robsko barked. "Any further outburst, like this, and security troops will be called in," his eyes fell hard onto Jossic and then Zare, "Councilors, take your seats!"

They did so. Robsko was not one to be trifled with. He did as he said he would — and has done so on incidents like this in the past. A stunned silence smothered the amphitheater.

"Acting Councilor Gisko still has the floor!" Robsko said, stepping away.

The visibly shaken white dragon stepped back to the podium. After another moment of silence, a sleek, gray clothed, silvery dragon with black, lifeless eyes, a head and upper body of a shark and the limbs and tail of a large lizard, stood and addressed Gisko.

"Who is on the trail of the attackers?" she asked in a cool, silky voice.

"Council-Leader Goldeye has chosen two... non-dragons."

Shouts and guffaws burst out from many representatives, both dragons and mammals, but died out as soon as Robsko moved toward the podium.

"This is preposterous!" Zare yowled, standing up again. "No disrespect intended toward our non-dragon colleagues, but this is a dragon affair. He should have hired dragons to do the job, especially one of this magnitude!"

Mutterings of agreement and disagreement

followed this remark.

"Well?" asked the silver dragon councilor, Deela. "Who did he select?"

Gisko's eyes locked with hers. "He has chosen Detectives Handoe and Sandstorm."

"What?" shouted Zare, launching out of his seat, looking as though he had just been asked to leave for no reason.

"A rabbit and a snow leopard?" muttered the red dragon councilor, Tabric, standing up and revealing his massiveness. "I must agree with Councilor Zare. Does Goldeye not trust his own kind?"

Jossic stood up.

"He has chosen wisely," he said, trading gazes with both Zare and Tabric.

Gisko looked sharply at Tabric, whose clan resembled the gold dragons with short, square-jawed faces, large, muscular bodies and horse-like ears. "He didn't do it out of spite or disrespect. He did it because he wanted the very best on the job!"

A tsunami of muffled whispers surfed across the chamber.

Gisko, no longer shaken, continued; "He wanted to prevent any kind of... contamination or favoritism —"

"He *doesn't* trust us!" the orange dragon, Sheema screeched.

Orange dragons were the smallest of the dragons and the most bird-like with round heads, beaked faces and piercing amber eyes and slender velociraptor-like bodies.

"Not true!" shouted the dragon and mammal representatives in the White dragon entourage.

Gisko waved them down trying to silence them before Robsko erupted again.

"Enough!" Robsko shouted. "We have other business to get to —"

"Just a minute," Sheema said, holding up two long and skinny, clawed fingers, her owl-like eyes set on Gisko. "Two final questions. Where is the egg? And, where are Detectives Handoe and Sandstorm?"

"The egg is safe," Gisko countered with a defensive tone in his voice. "And Detectives Handoe and Sandstorm are," he cast a glance at Councilor Zare, "on assignment."

CHAPTER THREE

-HANDOE AND SANDSTORM-

Buffer Zone

The Buffer Zone. A grassy, rolling hill plain that was hot and windswept in the summer and a muddy, impassible quagmire in the winter. This miserable eighty-five mile wide by seven-hundred mile long strip of desolation was the neutral-zone between the Griffon Empire and Dragonsrod.

This arid swath of land was ceded to the dragon republic after the war. Thousands, on both sides, died for this forsaken stretch that nobody seemed to want anything to do with.

The Buffer Zone was the real "Bad Lands." Nothing grew here except desperation.

Some roads connected dragon army forts with the few towns and settlements that were tough enough to survive here. This harsh land was, however, a haven for outlaws, gangs and any other ruffians that were on the run from the authorities, or just wanted to make themselves lost.

Handoe sat at a gaming table, in a grimy no-name cantina. His black fur gave him a shadowy appearance against the bar's dim and smoky lighting. He was playing a dice game called *Sixes and Tens* with a fat monitor lizard named Jinks. Handoe took a sip from his drink and set it back on the table.

"Your turn, Handoe," said the red dragon gamekeeper in low, scratchy voice, standing at one side of the table, between the two players. "Score's eighty-up!" he read from a small hand-held chalk board. "Handoe needs to roll a twenty to win the whole pot."

The rabbit casually picked up a small, clay jar that contained five, six sided dice and shook it before spilling the contents over the table.

"Nineteen!" called out the gamekeeper, etching the number with a white piece of chalk on Handoe's side of the board.

Jinks cracked a toothy smile and fixed his marble-like eyes on Handoe.

"Aw right, Jinxy," the gamekeeper croaked, turning his face to the monitor lizard and showing a long and ugly scar on the right side of his square jaw. "You need to roll a twenty to win."

Other beings in the cantina started to group around the table as the game drew closer to its climax. Handoe said nothing. His coal, black eyes met Jinks's gaze. The reptile's tongue flicked quicker, a sign he was getting excited, and his steely eyes glinted.

"Care to increase your bet?" he asked.

"What do you have in mind?" Handoe countered.

"How 'bout... your weapons?"

"Oh, is *that* all? What do I get if I win?"

Jinks flashed another smile.

"I'll give you mine?"

The onlookers exchanged mutters over the upgraded ante.

"Okay," Handoe said, unbuckling a belt that carried a sheathed, double-bladed sword and two razor sharp daggers. He, next, removed the straps across his torso that held a quiver of short arrows and a repeating, retractile crossbow. He dropped his "tools" on the table, with a loud thud, and knocked over a coin pot that splattered gold and silver change across it. "Your turn."

Jinks set down two long bladed knives, one of which looked as though it had seen better days, diseased with rust spots that formed on the blade and around the hilt. He then set down a small, hand-held crossbow and a few darts. The tension mounted as more patrons grouped around the table, looking eager to see what happened next.

Handoe's eyes coursed over the faces of the dragons, pig-like javilines, hyenas and several other beings that looked as though they expected, and hoped, blood to be spilt at any moment. He glanced above Jinks and saw the ash colored, black spotted face and gray-brown eyes of his friend and partner, Sandstorm, who was watching the activities going on around the bar.

"Well?" Handoe asked Jinks. "Are you gonna role the dice, or just sit there and slobber over my weaponry?"

A few onlookers laughed.

"You mean *my weaponry?*" Jinks countered, a very wide smile split across his face, highlighting a long, thin scar that ran over his nose and skidded to a halt under his left eye.

"Handoe leads, ninety-nine to eighty!" the gamekeeper called again. "First one to one hundred wins. Go over... you lose."

Every eye fell on Jinks as he picked up the jar and eagerly shook it. His tongue flicked faster and faster. He launched the dice on to the table expecting to walk away with his new weapons and a load of money to boot...

"Twenty-five!" bellowed the gamekeeper. "Jinxy went over — Handoe wins!"

Jinks' face dropped so fast, it looked as though it had bounced off the table and back on to his skull. He sat in a stunned silence, staring at his lost weapons and Handoe's like they were his best friends that suddenly wanted nothing more to do with him.

The crowd barked out its approval and seeing that no violence was about to happen, began to disperse. The gamekeeper slid the winnings to Handoe.

"Better luck next time, Jinks," Handoe said,

flashing a triumphant grin at the lizard.

"Mfleak!" Jinks cursed as he slammed a fist on the table then jumped to the floor and pushed patrons aside as he stomped to the door.

Handoe remained at the table. Sandstorm sat down across from him. They both inspected Handoe's newly acquired hardware.

"He didn't take very good care of his cutlery, did he?" Sandstorm asked, casting a scowl at the rust pocked knife.

Handoe picked up the little crossbow and studied it from end to end. "I underestimated Jinxy. This is a neat little toy."

The barkeeper, a white dragon with scruffy stubble around his jaws and a brown, leathery patch over his left eye, handed Sandstorm an ale and gave Handoe a drink that emitted a greenish swirling steam. He sat down where the gamekeeper had been only moments before.

"Oh, that Jinks," he chuckled. "He never seems to learn does he?"

Handoe grinned. "Someday he'll figure it out."

"That's what," Sandstorm said, grinning, "eighteen times now?"

The barkeep cast a concerned look to Handoe.

"Do you think he's waitin' for you outside?" His gaze shot to the door as he finished talking.

"Did you see that scar across his nose?" Handoe asked.

"Yeah?" the barkeep said.

"He tried to bushwhack me after our first encounter," Handoe said, taking a sip from his new drink. "*That* was the result."

The barkeep rested his elbows on the edge of the table and leaned forward. He looked around to see if anybody was eavesdropping. Handoe and Sandstorm traded glances and also leaned forward.

"I don't ask about anybody's business," the dragon began. "That could get one killed around these parts…"

Handoe and Sandstorm took swigs from their drinks and listened to the barkeep, seeming to know what was coming, as he spoke.

"… This place averaged one brawl every other night and usually, someone ended up dead. Since you two showed up, the place has been tame — almost like a church!"

Sandstorm flashed a fanged smile. "Grosh, you're not offering us another job are you?"

The barkeep straightened up and fixed his

eye on Sandstorm.

"Did I ask you this already?" he asked, his brow fell.

"This is the third time in the last five days," Handoe chuckled.

"That's funny," Grosh said, lifting his hand to scratch around his right ear. "I don't recall asking before. How did you know what I was about to ask?"

"It was your approach," Sandstorm said before drinking again from his mug.

"It's a good approach," Handoe added, grinning. "The drinks, a little idle chit-chat before getting to business…"

The corners of Grosh's mouth lifted into a hopeful grin. "Do you want security jobs here?"

Handoe gulped down the rest of his steamy drink and set the cup on the table. "I told you we need to think about it."

"Besides," Sandstorm added, "we need to finish the business that we're currently on."

Handoe nodded in agreement.

Grosh's grin sunk into a frown.

"Let us finish what we're doing and then we'll get back to you." Handoe said.

"Yeah, sure," Grosh sighed, sounding

disappointed. "Sounds fair enough."

Sandstorm fixed a serious gaze at Grosh. "While Handoe was playing *Sixes and Tens*, I saw three white dragons, who looked completely out of place here, walk toward your office. Know who they are?"

Grosh nodded before sinking a little further in his chair. "That's the other reason why I wanted to talk to you."

"Do they want us?" asked Handoe, looking as though he already knew the answer.

"Yep," Grosh grimaced, pointing behind the bar toward his office. "Probably shouldn't keep them waiting."

"Shall we?" Handoe asked Sandstorm as they both stood up.

"Thanks, Grosh," Sandstorm said patting the dejected barkeep on the shoulder as they walked toward the office.

CHAPTER FOUR

-MAXUM-

Eastern Buffer Zone

Handoe and Sandstorm were the best at what they did. In close quarters combat, it was a toss of a coin as to who was better. They possessed exceptional intelligence and could put two-and-two together faster than most. They could use most weapons with relative ease, and have, on numerous occasions over the years. Handoe and Sandstorm were so good they were dangerous. The criminal element feared this duo above all others.

They never underestimated their quarry. They knew all too well a fugitive can, and will, become so desperate to escape that he, she, or it, would resort to any measure to do so no matter how hair-brained the attempt was. It didn't really matter. Once Handoe and Sandstorm had you in their sites, capture or death usually followed within a few days.

As always, exceptions to the rule arose. One exception had evaded capture for the last seven weeks. Handoe and Sandstorm were no closer to catching him now than they were seven weeks ago. Maxum was his name, he was a puma. He knew the Buffer Zone badlands like the backs of his pawed hands.

Maxum didn't know Handoe or Sandstorm personally, but he had heard of them and of their incredible reputations. Maxum was aging. His younger years were dark and full of violence. He was not an evil or bad creature, worn around the edges and tired, maybe. A victim of bad luck and being in the wrong places at the wrong times, definitely! Maxum was a veteran of the last war. He lost everything — his wife and children, his home — all of it. He served as a scout in the Dragonsrod Army during the campaign in the Buffer Zone when he heard the news of the destruction of the things that kept him going.

Details were sketchy. Some said the griffons laid siege to Leezrone (his hometown in northeastern Gold Dragon Territory) after routing a dragon army and trapping the remnants of it there along with many civilians. Others said Dragonsrod forces were responsible for the town's destruction in a tragic case of friendly fire. Still other stories arose about a band of goblin raiders, who looted the town and burned it to the ground and killed the inhabitants before leaving. No matter who was responsible, Leezrone was gone. Maxum vented his anger at the griffons and all who sided with them. He knew how to use most kinds of weapons and had some pretty good hand-to-hand fighting skills. He also knew how to use the brain in his head and this is what made him a good match for his pursuers.

When the war ended, the tired puma was discharged from the army with honors. He spent some time wandering around Dragonsrod trying to settle down and live out the rest of his life in peace. Nothing worked. His services weren't needed. In some places, he was treated like an outcast and forced to leave. The angry warrior eventually drifted into the Buffer Zone and here, it seemed, he had found a home. In this forsaken land no one cared who you were or why you were here.

He still had not found the peace he longed for. He ran afoul of a gang of goblins and some rough looking javilines, who figured this solitary cat would be easy prey. Several gang-members fell on Maxum like vultures at a kill. When the dust settled, all the attackers lay dead or dying. Maxum did not escape injury, however, he had received a few good blows and left the scene battered, bloodied and exhausted. He went into hiding in some caves a few miles north of the White Dragon border to nurse his wounds. If Death were to come for him, so-be-it. He wouldn't fight it, in fact, he may even welcome it, an easy end for a hard life. Death did not come for him, and over time, his physical injuries healed.

The fight with the gang was not the event that landed him in hot water with the authorities. Violence happened all the time out here, it was literally kill or be killed. The trouble came a few months later. Maxum entered into a cantina near a black dragon fort to barter some old...

weapons and trinkets, he had found, for a hot meal. He sat alone, eating at a table, when four black dragon soldiers walked through the cantina doors. At first, they didn't bother the old cat and let him eat. However, after a few tankards of strong ale had been downed, the soldiers dander went up, and they wanted to cause trouble.

It wasn't long in coming, since Maxum was the only other one in the cantina. The senior ranking soldier, wearing two red stripes on his shoulder armor plates (indicating the rank of captain) approached Maxum. This had trouble written all over it. The bear barkeep seemed to sense it and tried to put a stop to it, only to be bullied and brow-beat into submission by the other three seriously intoxicated dragons.

The captain's name was Villic and he talked to Maxum in the same way an abusive master would speak to a servant. He ridiculed the puma and even flipped the remnants of his meal to the floor. Maxum only sat back in his chair and cast his dark, brown eyes up at the pickled dragon. Villic's verbal assault continued with little to no reaction from Maxum, while the other dragons laughed and drank and egged him on.

Then it happened. Villic, enraged by his victim's seeming lack of concern over these verbal attacks, drew his sword and cleaved it through Maxum's table. Maxum struck with lightning speed. He sprung from his chair and slashed his claws in to Villic's neck and head. Villic fell, face first, over the table debris, ruby red blood spurting from his wounds, and hit the floor with a loud, sickly thump — dead. Maxum had vanished before the stunned counter parts of the recently departed Villic really knew what happened.

Rumors and tall tales spread like wild fire about how four peaceful black dragon officers were viciously attacked by a malcontent drifter, who had it out for dragons. Villic was made out to be a hero in his native Black Dragon Territory and was laid to rest like one. Maxum had a large bounty put on his head by the Black Dragon Clan leader, Zare. Maxum had no way of knowing that Villic was Zare's little brother.

The stories of this seemingly unprovoked assault on a member of the black dragon military wing were told to Handoe and Sandstorm. They were told to be on their guard and to show no mercy when they caught up to this deranged assassin, now running amok in the Buffer Zone.

Skeleton Valley, the Buffer Zone

Maxum entered into a rocky valley looking for a suitable place to camp for the night. Something seemed different about this place. To the naked eye, this valley looked dangerous and forbidding. Tall pillar-like rocks jutted up from eroding hills with caves and crevices dotting the craggy slopes, giving this place a look like it was a very strange castle in which its creator spent too much time on towers and little else. With all the nooks and crannies in this canyon anyone on-the-run could hide out in here for years.

That uneasy feeling did not leave Maxum, in fact, it grew stronger by the moment. His ears were fixed to each and every sound. His whiskers flinched as the cool evening breeze blew through them. His tail flicked and swished in a way to suggest that he was on full alert. But from what? Were Handoe and Sandstorm in this valley closing in on him? Was he about to run into another band of marauders?

Maxum glanced down at his sword hanging from a belt around his waist and at two daggers sheathed on another belt strapped over his right shoulder and around his torso. If somebody, or something was waiting to jump him, they would soon realize the error of that decision...

Nothing happened.

Maxum was glad of it. He was tired of fighting, he was tired of killing. He just wanted to find a place to call home and disappear — to live out his final years in peace.

Darkness hung over the land like a thick blanket. Maxum's pupils were large and black and sucked in every ounce of light that a Dragonsrod settlement, three miles to the South, could give him. He found a small cave entrance and squeezed in to it. It seemed even darker in here than it was outside. Maxum's ears were pricked forward, his tail twitched in a stiff, nervous way. He heard something from somewhere up ahead.

"Great," he grunted. "I'm not alone in here."

Everything in him was telling him to stay where he was, or better yet, get away while he still could. No. He may be older and tired, but he was still very inquisitive. He cautiously moved forward.

The rock in this narrow tube-like tunnel was mostly smooth and cool to the touch.

Warriors of Dragonsrod

Maxum had no idea how far he had gone. The sounds he heard earlier were getting louder and a little more distinguishable.

"Somebody's chanting," he whispered. A flash of blue light briefly lit up the cave as it engulfed him and then faded away. "What the?"

He was hooked like a fish. He had to find out what was going on. The language of the chants sounded familiar. It was — *Griffonic*. Great, the griffons in here? This could be a blood-bath! He scowled as his fur bristled — another bright flash of blue light, much stronger than the last one, swamped him. Maxum's senses were getting confused, that last blast of light had done something to him. He stumbled out of one tunnel and into another. This tube was higher and wider, thus allowing him to stand fully erect. This cave may have more room, but it was every bit as dark as the last one was.

Maxum's eyes narrowed, he pulled his daggers from his baldric — he heard what sounded like *"DOP!"* Another blinding, blue flash of light punched through him. He sunk to his knees and dropped his daggers. He was in real trouble now and was starting to panic. He had never felt anything like this before.

"Dop, sceooze, floy!" he heard a voice bellow.

Maxum fell to the ground, unconscious, as a final wave of bright blue light blasted over, around, and through him.

CHAPTER FIVE

-THE SEER AND THE EGG-

"Up! Come on, get up! Rise and shine!"

"Huh?" Maxum groaned, groggy and blinking his eyes.

"Let's go, sleepy-head. Up and at 'em!"

Maxum slowly stood on his hind feet. His bleary eyes quickly came into focus and fell on to a griffon, casually reclining against a large rock. A small fire crackled and danced under two pieces of meat sizzling on a spit.

Maxum craned his neck up at the pale, blue sky. "How did I get out here?"

"Does it really matter?" the griffon asked.

"No," Maxum replied, watching the griffon

lazily draw shapes in the dirt with his formidable looking talons. "I guess not."

An awkward silence followed. Maxum slid a sideways glance to his weapons, holstered in the belts, laying a few feet away at the mouth of a large cave.

"You are not a prisoner," the griffon said in a casual voice, seeming to read Maxum's thoughts. "You are free to leave if you wish."

Maxum picked up his belts and slid them back on. The griffon's eagle-like eyes followed him as he moved around, stretching and flexing his body. "Feeling different today?"

Maxum stopped in mid-stretch, his eyes darted back to the griffon.

"As a matter of fact," he said, "I do. I haven't slept that soundly in years... I feel ten years younger!"

"That's because you *are,*" the griffon replied, the corners of his beaked mouth lifted into a grin.

A blended expression of shock, fear and confusion crossed the puma's face.

"What?" Maxum asked, staring incredulously at the griffon. "Are you a *Seer?*"

The grin on the griffon's face evolved into a

Warriors of Dragonsrod

full smile. "That's the universal translation for it, yes. My people would call me a *Gam-ka.*"

Maxum's face sunk into a frown. He was not stupid. No one would bestow on somebody this powerful of a gift for free. There was a catch — some kind of a favor to be owed — there had to be. Maxum's eyes narrowed as they met head-on with the griffon's gaze.

"Why?" Maxum growled, his brow sinking closer toward his nose. "What's the catch?"

"There's no catch," the griffon chuckled, seeing that the puma was starting to figure things out. "As I said, you're not a prisoner. You are free to leave anytime you wish."

Maxum wasn't buying it. His eyes glinted as they narrowed to slits and shooting the griffon a skeptical glare.

"So," he began, "you just did this out of the kindness of your heart. You just wiped ten years off from my life and expect nothing in return... I can go and relive these years... and you want nothing from me?"

The griffon cackled loudly at this. "Not quite."

He stopped laughing and spoke again, "I mainly wanted to see if I could still do the spell."

"And…?"

"It succeeded!" the griffon exclaimed.

"How?" asked Maxum, now more confused than ever about what he was hearing.

"It succeeded because you woke up," the griffon said with an 'isn't it obvious' tone to his voice.

Maxum sat down across from the griffon, who was checking on the progress of their breakfast. The puma was starting to feel like some kind of science project that had just come to a successful conclusion.

"I still don't understand," Maxum said.

The griffon Seer flashed another grin. "Powerful griffon magic. Emperors had this particular spell performed on them—"

"Being made ten years younger?" Maxum interrupted, an angry glint in his eyes. "Did it work?"

"At first, yes. Elderly emperors found out about this bit of magic and ordered Seersto perform it on them. Story goes, the last two emperors who had it done to them, didn't survive. They were *horribly* disfigured," the griffon chuckled, "Of course, the Seers were put to death for murdering the emperors! So the spell was banned. Seers were ordered, under penalty of death, never to perform it again."

"Thank you for that look into griffon history," Maxum growled, becoming impatient with the griffon's apparent stalling. "That still doesn't explain why you did it to me!"

The griffon sighed.

"Meat's done," he said, seemingly more to himself than to Maxum.

His eyes shifted to the scowling puma. "Hand me a dagger," the griffon extended a taloned hand to Maxum, "You eat and I'll explain what's going on."

"It's about time!" Maxum snarled, handing the griffon a dagger.

Maxum cleaned his dagger and sheathed it. He fixed a cold gaze on the griffon, who still hadn't told him what was going on. Instead, he just chewed on his meat.

"You said you would tell me what's going on," Maxum growled, "All you've done, so far, is to noisily chew on your food and burp a couple of times!"

"It's important not to be rushed while you eat," the griffon said, casually tossing away a bone and let out a deep and loud burp before fixing his amber eyes on Maxum. "Are you familiar with Council-Leader Goldeye?"

"We don't know each other personally."

"Well, he's heard of you."

"I'm sure he has," Maxum chortled. "I killed one of his officers!"

"It was self defense, was it not?"

Maxum stopped laughing and stared hard at the griffon. "Yeah, it was self defense."

"Why did you not just turn yourself in and plead your case?"

Maxum again burst out laughing, while the griffon sported a small, crooked grin.

"It was a black dragon I killed! Councilor Zare is brutal toward prisoners. I wasn't going to subject myself to any torture, especially at *his* hands!"

The griffon said nothing in response. He cast a thoughtful gaze at Maxum before speaking; "You know Handoe and Sandstorm?"

"I know *of* them," Maxum said sharply, "I know they've been chasing me all over this forsaken wasteland for the last two months," his eyes narrowed to slits again, "You have a hard time getting to the point. I'm tired of this dancing around. Tell me what's going on!"

The griffon chuckled again, but it seemed forced.

"You three have been selected by Council-Leader Goldeye for a very special mission."

"What?" Maxum said, his eyes widened and his mouth agape. "What kind of mission…?"

Grand Council-Leader Goldeye's office, Kublisa.

"…*What?*" gasped Handoe and Sandstorm in unison, their fur bristled.

The two detectives stood in front of Goldeye's desk. The old dragon sat behind it, looking back at them with a placid expression.

"Sir," Handoe began. "Do you know how long we've been chasing after him?"

"Seven weeks, four days, if I'm correct," Goldeye responded, he was expecting this.

"Sir," Sandstorm said. "It's going to be difficult to show this-this… fugitive any kind of trust or camaraderie. It would seem as though we just wasted these last few weeks."

Goldeye's eyes landed on Sandstorm, not with a harsh glare, but with a thoughtful considerate look. Sandstorm and Handoe were equal in rank so both could speak without being out-of-turn.

"I understand your concerns, gentle-beings," Goldeye said calmly. "That's something the three of you will have to work out. And you'll have plenty of time to do it."

Goldeye looked past the jack-rabbit and snow leopard to the doorway where a large, broad bodied, white dragon stood guard just outside it.

"Bard?" he called politely.

The dragon, named Bard, poked his massive head through the doorway.

"Could you close the door please?"

"Of course, sir," Bard said in a voice so low and guttural it sounded like a croak.

The door closed. Goldeye sunk into his chair. The gleam left his eyes and a look of worry and exhaustion spread over his age-lined face. Sandstorm and Handoe pricked their ears back to the door. Goldeye picked up on this and cast them a slight grin.

"Don't worry," he said, "Bard is loyal. He's no eavesdropper. You couldn't ask for a better dragon to have on your side."

Handoe and Sandstorm rotated their ears forward again. Goldeye rested his elbows on his desktop, he threw the detectives a look of the utmost seriousness. Handoe and Sandstorm stepped closer to the desk.

"Dragonsrod is in desperate trouble," Goldeye whispered.

Handoe's brow furrowed, "What kind of trouble, sir?" he asked just above a whisper.

"The worst possible kind, detective," Goldeye said. "I'm vulnerable. The destruction of my brood proved that. Dissension and mistrust are rampant in the council. No one outside the chambers can see it!" A dark expression flashed over Goldeye's face. "But, it grows worse by the *day!* Oh, it's normal for the councilors to have heated discussions," Goldeye sadly shook his head. "But *not* with the tensions that have been brewing in the council lately," Handoe and Sandstorm exchanged sideways glances. "I fear we could be headed for some kind of division... maybe even... civil war."

"Civil war?" gasped Sandstorm, cocking up his eyebrows.

"Why do you say that, sir?" Handoe asked, his brow still low over his eyes.

Goldeye leaned back in his chair and reached into his tunic and pulled out a key. He unlocked a drawer and lifted out a small, metal box with a long, rectangular hatch on the front of it. He set it on the desktop.

"Know what this is?" he asked, studying the quizzical looks on the detectives' faces.

"An incubator," Sandstorm said, his eyes and ears fixed on the metal box.

"Correct," Goldeye replied. "In it, contains my soul surviving chick. This thing has an Amorian fire crystal as its heat source to keep the egg warm. It will buzz when the egg is about to hatch. Other than that, I don't really know how it works."

The old dragon paused for a moment and drew in a deep breath and let it out slowly. "It may be the only chance we have to avoid civil war."

"Again, sir," Sandstorm asked, "why do you say that?"

"You know the laws of this country," Goldeye said, this was not a question.

Handoe and Sandstorm nodded.

"My heir is in here," Goldeye revealed, gently patting the incubator. "If I die, or am removed from office, and have no family to take my place for the rest of my term, the second in charge — in this case, Robsko — takes over for the final years or months of my term. The white dragons will lose the lead spot in the council."

"What about your wife, sir?" Handoe asked. "Wouldn't she take your place?"

Goldeye's mismatched eyes fixed on the rabbit. "She's in too much danger here. Whoever the attackers were won't stop at just our egg clutch. I'm afraid they are going to target her next. I can't have that — I *won't* allow it!"

"But if Councilor Robsko is left in charge," Sandstorm asked, "Who would be his number two?"

Goldeye's slid a dark gaze to the snow leopard. *"That's* the problem. Councilor Zare would be second in line."

"Okay?" Handoe asked, first glancing at Sandstorm, than to Goldeye. "Why is that a problem?"

Goldeye's brow sunk as he shot a hard look at Handoe. "Haven't you been reading the news prints, Detective? They don't like each other! A power struggle would almost certainly ensue. I have all the faith in the world in Councilor Robsko, but I don't think many others in the council do. Zare is too manipulative. He would have the other councilors at one another's throats in no time if he could benefit from it."

"Where are we supposed to take the egg, sir?" Handoe asked.

"I've made arrangements for both my wife and the egg to be safely removed from this country to the city of Gane, in the Cannis Republic."

"Are we taking them together?" asked Sandstorm.

"No," Goldeye said. "Just the egg."

A short pause followed.

"As long as Moira and our child survive, the White Dragon Clan will remain in power for the next few years and will keep this country together. They are in too much danger right now and can't stay here because my enemies *will* find them, eventually, and destroy them. You will take the egg and depart with it as soon as we are done here."

"Yes, sir," Handoe and Sandstorm said together.

"Another question, sir," Sandstorm spoke. "About the crystal, how long will it last in the incubator?"

"I was told it lasts about thirty days before it needs to be re energized," Goldeye said.

"How do you re energize it?" Handoe asked, his eyes sunk to the device on the desk.

"You pull it out from the bottom and either set it in the sun for a bit or place it in a fire, it'll glow bright red when it's ready. Don't get it wet! Water will destroy it," Goldeye flashed another smile, "Don't worry too much about it, you should be in Gane before any recharging will need to be done."

Goldeye reached into another drawer and pulled out a piece of paper and a pencil and scribbled on it — folded it — and handed it to Handoe.

"What is this, sir?" Handoe asked.

"It's for your new partner," Goldeye said, leaning back in his chair.

Handoe opened his mouth to speak, but Sandstorm spoke first; "One last question, sir. Why not just leave the egg with your own clan? Wouldn't it be safer with your white dragons instead of being trekked across the continent?"

Goldeye studied Sandstorm for a moment as if trying to be careful with what he was about to say. He drew in another deep, sad sigh.

"Alas, no," his face drooping into a regretful expression. "I can't trust *any* dragons. They can be too easily manipulated to do the bidding of others. Especially if the price is right. If I handed the egg to any of my friends, other clan leaders would bark about favoritism. You two have solid reputations for getting things done. Maxum will probably be happy to have the fugitive label removed from him. He has no loyalties and seems to be good-of-heart. The three of you are perfect for this."

"Okay," Handoe said, glancing at Sandstorm before shifting his attention to Goldeye. "Where do we find Maxum?"

Goldeye smiled and leaned further back in his chair. His face lifted with a relieved look on it. "Go to the city of Borq, in Black Dragon Territory, to the *Lucky Gambler Inn*. My contact there owes me some favors. He knows you'll be coming and is expecting you in the next few days," Goldeye reached into his desk again and pulled out a gray, leather pouch and put the incubator in it and pushed it to the detectives. "Guard the egg well, Detectives, I fear more than just my future is at stake here. Our very existence could be at stake."

CHAPTER SIX

-ZARE-

Council Dragon Zare lay sprawled across his king-sized bed. He rested his left hand on his chest and held a lit, long, green cigar close to his lips, with his right hand. The tiny red-orange glow from his cigar shined against the pitch-black bedroom like a beacon. He loved the darkness, it was like his mistress. He was all too willing to let her wrap her arms around and envelope him. He learned, long ago, not to fear the night. Dragons have good night vision. Nothing hid in the dark that he could not see in the day. He owed much of his success to this natural gift. During the war, he used it to launch many night attacks on the invading griffon legions with devastating results. Yes, the night was good, darkness was a powerful partner.

Zare drew in a deep inhale from his cigar and slowly exhaled a long and puffy, cloud of smoke that had a thick, peppery-sweet smell to it. He was in a pretty good mood. His old rival, Goldeye had been knocked for a loop by the attack on his nursery. Now, he was running scared, falling back to protect what he still had. Pity. Well, not really, considering that the old white dragon had been a very irritating thorn in his side since they first met, during the war.

Goldeye was the over-all commanding officer during the bitterly fought Buffer Zone campaign. Zare's troops overran a valley defended by a rat-like race known as the zaltee, allied to the griffons. Many of the filthy rodents were captured. Zare was going to have them executed and be rid of. But no, that old *son-of-a-berk*, Goldeye, intervened and sent them to the rear as prisoners.

Goldeye kept those annoying, mismatched eyes very close on Zare after that. He even had the audacity to threaten him with dismissal if he ever did anything like that again. That episode was still a sore spot with him. Now the old dragon had been hit where it hurt the most and it suited Zare just fine. In fact, this is exactly what he wanted, it only added more sweetness to his satisfaction.

After the war, Zare returned home to a hero's welcome. He ran for, and easily won, the election for the vacant council-leader's position of the Black Dragon Clan. The war had devastated this territory in just about every way. The land was wrecked, cities destroyed, many black dragons had been killed or wounded. It was time to rebuild.

Zare made promises to rebuild this shattered land from the ground up — and did so. He promised his people a return to dignity and self-respect by a renewal of wealth and power — it happened. He, and he alone, did this for them. All he asked for in return was obedience. *Complete* obedience. Most complied. He had his people firmly under his clawed thumb. Some, however, became skeptical and gave warnings and said *'Beware of what Zare asks, it is total control!'* How dare they do this after all *he's* done for them! The insolence of it all! They'll pay for this. Zare's alligator-like face lifted into a crooked, sharp toothed smile. Pay for it they did.

The dissenters and troublemakers were hunted down by black dragon troops, police and mercenaries. Those caught were sent to prisons, executed or vanished "mysteriously." Few escaped. The ones that did went into hiding or fled to other territories. Zare's message was received loud and clear by his people, speak out and disagree... suffer the consequences.

Zare blew out another long cloud of sickly sweet smoke and crawled out of bed. His schedule was full today. First on the agenda, was a hearing he had to attend, a meeting with the green dragon leader, Robsko. That pompous windbag was up-in-arms over something and has assembled other councilors to hear his complaints. Probably that stupid wall issue again. Not much good was going to come from this one.

Dragonsrod Council Building; Securities Division Chamber.

Zare entered the Securities Division Chamber

in his usual heavy cloth, black jacket resplendent in rows of colorful medals, sashes and badges of honor. His gold epaulets and lacing glistened in the chamber's light. He looked every bit like someone of great importance and had expected to be treated that way.

    Councilor Robsko, on the other hand, gave the impression that he was some commoner, who had just come in from the street, dressed in a simple, everyday shirt and vest. He sat at one end of a long, stone table. His large, muscular hands clamped together and rested on the table's surface. He probably envisioned Zare's head being squished between them. He would never be given the satisfaction, not willingly anyway. Robsko's red, snake-like eyes followed Zare as he sat at the other end of the table. Since this was a security issue, Councilor Jossic, who was the security chief, presided, sitting in between the disputants. Great! An enemy presiding and an enemy bringing up charges. Who were the neutrals? Whenever one dragon clan leader had a compliant with another leader, three other clan leaders were to act as a "neutral" jury. In this case, it was the bird-like orange dragon, Sheema, the square-jawed, horse eared gold dragon, Zhangi and the shark-faced silver dragon, Deela. Jossic, his medals gleaming from his blue jacket, turned to Zare.

"Councilor Zare," he began in a formal tone of voice, "you have been summoned here to—"

Zare stood up, completely ignoring Jossic, leaned his hands on the table and returned Robsko's glare with one of his own. "What is it this time, *Councilor?*"

"What is it always — *Councilor?*" Robsko growled, clamping his hands even tighter together.

"Not that stupid wall again?" Zare yelled.

"Only the stupid wall that your kind haven't been working on for the last three months," Robsko shouted, shooting up out of his chair.

"Order!" Jossic yelled. "Councilors, you will retake your seats. This is a meeting hall, not a fighting arena!"

Zare plopped into his seat. Robsko slowly sat back down, his eyes coursed over Jossic and the stunned Neutrals Panel.

"I apologize to the judge and the panel," he said through clenched teeth.

Zare let out an angry grunt.

"Is it true, Councilor?" Deela asked, turning

to Zare. "Your people haven't been working on your portion of the wall in three months?"

"We've had delays," Zare hissed, flashing a contorted smile at Deela.

Robsko coughed out a contemptuous grunt. "Delays, I'm sure! Our section has been completed and stationed with a full compliment of troops!"

A relaxed look spilled over Zare's face as his eyes kept on Robsko.

"What of defensive fortifications?" he asked, more to the panel than to Robsko. "One earth-and-wood wall won't hold for long against a massive attack."

"My people are working on trenches, abates, and forts as we speak," Robsko countered, seeming to have anticipated this being brought up. His eyes narrowed, his nostrils flared as he pointed a clawed finger menacingly at Zare. "All your kind has been doing is to pile up a mound of earth, so small, that a chick on a tricycle could ride over it in two minutes."

Zare sat back for a moment, silent. He was ready for this one. "As I said, a wall will do no good against a massive attack. My people are working on defensive fortifications that will...

enable my troops to lay down a cover fire much more effective than — a *wall*."

Zare's alligator-like face lifted into a toothy, crooked smile as he watched Deela, Zhangi and Sheema lean into each other and converse quietly. That should shut the green windbag up.

"I was out there just last week," Robsko said slowly, his eyes flashed even harder. "I saw no such work being done."

He just won't quit!

Inside, Zare was boiling over. He wanted nothing more than to pull out a crossbow and turn Robsko into a pin cushion. That will have to wait — for a little while longer anyway.

"One more thing," Robsko said. "My scouts said they saw several dark colored, bipedal figures only about a mile from your border," his eyes glinted and narrowed, "they seemed to be taking a particular interest in the lack of work being done on your wall."

"What kind of creatures were they?" chirped Sheema, her owl-like eyes sliding to Robsko.

"Vordral."

Zare's face tightened. Sheema and Zhangi flinched.

"Vordral?" Jossic said, his indigo eyes widening. "Are you sure?"

The chamber echoed with a loud burst of laughter from Councilor Zare. The eyes of all the other councilors fell on him.

"The vordral haven't been seen in three-hundred years!" he cackled.

"That does not mean they are extinct," Zhangi said, keeping his shocked gaze on Zare.

"Does that make them a threat if you see a couple of them standing in a field?" asked the black dragon councilor.

"OF COURSE IT DOES!" shouted Robsko, slamming both fists on the table, causing it to shake.

"Enough!" Jossic ordered.

He looked at the three councilors on the Neutrals Panel. "Councilors — what say, you?"

The three again leaned into each other, whispering and hissing in deep conversation. Moments later, they cast their eyes to Zare who was casually leaning back in his chair, watching them, feigning interest in their decision, whatever it may be.

"Councilor Zare," began Zhangi. "May I remind you, that wall is of critical importance to our national safety. It needs to be completed. If your section is not finished during the time tables set, we, the Neutrals Panel, will send someone there to make sure that it gets done."

Zare smiled and gazed coldly at Zhangi. Everybody was expecting an outburst from the hot tempered black dragon. "The work has already begun. Are we done here?"

Robsko snorted.

"Dismissed!" Jossic said as everybody stood up, exiting the room from different doors.

The look on Zare's face did not show how furious he was. That humiliating affair did not have to happen. The officer, in charge of the wall project, was getting reckless, his officers, in general, were letting their guard down. A message of Zare's displeasure needed to be sent. An evil grin stretched across his face. He knew exactly who to send. He needed to send his most loyal *and* ruthless subordinate to take this message. One, who would stop at nothing to get the job done. Heads would probably fly for this failure in secrecy. General Zmoge would be the perfect tool to whip his troops back in to line.

CHAPTER SEVEN

-THE LUCKY GAMBLER INN-

Borq was an ancient city, located in the northwestern corner of Black Dragon Territory. White Dragon Territory lay six miles due West, and the Buffer Zone, only four miles north. Like most of the cities in northern Dragonsrod, it took a lot of damage during the war. Borq withstood two years of griffon occupation only to be leveled in battle when the Dragonsrod Alliance retook it early in the war's third year.

The citizens took great pride in the fact their city was nearly a thousand years old and one of the oldest in Dragonsrod. After the war, the surviving residents said they wanted it to be restored to the way it looked before the conflict. Zare said they could have anything they wanted, but with a few conditions. It was, for the most part, restored to its former glory.

Northern outskirts of Borq.

A lot was going through Maxum's mind. Just a few short hours ago, he was a fugitive, hiding out in the badlands and living like a nomad. Now, he could possibly become a hero. A hero to a country that shunned him after he sacrificed so much for it. A hero to a country he didn't particularly like anymore.

His reasons for taking this assignment were all his own. Glory and riches meant nothing to him. The only thing Maxum wanted was a place he could call home. Borq would *not* be that place.

He was in enemy territory. The bounty, Zare put out for his capture, was still active here. He knew quite well of the danger he was in. He knew the only chance he had was to rely on his scout experience — play it cool, blend in — be inconspicuous. That seemed easy enough in this town for beings of many shapes and sizes walked the narrow, cobblestone streets, wrapped up in their own affairs. Maxum certainly looked like a traveler, being dressed in an olive green traveling cloak and carrying a walking stick. He had no idea where that crazy griffon got this stuff. After giving it a little thought, he didn't really want to know.

Maxum took in some of the sights as he walked. Nearly all of the buildings were made from stone with wood roofing with the tallest structures only being four to five stories high. A peculiar feature about these buildings were none of them had glass in the windows. Curtains provided some privacy with wooden shutters flanking the rectangular shaped holes.

His eyes fell on some things that made him cringe. Cold, gray statues of Councilor Zare jutted up on many street corners in several different poses like ugly, gnarled trees. Some depicted him pointing forward with either a finger or a sword. Others showed him looking backward, while pointing ahead as though he were leading his people toward some unseen destination.

Maxum tore his eyes away from these grotesque and ridiculous statues to something even more chilling. On every building's ground level, between windows, and on every tree trunk were posters of Zare's ugly alligator-like face with his eyes fixed sternly ahead in an unblinking glare. *I'm watching,* is the message Maxum got from this. His eyes narrowed and he let out a derisive grunt at this narcissistic display of totalitarianism.

For as busy as these streets were with foot traffic, it was strangely quiet. Tension hung in the air as thick as the sweet smells of the blossoming trees that lined the sidewalks of this ancient town. Maxum slid his eyes to the sidewalks, in front of the buildings, to see the source of the unease. Standing here-and-there in small groups of twos and threes, were dog-like creatures called Cannidene. Maxum had a special dislike for these beings. Everything about them he despised. Everything from their short, orange and black fur to their beady, coal black eyes that scanned all passers-by with suspicion. He dodged cannidene guards at the boarder last night to get here. He knew their eyesight wasn't the greatest. Their hearing was pretty good, so he had to be very quiet while sneaking by checkpoints. It was those black, bulbous noses that concerned him most.

Warriors of Dragonsrod

Cannidene had a sense of smell that was second to none. So keen, in fact, it was believed they could even smell fear.

What made Maxum dislike them the most was their reputation. Cannidene were good fighters and incredible trackers, but they had a history of selling themselves to the highest bidder. The cannidene were so untrustworthy and seemingly treacherous that even their fellow Cannis Republic citizens, the junglewolves and the hyenids didn't even like them.

This lot seemed satisfied. They all wore black shirts with chrome colored badges on the right side and shinny black helmets on their heads. Zare has granted them authority. With authority comes power, with power comes wealth. How could any self respecting mercenary pass up on that?

Maxum tightened his grip on his walking stick, his claws slightly digging into it. He wanted to take this stick and crush those pretty helmets into their skulls. One of them shot a sharp gaze at him as he walked by. Could they smell aggression too? Better not to find out. He relaxed his grip on the stick and moved on. The cannidene's beady eyes darted off at something else.

"There it is," Maxum whispered, his eyes landed on a weather-beaten wood sign hanging over the doorway to a rundown looking tavern. *"The Lucky Gambler Inn."*

Western outskirts of Borq
Handoe and Sandstorm had a bit harder of a time with the cannidene guards stationed at the White Dragon/Black Dragon border.

"You realize we might have to fight it out if they don't believe us," Handoe said, looking ahead at the guard post down the road.

"Give me your crossbow," Sandstorm demanded.

"Why?" Handoe said testily. "You have your own. Besides, they're too far away."

"That's not what I have in mind," Sandstorm countered, taking off his traveling cloak, revealing the square shaped pouch, nestled next to his crossbow, strapped over his shoulders. "I want to set the incubator between our crossbows. Then I'm going to stoop forward, making me look hunchbacked."

Handoe grinned as he seemed to catch on to

Sandstorm's plan. "Put the hood over your head. Scrunch up your face. Smack your lips a few times... give the impression you don't have any teeth."

Handoe helped Sandstorm with the crossbow and cloak and then the two walked slowly toward the checkpoint.

"Where are you two... going?" asked a bewildered cannidene guard to Handoe.

The guard cast a revolted gaze at Sandstorm, who just stared blankly ahead, smacking his lips.

"He has a sister in Borq," Handoe said. "She's very sick."

"Yeah," the guard responded, still gazing at Sandstorm as though he were morphing into some kind of hideous creature. "I bet."

"I musht she my shishter," Sandstorm wheezed in a soft voice, a trickle of drool oozing from his mouth.

"Can we go?" asked Handoe, shooting the guard a look of mocked concern. "She's probably withering away as we speak!"

Two other guards approached and looked Sandstorm up-and-down. They seemed afraid to really get close to him. One of them looked to the lead guard and shrugged his shoulders. The other dipped his head and darted his eyes toward the town.

"Uh, yeah," the lead guard said, a look of total confusion splashed over his face. "Go ahead... *please!*"

The two trudged eastward and away from the guard post.

"Your crossbow's digging into my ribs," Sandstorm muttered.

"You can't take it off just yet," Handoe replied in a loud whisper. "They're probably still watching us."

"After we round this hill, I'll give it back to you."

Handoe nodded. "We're almost in town. What's the name of that place again?"

"The Lucky Gambler Inn," Sandstorm replied testily.

The Lucky Gambler Inn looked like most other buildings in Borq. One exception was It had glass windows as opposed to open air holes cut into the walls. The owner of this dive apparently didn't share the locals' views on keeping the ways of old.

Maxum had just sat at a table near the bar. This looked to be the quiet time of the day for only two black dragons sat at one table, two elephants were at another table near the door. A golden junglewolf, with a leather patch over his left eye, sat at the bar and so did a fat monitor lizard, a few seats down. An old black dragon barkeep stood behind the bar. His face and snout seemed to have more scars than wrinkles and bore testament to many past scraps with drunk and unruly patrons.

A young black dragon female emerged from the kitchen (behind the bar) toward the barkeep.

"Jessa," he called to her, while pointing a long, bony finger at Maxum. "You have a customer."

Black dragon females have similar features as their white dragon cousins, slightly larger eyes, short snouts, and slender bodies. This one, Jessa, had fierce looking pale, yellow eyes that fell hard onto Maxum as though he had insulted her by just walking into the inn. She was not the only one looking at him. The fat monitor lizard cast his beady, marble-like eyes on the him as he sat down.

"Can I get you something?" Jessa asked in a

polite way that sounded forced.

"The house special soup," Maxum responded calmly. "Some sweet bread and some ale. Plus two menus, I'm expecting friends."

Jessa whipped away from Maxum's table and stormed behind the bar and into the kitchen.

Maxum continued to look around. His eyes eventually landed on the monitor lizard, who still stared at him. The reptile's tongue flicked faster than before and his tail swished back-and-forth in an excited way. Maxum nodded his head once at the lizard and continued his visual tour of this dusty and slightly gloomy inn.

"Here," Jessa spat, setting down a bowl of hot, sour smelling soup, a plate with a few slices of bread and a gray tankard full of ale, which slopped over the edge of the table.

Maxum's eyes sunk to the soup, which had white, meat cubes, some vegetables in a yellow broth with little, green flakes floating in it.

"Jinxy, no!" the barkeep yelled.

Maxum cast a sideways look at the creepy lizard, who was sliding off his bar stool to approach him. The barkeep clapped a hand on Jinks's shoulder to try and stop him.

"Let me go!" Jinks demanded as the struggled

to break free.

Two figures, dressed in brownish-gray traveling cloaks, with the hoods over their heads, entered the inn. Both were tall and one looked to be hunchbacked. All eyes in the place fell on the new arrivals as they glided toward Maxum's table. Thinking fast, Maxum stood up and faced the two. He contorted his face into a toothy smile and extended his hands, which peeked out from under his traveling cloak.

"Ahh, my friends," he called loudly. "You're here at last. Come and sit down!"

Jinks froze in his tracks and watched as Handoe and Sandstorm removed the hoods from their faces. Both wore smiles that looked as strained as Maxum's was. Jinks quickly turned around and crawled back onto his bar stool and took a sudden interest in the bottom of a glass that sat in front of him.

"Want another one?" the barkeep asked, his eyes gazing coldly at Jinks, who nodded and flashed a stupid grin.

An awkward silence fell over the table as Maxum returned to his meal and Handoe and Sandstorm settled in and picked up the menus. The other patrons had since returned to their own business. This was good, because anybody with a keen eye could see by the body language of these three, they were *not* friends. Tensions hung over this table like a thick, black cloud. No doubt this trio harbored similar feelings about how they were supposed to just drop everything, all those building emotions and frustrations and anger and become friends — or a team — just like that. In time, maybe.

"Have a good journey?" Maxum asked, lifting his eyes from his soup to his "friends."

"For the most part," Handoe replied from behind his menu.

"Jessa!" the old barkeep called. "Two more guests."

Jessa poked her head out of the kitchen. Her eyes narrowed and glinted as they fell on the new arrivals at Maxum's table.

"So," Maxum asked, just above a whisper, "Where are we going from here?"

"You weren't told?" Sandstorm looked taken aback by the question.

"My contact had problems getting to the point," Maxum spat, flashing a fake smile.

"This should explain everything," Handoe said, reaching into his traveling cloak and pulling out a folded piece of paper and flicked it across the table at Maxum.

He grabbed the paper and opened it. Handoe and Sandstorm peaked above their menus and watched Maxum's face as his eyes slid down the page.

"What would you like?" Jessa asked as she approached the table.

"I'll have what he's having," Sandstorm returned, glancing at Maxum's bowl and plate.

"Just a plate of greens and an ale for me, thanks," Handoe told her.

Jessa grunted and turned away.

"The Cannis Republic?" Maxum gawked, his eyes not leaving the paper. "Does he have any idea how far that is from here?"

"I'm sure he does," Handoe replied. "Keep reading."

Maxum blew out what sounded like a relieved sigh. "A *pardon!*"

"*If,*" Handoe quickly said, "we successfully carry out this mission."

"Well," Maxum spoke setting the paper on the table, "we probably die if we fail. What else am I supposed to say but yes."

Jessa emerged moments later carrying food

and drinks for Handoe and Sandstorm, yet her steely gaze was fixed firmly on Maxum. Did she know something about this? The old barkeep also stared at him with seeming interest. So did Jinks.

CHAPTER EIGHT

-INTO THE SHADOWS-

Council-Leader Goldeye's mansion, Kublisa
Goldeye paced back-and-forth on his balcony. The cool night air and the beautifully lit skyline of Kublisa was no comfort to him this time. Much was on his mind. The griffons were arriving tomorrow still nagging with questions about security. The old dragon had lost count of all the reassurances he had to make before the griffon ambassador finally agreed to stay with his scheduled visit. The *absolute* last thing Goldeye needed right now was an international incident and a renewal of hostilities with the

Griffon Empire.

Dragonsrod was splintering and about to fly apart at the seams before his very eyes. He didn't know how, or why it was happening. He felt vulnerable, exposed and scared. Worse yet, he feared he was powerless to stop war from returning to his beloved country. Everything he had worked, bled and sacrificed for over the last few years was about to be wiped away in a single stroke. Who was responsible for all this? Was somebody on the council trying to depose him? If so, they had made it *very* personal. Goldeye had his suspicions, but so far, that's all they were. He couldn't prove anything and was not about to risk his reputation by throwing fingers of blame around with no evidence to back it up.

He took some comfort in the fact that his surviving egg was in safe hands. He felt confident that Handoe and Sandstorm were the right choices. Maxum should have received his pardon by now. That should help ease things a bit between them since Handoe and Sandstorm have no further reason to chase him. His thoughts returned to his sole-surviving egg. Something felt different to him about it as he held it on the night of the attack. It seemed like it was picked to be saved. No damage to the shell at all even though some of it was exposed to the attacker, or attackers. That's the part he couldn't figure out. Were they drunk? Were they high on something? Were they just stupid? What? It appeared as though the gods had something in store for this child. It was meant to survive. But why only it? What made it different from the rest? Why couldn't they all have survived?

The egg was on its way to safety in the Cannis Republic, far to the South, and out of danger. Two issues down — a thousand more to go. Yet the most painful one was still to come.

"Can't sleep again?" Moira asked from behind him.

She emerged from the darkness and on to the balcony next to her husband. She gently placed her arms around him. He turned to her, closed his eyes and returned the embrace.

"No," was all he could say.

Their eyes locked. He drew in a deep, heavy sigh.

"What?" she asked, studying the pained expression on his face and his misting eyes.

"What's wrong?"

Goldeye opened his mouth to speak, but nothing came out.

"Talk to me *Golds!*" she pleaded.

"It's been a week since-since the attack," he started, his voice cracking. "I wasn't able to protect them… I don't know if I can protect you anymore either."

Moira's brow furrowed. "What are you saying?"

She kept staring into his eyes, hoping to find an answer from them.

"Dark times are ahead for this country," he said, "the signs are everywhere. Tensions in the Council Chambers are as high as they've ever been. The councilors are at each other's throats. Someone, I think, is trying for a forceful take-over and I may not be able to stop it."

She looked at him, aghast, was this some kind of a joke? What a horribly outrageous thought! This land had known peace and relative prosperity since the war with the griffons ended. She knew who was responsible for it. She was standing in front of him — holding him. She loved him deeply. She would die for him if need be! "You-you think we could be heading toward war?" a fearful look spread across her face.

"I'm almost certain of it," he spoke softly.

"I'm staying with you!" she said defiantly.

"You will *not*," he countered with a firm, but calm, voice. "You must understand, I cannot guarantee your safety. As long as you are here, you're too big of a target for my enemies. I cannot lose you because of my own weaknesses."

Moira stepped away from him, her greenish-gray eyes were still fixed on his mismatched ones. She couldn't understand why he was telling her this. She saw in his pained facial expressions, he was having difficulties with it too. "There's nothing I can do to change your mind?"

Goldeye only shook his head, tears started to stream down his cheeks.

Moira turned and faced the cityscape that sprawled out before them. She rested her arms on the balcony railing, gazing at the colorful city lights, trying to rally her thoughts. Goldeye watched her. The words he wanted to say got stuck in his throat and could go no farther. He took no pleasure in looking at the hurt and confused expressions on her face. He didn't want her to leave anymore than she did.

However, it seemed to be the only logical thing to do.

"Where am I to go?" she asked with a cry in her voice. "What am I to do?"

He stepped beside her and placed his right arm over her shoulders and looked at her. "I've given this a lot of thought, believe me, it wasn't an easy decision. I have friends, who live in the city of Gane, on the east coast of the Cannis Republic," She shot him a fiery glare. "I talked to them, through the tele-wires, and they have agreed to look after you until things settle down up here."

"The Cannis Republic?" she muttered, still not believing what she was hearing.

"I have a contact who'll meet you in Drallics and escort you to Gane. My friends will meet you there in a few days." he said in as reassuring of a voice as he could muster up. "Handoe, Sandstorm and Maxum will be there eventually with our child."

Moira let out a derisive grunt. "Why couldn't you just let us leave together?"

Goldeye shook his head, his heart ached at the waves of frustration he knew she was feeling. "You would be too big of a target. If one of you were to be lost — both of you would probably be lost."

She wanted to shout and protest and vent out the outrage that was blasting through her body. His mind was set, there was no swaying him. Tears streamed down her cheeks.

"When do you want me to go?"

"As soon as possible. I've written out a route for the driver to take and he'll get you to Drallics safely."

She let out a sigh, her eyes sunk to the ground. The reality of it all was soaking in.

"Okay," she whispered, giving in. "W-What about you?"

Goldeye's face lifted into another sad grin.

"I'll be fine," he said, wrapping his arms around her. "With Gisko and Bard at my side… I'll be fine."

She threw her arms around him and sobbed. Nothing more was said.

Councilor Zare's mansion, Kublisa

General Zmoge casually rode his tyrocc (a large, gray animal with rhinoceros-like body and a horse-like head and neck) through the

empty streets of Kublisa. He stopped
at a small checkpoint leading to a long, narrow
concrete walkway to Councilor Zare's castle-like
mansion. The general's body armor clinked and
clanked as he nimbly stepped down from his
mount. A black dragon guard stepped toward
the tyrocc and grasped the beast's reins. Zmoge
strutted casually to the mansion's two large,
metal doors as two guards opened them and let
him pass through. He entered the foyer and was
met by a much smaller black dragon female.

"Inform Councilor Zare, General Zmoge is
here," he said in a whispery, raspy voice.

The attendant curtsied and rushed off to do as
she was told.

General Zmoge was not an imposing dragon.
In fact, he was kind of a runt. He was small and
thin and spoke in whispers due to a throat injury
he suffered during the war. Yet, he was as
deadly as they came. He was vicious, he was
lightning fast with a sword and he was brutally
efficient.

Councilor Zare appeared in the foyer clad in
his black, medal-heavy jacket. Zmoge stiffened
to attention.

Warriors of Dragonsrod

"Stand down, my friend," Zare said, standing in front of the general. "I trust all went well?"

"Yes, sir," Zmoge hissed.

"Who did you put in charge of the border project?" Zare asked in a lazy, uncaring tone of voice.

"Captain Tolic, sir."

"Good. Tolic's not the sharpest sword in the arsenal, but he's loyal." Zare's eyes slid from Zmoge's face to his blood spackled chest armor. "I trust you dealt with Captain Irmis?"

"Captain Irmis will no longer be of any concern, sir," Zmoge whispered, a twinkle glinted in his pale, dead-looking eyes.

"Good!" Zare barked. "Irmis was getting sloppy. He was jeopardizing the whole operation," he paused for a moment and then spoke again, " What of our *friends?*"

"I spoke to the chieftains," Zmoge croaked. "I was assured the ones, who were spotted will be eliminated."

"You've done well, my friend," Zare declared with a crooked smile stretching over his face and patting Zmoge on his right shoulder plate. "I have a new mission for you."

"Yes, sir. What do you wish done?"

"My contacts in Borq have told me that the three *fur-balls* have left the city heading south. One of them arrived in the city… hunchbacked."

"Hunchbacked?" Zmoge's brow wrinkled. "How is that unusual?"

"Because he is no longer," Zare countered. "One of the others is. They have Goldeye's last egg and are trying to move it out of the country, I'm certain of it!"

"Yes, sir."

"Your mission, my friend, is to put out word to all the slums and dives throughout this country that a reward is being offered for the capture of the egg. It is to be brought to me — intact — and whoever captures it will be *handsomely rewarded.*"

"What of the egg's guardians?"

Zare shot Zmoge an 'isn't that obvious' glance.

"Yes, sir."

"I'm giving you free reign on this one. Do what you must, but *do not* link it back to me or to our clan."

"Yes, sir!"

"Goldeye has many enemies," Zare said, his face lifting into another twisted smile. "We need to keep him guessing."

Zmoge was silent.

"You have your orders," Zare said. "Get to them."

"One more thing, sir," Zmoge hissed. "I saw a carriage with one, who looked like Council-Leader Goldeye's wife. She, too, was moving southward."

Zare stared at Zmoge for a few moments. This was unexpected, but interesting news, very interesting news.

"Out of the city?' he asked, cocking up an eyebrow.

"Yes, sir," Zmoge said.

"The old *zoof* is afraid for her safety," Zare tooted, his smile widening. "Rightfully so!" A short pause followed, he looked to Zmoge again. "She's my concern. I have contacts who can watch her and see where she goes."

"Very well, sir."

"It's clever of Goldeye to hide his family in the shadows. But not clever enough! They'll be destroyed and so will he. Good hunting, my friend."

Zmoge saluted, turned and exited the house. The hunt had begun....

CHAPTER NINE

-BURYING THE HATCHET-

The Griffon caravan snaked through the streets of Kublisa amid no fanfare. The thunderous echoes from the clomping of tyrocc feet and the rumbling of carriage wheels roared through the deserted streets. A lot of animosity still festered between the dragons and griffons. Security had to be ultra-tight. The route was top secret, known in advance, only to Goldeye, Jossic and the griffon ambassador. Nothing could be left to chance. If the public knew of the route, someone might be angry or dumb enough to try and attack the griffon party. The caravan streaked through the city on a preset course

Warriors of Dragonsrod

and nothing was going to stop it.

All of the Dragonsrod councilors stood on the steps outside the Grand Council Chamber building. No one spoke above whispers. Anticipation and curiosity was as high as the tensions. Some of the councilors brought family to see the griffons when they arrived. Robsko's two sons, Garth and El, stood on either side of him. Sheema and her mate had their entire brood of eleven chicks herded together at the top of the steps in order to see the griffons. Zhangi, Jossic and Zare all wore military jackets, bedecked with the records of their individual glories. Tabric conversed quietly with Deela. Goldeye and Gisko stood on the bottom step, in front of all of them.

"Sir, here they come," Gisko said, pointing to his right.

All heads craned to the right as the rumbling caravan came into view. A cavalry squad of eight heavily armed hippogriffs, riding two-by-two, clad in red coats with black sashes strapped around their shoulders and waists and shiny black helmets on their heads, stopped in front of the councilors. Behind this squad were four, boxy coaches followed by eight more hippogriff troopers. The carriages stopped. The zaltee drivers, all wearing red, long tailed coats with white, lace around the neck and sleeve cuffs, sprang from their seats and hurried to the carriage doors and opened them.

Out from the first and last carriages, emerged an honor guard of griffon soldiers, all wearing dark, blue jackets with black, pith-style helmets that gleamed in the sunlight. These soldiers lined up and faced each other in front of the two middle carriages. Two high ranking griffon officers stepped out from the second carriage and took their places in front of the honor guard. Finally, two tall, fierce looking griffons emerged from the third carriage and stood at attention on either side of the door. Last, a tall, black headed griffon with a broad, hooking beak and glaring eagle-eyes stepped out from the carriage. He wore a blue jacket covered in medals, sashes and badges that made Zare look under dressed by comparison.

His steely eyes coursed over the dozens of reptilian, furry, and bird-like faces that stared back at him. Goldeye's blood ran cold at the sight of the griffons. A flood of bad memories splashed through his mind from the war. A sobering thought then doused his fires of hatred and fear — the griffons are probably having similar thoughts and feelings. No griffon has been on these hallowed steps since the war. Privately, Goldeye would have preferred that to continue. However, this was a time to bury the hatchet. This was a goodwill visit and all must be on their best behaviors for a lot was riding on this visitation. More than, perhaps, anyone here could possibly know.

The griffon ambassador stalked up to Goldeye.

"Council-Leader Goldeye, I am Ambassador Romar, Highest Confidant to His Majesty, Emperor Parshan the First. I am pleased to make your acquaintance at last."

Ambassador Romar extended a clawed hand to Goldeye, who returned the shake. The old dragon had his doubts. One cannot just shake off seven years of hurt and hard feelings about another creature, who at one time was a bitter enemy, just like that. Such is politics. Goldeye discovered early in his political career that public shows, as this was, was as much acting as anything else. He had to put on the best welcoming face that he could regardless of how he truly felt.

"And I, you, Mr. Ambassador!" he said, his crocodile-like face lifting into a toothy smile. "I hope your trip here was uneventful and safe."

Romar's face was expressionless. His eyes seemed to bore through Goldeye.

"Council-Leader Goldeye," he said in a low tone of voice, " I am not much for small talk. I am here for other reasons than just a goodwill visit. We have an urgent matter to discuss."

The smile faded from Goldeye's face, but not in a way to indicate that something was wrong.

"Of course," Goldeye returned. "What is it?"

Romar shook his head. "I must address your council as soon as possible. It is a matter that involves *all* beings in our two countries."

The old dragon didn't miss a beat. He motioned with an open hand toward the colonnades and pediments over the Halls of the Grand Council Chambers, at the top of the steps, and flashed another smile at the griffon. "Right this way, Mr. Ambassador."

The dragon clan representatives took their seats. The atmosphere had become even more electric, more tense, more volatile. Goldeye and Romar approached the podium. The two said nothing to each other, in fact, they didn't even look at each other. Goldeye reached inside the podium and grabbed the new stone gavel and faced the captivated audience. He tapped it on the podium a couple of times to call every one's attention to them. He didn't need to. All eyes were glued to the ambassador already.

"Councilors and representatives, this is Ambassador Romar," Goldeye craned his neck toward the griffon. "Mr. Ambassador, the podium is yours."

Goldeye left the podium and took his seat next to Gisko.

Romar's black talons clicked as he rested them on the podium. He gazed at the deathly silent audience. "Councilors and staffs," he began. His voice was a deep baritone and it echoed off the walls of the meeting chamber. "I have come bearing a message from His Majesty, Emperor Parshan the First. He sends a warning — not as an enemy — but as a potential ally. We *both* have an enemy massing on our borders to the East," hisses and whispers echoed through the hall. Heads turned in every which direction, their faces flashed quizzical and dumbfounded expressions. Romar paused for a moment and resumed talking. "It's an ancient enemy. It's one both of our peoples have fought in the past. It's a *united* enemy and it represents an even bigger threat to us than it has ever been."

"Who is this enemy you speak of?" asked Tabric, now standing.

Romar's eyes landed on the massive red dragon councilor. "The vordral."

The whispers and hisses grew louder. Goldeye studied the expressions on the faces of his colleagues. He saw fear and confusion on some. Wonder on others and a few were blank and stone-faced.

Sheema, the orange dragon councilor now stood. "It has been three hundred years since we've seen the vordral. Why would they pick now to attack us?"

Romar's eyes slid over to her.

"Their people were scattered into small tribes and introverted from one-another for most of that time," Romar's voice was calm and quite composed. "However, within the last few years, things have changed. They are becoming more aggressive. They have been attacking and, and all, they come close to, including — most...

recently — two of our outposts on our easternmost boundaries."

Goldeye remained silent. He was curious to see how the ambassador would hold up to the barrage of questions, he was sure his fellow councilors were going to throw at him...

"What makes you so sure the vordral *are* uniting for war?" Zare asked, standing up, all eyes now focused on him. "Could it have been a random attack from a small group of marauders? A band of criminals? We don't really know what lives out in the wastes. It could've been *anything.*"

"My scouts saw some just two weeks ago," Robsko said, standing and shooting a dirty look at Zare. "They seemed to be studying us and turned and ran once they were discovered."

Romar seemed to ignore Robsko and fixed his eagle-eyes on Councilor Zare.

"It was the way they attacked and destroyed the outposts and the massive casualties they suffered. We know for certain it was the vordral." Romar replied, but with a hint of bitterness in his voice. "Nothing was spared, the beasts overran our defenders and slaughtered them."

"What about their tactics?" Jossic asked, standing up.

Romar's gaze slid to the blue dragon councilor.

"They attack as a horde," Romar replied, calmly. "It is a swift and lethal assault."

Another wave of whispers and cricket-like hisses rippled across the chamber…

"Did your outposts provoke the attack?" Zare inquired.

Romar shot a sharp gaze to Zare. "No! Our outposts are *strictly* defensive in nature."

Zare began to slowly pace back-and-forth.

"How many outposts do you have on your eastern boundaries?" he asked.

"I am not at liberty to give a precise number," Romar countered. "But our defenses are more formidable than your wall," he shot an icy glance at Goldeye before fixing his attention back at Zare. "Or, those pathetic little forts being built on *your* eastern border!"

Zare froze ever-so-slightly, paced for another moment, and sat back down. Robsko and El chuckled as did Jossic.

Goldeye now stood up. "What would you suggest we do, Mr. Ambassador?"

Romar faced him.

"Arm your peoples," the griffon returned. "Strike first!"

A collective gasp spewed out from the audience...

"I know there is still much animosity between your peoples and mine," Romar admitted. "This is no time for division... we must leave the past in the past and come together against a common foe. Make no mistake, councilors, the vordral's intentions are hostile. They are moving toward your borders and they will attack once they reach them. Prepare yourselves while you still can!"

Goldeye sat alone in his office. His desktop was covered in hard-back books on history, science, and geography that may mention the vordral or anything about them. Ambassador Romar had sounded worried. Goldeye's ears were pricked up to this. Something that could worry the mighty Griffon Empire was worth taking note of. Goldeye had Gisko and Bard looking for more material. They had been to the libraries and to the Dragonsrod archives. He also contacted a few historians and experts in the biological sciences. He wanted to understand as much as he could about the vordral. So far, little to nothing had been found.

His own research into the matter was also proving futile. He had sifted through about a dozen books with no results. His eyes were burning and a painful throb was forming in his head. He had to continue. His frustration mounted as he flipped through and discarded two more books. He considered calling it a night and getting some needed sleep. Just one more book and then quit after that. He reached for a gray, hard-back book that smelled slightly musty and was thick, probably over a thousand pages, if he had to guess. It was entitled *Ancient Military Campaigns of the Dragonsrod Vol. 1.*

This had promise. His tired, irritated eyes slid through the pages of his country's painful and bloody military history. He read about the numerous border clashes between the clans. Two conflicts with the pre-imperial griffons and one very nasty, long lasting civil war. This made for interesting reading, but it still wasn't what he was looking for.

His eyelids grew heavier and his brain felt as though it had turned to mush. He was about to close the massive book, when he glanced at the title of the last chapter: *Campaigns of Gortha the Great.* Gortha the Great was the most revered leader in Dragonsrod's long history. He was a green dragon, to whom Robsko claimed he was descended from. Gortha united the eight clans into a strong country. He gave it purpose, meaning and pride. He was also credited with forming the Dragonsrod Grand Council. Gortha the Great was a hero of Goldeye's. Gortha waged three campaigns against the vordral. All were savage and bloody and were brilliant strategic masterpieces (at least according to the book.)

Goldeye was no stranger to Gortha's tactics and strategies. They were taught at the academy almost as gospel to the students. Yet nothing in his training mentioned anything about the vordral or how Gortha got rid of them. So secretive were the vordral, no one really knew much about them. They were bipedal, with an ape-like head and upper body with goat-like legs and cloven hoofed feet. They had horns on their heads that sprouted up, or hooked down, or curved backward. The vordral were very secretive creatures and all attempts to study them have met with failure. What was certain was they lived in the vast empty wastes of hilly, grass lands, east of Dragonsrod.

Goldeye finally tore his gaze away from the book. His eyes and his head were protesting too painfully for him to continue reading. He looked out a window and over the skyline of Kublisa. The sun was peeking over the buildings in a steady climb up. He tried return his focus to the book. No luck, his concentration was shot and the pain he was feeling was too much to bare. He found some useful material, but it was scant and three-hundred years old. He needed new information on this seemingly resurgent enemy. There was only one place he could get it from, the only ones, who have faced the vordral recently — the Griffon Empire. They were offering aid, he had best take it, while he still could.

CHAPTER TEN

-CRANCH HOLLOW-

Handoe, Sandstorm and Maxum wasted little time in getting out of Borq. They knew hostile eyes were upon them and the sooner they left this ancient city, the better. The route they took only led them deeper into Black Dragon Territory. The road they trudged down was a winding path that meandered southward through dense, gloomy thickets, along streams and through villages.

The three encountered no fellow travelers, which was strange. The towns and villages they passed through seemed deserted, cold and unwelcoming. Fear saturated these places like a monsoon. Each settlement had at least one of those ugly statues of Zare posed on a pedestal in the town square or along the main street. The eyes of the statues were always set as if looking down at the towns-folk. The stone and bronze facial expressions spoke the same thing, *'I'm watching you.'*

An uneasy feeling tugged and pricked at their senses. It was a certainty someone, or something was tailing them. But who?

"We have to get off this road," Handoe said.

"No argument here," Sandstorm replied.

They had just entered into another "ghost town." Not a sound was heard outside of the wind blowing through the trees, causing occasional creaks, or whistles around the corners of houses and other buildings.

Maxum was now carrying the incubator on his back. He glanced over his left shoulder at a house, which he thought for sure, he saw the curtains in a front window roll slightly back. He couldn't see who, if anyone, was watching them. A tingle shot up and down his spine. The fear in this gloomy place was thicker than the dense scrub that surrounded it. The curtain fell over the window sill again. Wind? He doubted it.

"Do you know this country?" he asked Handoe, his eyes still fixed on that window.

"I do," Handoe replied. "I spent a lot of time here as a pup."

"Whatever you have in mind, don't keep it a secret," Sandstorm said, the uneasiness clear in his voice, his eyes sliding around the buildings as if expecting something to come charging out at them.

"We'll turn in to the scrub after this next bend," Handoe announced. "We can throw any pursuer off our trail in there."

"The sooner the better," Maxum said, his fur bristled and his tail twitched nervously.

Turning in to the scrub from the road, was the easy part. Stunted, gnarled pine trees hid thorny bushes that seemed to reach out like clawed hands and snag their cloaks and scratch any uncovered parts of their bodies. Their senses were on full alert for any sound, any smell, any feel or any change in the breeze that didn't seem right. It would be an ideal place if something wanted to attack them, using this tar-thick darkness where the sun could only poke through in thin beams of dusty white light, as cover.

After what seemed like an eternity of being prodded, stabbed and scratched by the seemingly hostile undergrowth, the three emerged from the thicket into a clearing of high elephant grass, which grew higher than they stood tall.

"So," Sandstorm said to Handoe. "What's the wildlife like around here?"

"Big," was the reply. "Dangerous. If it's not big, it's still dangerous."

"Care to elaborate on that?" Maxum asked.

"The predators resemble dragons, but bigger," Handoe spoke as if he were talking about the weather. "They're bipedal, have huge, sharp teeth and they're vicious."

"That sounds lovely," Sandstorm said, a hint of fear creeping into his voice.

"The predators come in all different sizes," Handoe continued, "but, the prey animals are as bad."

Maxum glanced over his shoulder at the incubator. "Did you hear that, little egg, Uncle Handoe is going to get us all killed."

Handoe ignored Maxum's verbal jab and continued; "The plant eaters herd together for protection. What makes them especially dangerous is that they will try to run over you first, then run away."

A thunderous roar echoed from somewhere, causing the fur on all three to bristle. Maxum and Sandstorm's tails flicked much harder than normal.

"Let me guess," Maxum said, "either one of us is really hungry, or that is one of those friendly creatures you have told us about."

"No wonder why we haven't seen anybody," Sandstorm piped out. "With these kinds of things patrolling about, I don't think I'd venture out much either."

The three scurried through the tall, thick grass with Handoe leading the way. A short time later, they were standing on the East bank of a shallow and gentle flowing river.

"The Cranch River," Handoe reported.

Sandstorm looked to the left, down stream, toward a bend in the river. He saw a bloated carcass of a large, plant eating creature with three horns on its face, being scavenged by over a dozen small, bipedal, sickle-clawed creatures. He nudged Handoe on the left arm and pointed to the scene. Maxum's eyes were fixed on the river. He watched several large scorpions float, lifeless in the lazy current.

"Look," he said to Handoe, pointing at the bodies.

Handoe sighed. "There's another danger," his eyes followed the carcasses as they drifted by, "Those things run in packs, anywhere from a few to hundreds. They average two feet in length. Individually, their venom isn't strong, but get stung by a bunch of them and it will do you in."

Another loud roar. This time the three could feel the vibrations in their foot pads. Whatever made that roar was big, most likely dangerous, and moving toward them. No one felt like finding out what the creature was. It was probably heading to the carcass, better it than them. Without further hesitation, the three crossed the cool, clear water and vanished into the grass and scrub on the western bank.

To say this patch of thorny, scrub strewn land was dangerous would be a gigantic understatement. It was not the place to stop and have a picnic or to camp out in, unless the one doing it had a death wish. Handoe, Sandstorm and Maxum kept a steady pace, not daring to stop.

The sooner they get through this forsaken valley, the better.

A strange clicking noise seemed to be following them as they struggled through another stretch of thick, head-high grass. It wasn't going unnoticed. The travelers' ears were getting a real workout, turning and flicking in every which direction. The clicks were getting louder and more rhythmic, whatever was pursuing them seemed to be in communication with each other. *Great.*

Handoe suddenly froze, Sandstorm and Maxum nearly fell on top of him.

"We have to get out of here!" Handoe said, a horrified look spread over his face.

"What is that clicking?" Sandstorm asked.

A wave of finger snapping-like clicks brushed through the grass.

"Is it those scorpions?" Maxum asked, drawing his sword.

Handoe and Sandstorm drew their swords. All three turned their heads trying to see what moved here, or what rustled over there. The clicking was everywhere. Several large, grayish-brown, fat tailed scorpions with thick, black, fishhook-like stingers lunged out of the grass at the trio. Maxum swiped his sword in a downward, diagonal angle and slashed one of the creatures in two.

"RUN!" shouted Handoe.

No one needed to be told twice.

The predatory chase and kill mode had been triggered in the scorpion pack. Scorpions were emerging out of the grass from seemingly every crevice and nook, launching their tails like missiles at the three as they fled. Grass fell like trees, swords swished and swiped, yellow scorpion blood and body parts flew through the air. The trees and shrubs seemed to sprout scorpions, trying to get at their prey as they sprinted passed…

"Look!" shouted Maxum, pointing to a clear path to their right. "We can go that way!"

"No," Handoe answered. "There is a cave on that rocky knoll to the left. The climb might slow them down."

"It might slow us down, too," Maxum shot back.

Sandstorm had shed his traveling cloak, which was crawling with scorpions. He had escaped being stung, due to the combined thickness of his fur and the cloak's material.

The three sprinted by a few large rocks, just in front of the knoll. The once frenzied scorpions appeared to be giving up the pursuit. Two scorpions jumped onto Maxum's back, but quickly bounced away as though jumping on to something super hot. A large scorpion — over three feet long — lunged at Handoe's head. The rabbit ducked to his right, while swinging his sword in an upper diagonal motion, cleanly chopping the scorpion in two.

The three sheathed their blood drenched swords and proceeded to climb up the rocky face toward the cave. The scorpions vanished into the grass.

"Do you know what's in this cave?" Maxum asked Handoe.

"Nope," he returned. "I think we'd do better against whatever is in there than what we just got away from."

Maxum grunted. He had his doubts.

A small dragon with blue-gray skin, big, nearly bulging, blue eyes, and a narrow snout leading to a broad nose with small, spikes for horns on its head, peaked out from the mouth of the cave. Its eyes and its small, pointed ears fixed on the blood stained trio. Its mouth lifted into a welcoming grin.

"Welcome," it said in a feminine, misty, high-pitched voice. "We've been expecting you."

Handoe, Sandstorm and Maxum gazed dumbstruck at the little dragon.

"Come in, please," she invited.

They reluctantly followed her.

"Great," Maxum growled. "Another cave."

CHAPTER ELEVEN

-MOIRA-

Moira's heart ached. The loss of her egg clutch was still a fresh and open wound. She was angry. She was frustrated. She was confused — it had all happened so fast! She felt as though some unseen force had reached into her chest and pulled out her heart and soul and left an empty shell in its place. She wanted nothing more than to be with her husband as they prepared to welcome their yet-to-be hatched chick into the world.

Moira was angriest at her husband for rushing her out of her house and out of her country. Why the Cannis Republic? It was so far away. All he told her was she would be safe there with some of his friends. Her anger fanned out at Handoe, Sandstorm and Maxum as well. Who were they? What made Goldeye trust them so much? He said they were dependable. She felt uncomfortable with how he placed their lives in the hands of complete strangers. Moira didn't share the haughty air of superiority that many dragons held toward other races, yet she did not trust the trio with *her child.* For all she knew, they had decided to scramble the egg — eat it — and go their separate ways. Her anger at them was because *they* had her egg and *she* didn't. Was it right for her to feel this way? Probably not, but she didn't think it was right about what was happening to her either.

    The carriage she was riding in was comfortable. She didn't feel too many bumps along the way. She had her two nurses come with her. She will need help with her child once they are reunited. May that time come soon.

    Drallics, Port city on the eastern shores of Green Dragon Territory.

Drallics was a sprawling, bustling city, with one of the busiest seaports on the continent. Where Borq prided itself in being old and historic looking, Drallics seemed to be leading the charge toward the future. This city was about as modern, for its time, as it could be with its large, concrete, metal and wood buildings, clean, paved streets and trees growing on the outer sidewalks. Everything was neat and orderly. As with Borq, the streets teamed with beings moving around conducting their daily business. The atmosphere was not subdued as it was in Borq. In fact, it was quite the opposite. Little to no tension hung in the air, creatures met and talked openly with no fear of being arrested or broken up. No, this place was lively and open and seemingly friendly.

Moira and her two nurses were huddled together on the wharf. They were awe-struck by the size and number of the ships moored here. The clippers had their masts stabbing at the sky. Ropes ran every-which-way from their rigging as if a spider had gone berserk while spinning its web. Steamer ships and paddle-wheel boats had tube-like smoke stacks that jutted up like horns. Beings of all kinds moved around the wharf. Crew members, deck hands and dock workers scurried on and off ships, carrying various cargoes. Passengers walked around with clueless expressions on their faces, while looking around for whatever ship they are supposed to be boarding.

Moira and her nurses were so taken in by the activities around them, they didn't notice a zaltee step up to them.

"Take your bags, ma'am?" he requested.

Moira swung her head around looking for whoever was addressing her.

"Uh — down here," he said.

Moira's eyes fell to a sandy colored, rat-like creature with bright red eyes looking up at her. He wore a tattered, sleeveless red shirt and brown pants that resembled jaggedly cut shorts where the pant-legs had been torn away at his knees.

"I'm so sorry," Moira said, smiling as her face turned red.

"Think nothing of it, ma'am," the zaltee returned politely. "Can I take your bags on board?"

"By all means," Moira replied.

She stooped toward the zaltee, who only stood up to her middle. Her eyes bounced from side-to-side.

"Are you my contact?" she whispered.

The zaltee also looked from side-to-side, he stood on his tip-toes and pointed his long nose up to hers.

"Maybe," he whispered back. "Maybe not."

Again her face flushed as she returned to her full height. The zaltee bent down and hoisted a bag on his back and carried it up the gang-plank and onto the deck of a paddle-wheel steam ship moored in front of them. Moments later, he came back for another bag.

"Thank you, Mister — uh?" Moira said.

"Friends call me River Rat," he replied with a smile. "My zaltee name isn't easy to pronounce, it's full of squeaks, squeals and clicks."

River Rat picked up another bag and hauled it on to the boat. Moira watched as a wrinkly-faced orange dragon in a dark, blue jacket and a black cap on his head, called River Rat over to him. She couldn't hear what was being said. Since River Rat's eyes and the captain's owl-like eyes frequently rested on her and her nurses, she figured it was about them. After a few moments, the old captain tipped his hat to Moira and her nurses and flashed them a pointy toothed smile. Moira nodded her head in return. River Rat raced back to grab another piece of luggage.

"We could carry our remaining bags," Moira said, looking down at River Rat, who had just hoisted another bag on his back.

"Oh, no, ma'am," he said, "we zaltee are stronger than we look. Besides, this is one of my roles on this ship."

"Was that the captain you were talking to a few moments ago?" she asked.

"Yes, ma'am," came his reply. "He wants to talk to you when we get underway."

"This vessel is going to Gane, is it not?"

"Yes, ma'am... eventually."

Moira and her nurses exchanged glances. River Rat carried another piece of luggage on board and hurried back for the final bags.

"What do you mean by — eventually?" Moira asked him.

"Well," he replied, "we have a couple of stops to make in Silver Dragon Territory. Then we go out to sea to the Vulcria Islands. Next we go to Abysinna... Finally, we go to the Cannis Republic, and the city of Gane."

Moira again exchanged glances with her nurses before looking back at River Rat.

"How long will this trip take?" she asked.

"About a week," came his matter-of-fact reply.

The captain stepped to the front of the boat and again tipped his hat to Moira.

"Good day, me lady," he said in a scratchy voice.

"Hello," Moira replied politely.

"We'll get underway as soon as River Rat finishes with your luggage."

"Thank you, Captain."

The captain turned and walked toward the back of the boat and started talking to some of his crew.

"His name is Ako," River Rat said. "He's a little… eccentric."

"Oh," Moira replied, her eyes shifted from River Rat to Captain Ako, who was still chatting with his crew.

As River Rat finished with the luggage, Moira studied the boat's features. She looked at the oar-like paddles in the back. Boxes and crates were staked and tied down. She gazed at a structure behind the pilot house. She assumed

that was where the crew quarters were and also
the boiler room since the tube-like smoke stacks
jutted up from it. She glanced at the side of the
ship and its name *The Mudskipper*. River Rat
stepped over the gang-plank once more.

"Why *The Mudskipper?*" Moira asked.

"Well," he replied, "we were going to name
her either the *Sea dart* or the *Wave hopper*. But
she doesn't dart and she doesn't hop. She skips
over mud pits and sandbars really well, so we
called her *The Mudskipper*."

"Oh," Moira said, nodding her head.

"Your bags are packed, ma'am," River Rat
said, standing to one side and pointing an open
hand to the boat. "I'm to usher you on and
welcome you onto the ship."

"Thank you, kind sir," Moira said.

Her nurses walked on first, she followed close
behind. River Rat dragged the gang-plank on
deck and shouted to Captain Ako that all were
aboard. Minutes later black smoke streamed
from the stacks and the paddles lifted out of the
water in a counter-clockwise motion.

Moira and the nurses stood by the cargo hold
and watched River Rat and his crew-mates at
work. It had been a long time since she felt the

cool sea air caress her skin and face. She took a deep breath of the salty air. It reminded her of how much she loved the ocean. The memories of the cruises she took with her family, as a girl, sailed through her mind. She and Goldeye took a cruise a couple of years ago. A sorrowful feeling swept over her again. She tried not to think about her husband too much, it only made her miss him all the more. Moira was confident that she would be reunited with him soon. She also realized that she had to trust his decision to make her leave. She had to trust his faith in Handoe, Sandstorm and Maxum to do his bidding. Yet, she would remain fearful.

CHAPTER TWELVE

-THE CLOUDS OF WAR APPROACH-

Goldeye tested the griffon, Romar's, claim that he was the *'Highest Confidant to His Majesty, Emperor Parhsan the First.'* Goldeye wanted to see for himself the destruction of those two outposts. To his surprise, the griffon agreed. Before leaving Kublisa, Goldeye met with his two most trusted councilors, Robsko and Jossic.

"Are you sure this is a good idea?" Jossic asked, a look of concern on his face.

"I can think of no better time," Goldeye calmly returned. "Council is out for the season. There's little of importance going on right now. Gisko can handle the White Clan affairs until I return."

"Do you want me to come with you?" Robsko asked.

Goldeye's face curved into a grin.

"I'll be fine, my friends," he said, almost laughing. "Bard is coming with me."

His grin faded, replaced instead, with a look of the deadliest seriousness.

"I have to see what happened up there," he patted his friends of the shoulders. "Guard yourselves well. Keep your eyes open."

Days later, Goldeye, Romar and Bard stood in front of one of the destroyed forts. The three surveyed the damage. Ramparts were charred black, burnt arrow shafts stuck out like spines from a large cactus. Arrows stuck up from the ground and out of the mummified remains of what Goldeye assumed were the vordral. He had witnessed too many scenes like this to be visibly shaken by it. However, his nightmares of the war were just as fresh and vivid as they had ever been.

"The vordral do not care for their dead the way we do with ours," Romar snorted, disgust clear in his voice.

"Did they move any further than this area after the attacks?" Goldeye asked, looking to Romar.

"No," he replied, shaking his head. "We believe this to be a message — to let us know they are back."

Goldeye slowly walked around the carcasses. Hundreds of them lay over the grassy field. A message? Sacrificing this many of your soldiers just to say, *'hello, we're back and we're going to kill you?'* He watched Bard pick up and swish around a cutlass sword.

So this was a raid? All these dead? Thousands must have charged these forts! Apparently losses were of no concern to these beasts. Romar was right. His defenses on the eastern borders weren't just inadequate — they were *woefully* inadequate.

"Sir!" Bard croaked, pointing at a thick pillar of smoke rising over some hills directly to the East.

Goldeye and Romar's eyes followed where Bard was pointing.

"Are they attacking another outpost?" Goldeye asked.

"We have nothing out that far," Romar replied. "Only vordral settlements lay out there."

It was a very disturbing sign. If they were attacking their own people, nothing was safe. The vordral were restless. They were whetting their appetites for war.

"I have to get back to Kublisa as soon as possible!" Goldeye demanded.

Dragonsrod Grand Council Chamber; Kublisa, three days later.

Upon returning to the capital, Goldeye summoned the councilors together for an emergency meeting. The days it took for them to arrive seriously tried his patience. Yet he knew waiting was about all he could really do. During high priority meetings, like this one, the councilors brought only their most senior ranking confidants or lieutenants.

Goldeye stood behind the podium. He studied his subordinates for a moment. Gisko; Robsko and his sons, Garth and El. Zhangi and what looked like his oldest son. Jossic and two of his lieutenants. Sheema and two of her aides. Deela and an adjutant, Tabric with a general

officer from their military wing, Zare and...
Wait a minute, where was Councilor Zare? Only one black dragon was present. He looked young and had a wiry mustache. He sported the typical black jacket with silver epaulets on his shoulders. He wore no medals or sashes. The only thing he did wear was the look of importance, though his rank suggested otherwise.

"Where's Councilor Zare?" Goldeye asked the young dragon. "Where are his senior staff? Who are you?"

"Councilor Zare sends his apologies, sir," the young dragon said, standing at attention. "He has unavoidable business to tend to at the eastern defenses. My name is Walker, sir."

Goldeye gazed unbelievingly at Walker. How could Councilor Zare blow off an emergency session as if he were canceling a dental appointment? How could he send someone so raw and who looked like he should still be in an academy class? No one else was here from Zare's clan. This was a clear breach in protocol, Zare *will* answer for this. But for now...

Goldeye masked his anger and kept a neutral expression on his face as he began to speak; "I recently visited the attack sites that Ambassador Romar told us about. During that time, we witnessed the vordral attacking what appeared to be one of its own settlements. They burned it to the ground. Losses do not concern this race! I saw hundreds of their dead scattered over the field in front the griffon forts and they still managed to destroy both of them."

Goldeye paused while the councilors whispered to each other. His gaze fell on Robsko. "Double your defenses!"

The burly green dragon nodded.

Goldeye shifted his attention to Walker. "Tell Councilor Zare to make *every* preparation he can on his section of defenses!"

"Yes, sir."

The old dragon's mismatched eyes coursed over the rest of his colleagues.

"The vordral are restless," he said quietly. "There could be *millions* of them. They are coming. I'm announcing a call for mobilization of Dragonsrod's troops," the other councilors gasped and the color drained from their horror-struck faces. "We need as many bodies, regardless of the clan, on those defenses or they will be overrun *when* the vordral attack."

"That could unleash a general panic!" Deela exclaimed.

"Then use subtlety," Sheema countered, shooting a cold gaze at Deela.

"I have troops at the ready," Jossic said. "They just await your orders to move."

Good old Jossic.

Loyal, almost to a fault, a good friend, a good soldier. One definitely to have on your side when the swords start to swing in anger.

"My people may not support such a move," Tabric said. "They are very peace-loving."

"Your people are too peace-loving!" Zhangi snapped, his brown eyes narrowed and his nostrils flared.

Tabric faced him, his hands balled into fists.

"ENOUGH!" shouted Goldeye. "This is not the time for a renewal of internal divisions! We *must* come together as one country. I fear our existence is at stake here. The call for mobilization *has been made!* We all have work to do, so get to it! Spread the message to the people. We will convene again in two weeks — meeting adjourned!"

The councilors departed in a stunned silence. Robsko placed himself between Zhangi and

Tabric, who exchanged dirty, poisonous glares. Everything Goldeye feared would happen seemed to be unfolding before his very eyes. Only he, Robsko and Jossic appeared to recognize the danger signs. What about the others? The issue at the border over the wall, that Goldeye once dismissed as being trivial, had now turned into a problem… a potentially fatal problem.

CHAPTER THIRTEEN

-PROPHECIES OF THE MYSTICS-

"We are known as the Mystics," the little dragon said as she led Handoe, Sandstorm and Maxum down a narrow tube-like tunnel that was barely high enough for them to stand up in.

"Mystics?" Handoe asked.

"I've heard of you," Sandstorm spoke. "I've heard stories about a ninth tribe of dragons that shunned the ways of the other clans. So they retreated — deep into the country to where no one would bother them."

"Those stories are true," the little dragon's voice carried in a misty, dreamy tone.

"Oww!" Maxum yepled as he hit his head

against the low hanging ceiling. "What is it with you magic-types and caves?"

"For protection, brave puma," the little dragon said. "For privacy as well… my sisters and I are highly respected by our people."

"Does anyone come here for visits?" Sandstorm asked.

"Our people, yes," she responded, casting her big, blue-gray eyes at Sandstorm. "Outsiders, rarely… you are among the first in many years."

"You said you were expecting us," Handoe asked. "How?"

"We are telepathically linked to other Mystics and Seers," the little dragon revealed, sliding her gaze to Maxum.

"The griffon," he hissed, annoyance in his voice. "I hope he was clearer with you than he was with me."

The four entered into a vast, pitch-black chamber. As if on queue, a cauldron appeared spewing out bright, bluish-white light in a steamy vapor that vanished as it rose into the thick, musty air. Behind the cauldron, appeared six dragons that were bigger versions of the little one. Their horse-like faces and reptilian upper bodies were bathed and highlighted in a blue light. Their eyes were the attention catchers, black with white vertical slits — all fixed on the three travelers.

"Welcome," the one furthest to the to the right said in a high-pitched, misty voice, identical to the little one's voice.

"Bring them closer," ordered the one in the middle, her voice the same as the others.

The little dragon stopped and ushered the trio closer to the cauldron. The glow illuminated their facial features, licking them in a soft blue shimmer against the darkness.

"The puma has the egg!" screeched the one furthest to the right.

"Guard the egg well," the little one said, her eyes were now black with white, vertical slits. "This child is the key to Dragonsrod's future... without him, the country will be destroyed from without *and* from within!"

"You have questions?" the one furthest to the left said in a calm, but no less misty voice.

"Yeah," Maxum barked. "How did Goldeye know how to contact the griffon Seer?"

"He didn't," the little one said.

"Council-Leader Goldeye has a telepathic ability he is unaware of," told the middle dragon

"The night of the attack on his young, he mentally — and quite involuntarily — made a distress call."

"The griffon Seer happened to be the first one to pick up on it," the one furthest to the right said.

"Great trust in you, the council-leader has," spoke the one furthest to the left.

"You *must* deliver the child to the Cannis Republic as soon as possible!" the middle one barked.

"You are being followed," the little one said.

"By more than one party," spoke the dragon, third from left.

"Word is being spread of a ransom for the egg," the middle one stated.

"The guardians of the egg are to be exterminated!" yelled the one furthest to the right.

Handoe, Sandstorm and Maxum exchanged glances.

"On whose order?" Handoe asked.

"Councilor Zare," the seven sisters said in unison.

"Beware of him!" warned the little one. "He is planning a rebellion and has influences from outside the country."

"Griffons?" asked Sandstorm.

"No," all seven returned, again in unison. "Creatures from the East."

"Dragonsrod — and all living in it — are in mortal danger!" yelled the one furthest to the left.

"Wait a minute," Sandstorm said, holding out his hands. "You said something about us being followed — by who?"

"The brave snow leopard asks a valid question." the one in the middle said.

"By two parties," returned the dragon, second from right.

"One organizes those to come after you, to destroy you," spoke the one furthest to the left. "The other is a member of a resistance cell versus Councilor Zare and seeks to assist you."

A short pause followed. Handoe, Maxum and Sandstorm seemed to be attempting to digest what the Mystics were telling them. Handoe folded his arms, his ears sunk behind his head, and paced slowly back-and-forth.

"So," he said, "Goldeye is telepathic — Okay. Zare wants us dead… Death marks are nothing new to us... And we're to avoid every public

place between here and the Cannis Republic —
Anything else?"

"Do not treat this lightly, brave rabbit!" snapped the second dragon from left.

"I'm not!" Handoe shot back, his eyes glinted a pale blue.

Another silence followed...

Only the bubbling and hissing of the cauldron could be heard.

"Please," Maxum said, throwing Handoe a sharp look, "continue."

"The child must be delivered to the Cannis Republic!" all seven said together. *"The child will become powerful over time. Powerful enough to unite all species together against those who seek to destroy us!"*

Handoe, Sandstorm and Maxum seemed glued to the spot. This was a prophecy they were hearing.

"The mother and the father have powers they are unaware of," the seven said in a chant-like tone. *"The hatching of the child will unlock these abilities in them both."*

Maxum glanced over his shoulder at the square-shaped pouch.

"The child has developed a bond with you,

brave puma," said the little one.

Maxum flashed an uncontrollable grin. Handoe and Sandstorm briefly looked at him before returning their attention to the sisters.

"Fras and Fray," the sisters hissed in unison.

Handoe's fur bristled and his ears shot straight up. "What did you say?"

The eyes of the sisters fell on him.

"A grave injustice had been committed against you, brave rabbit. You will confront those who have wronged you. The brother's Fras and Fray are treacherous, You must destroy them... or they will destroy you."

Handoe dipped his head toward his chest. Sandstorm passed him a concerned look.

"He's never talked about his past," Sandstorm said, his eyes lifting to Maxum.

"The prophesies you've heard *must* be fulfilled," the little one said. "If you fail, the life you know it to have been will be over. Despair, darkness and the gloom of evil will dominate Dragonsrod's future."

Handoe, Sandstorm and Maxum stood in a stunned silence.

"Seek out the resistance fighter," the Mystic furthest to the right said.

"Beware," warned the one furthest to the left. "Enemies lurk everywhere."

"I have a question," Maxum said, holding out his left hand. "Will the child survive outside this incubator?"

The eyes of the sisters slid to him.

"In its present form, no," they said. "If it hatches… yes!"

"When will that be?" Maxum asked.

"Only the child knows," the little one said.

"How will we know when it has hatched," Sandstorm asked. "It's not as though we can pop open the hatch and look in on him every other hour."

"The incubator will let you know," the dragon furthest to the right answered.

"How?" asked Maxum, not hiding the irritation in his voice.

"You will know," said the middle dragon.

"No more can we tell you," the little one finished.

"Where do we go from here?" Maxum blurted out.

The eyes of the sisters fell on Handoe. His eyes narrowed as he lifted his head.

"Elmshir," he growled.

"Beware, brave travelers," the sisters said in unison. "The Elmshir Warren is controlled by Fras and Fray. They are very dangerous and they will stoop to the lowest levels to keep what they have."

Maxum turned to Handoe. "What's so important about this Elmshir place?"

"I was banished," Handoe snarled, lifting his eyes to meet Maxum's. "And told never to return—"

"Return you shall!" the sisters chanted in unison.

The sisters departed almost as dramatically as they appeared. The little dragon's eyes returned to their blue-gray color. She escorted Handoe, Maxum and Sandstorm to the cave mouth. She assured them safe travel out of the valley. She bade them goodbye and vanished inside the cave.

The trio stood atop the rocky hill and looked down at the valley. It appeared calm and tranquil, but that was the deception. It seemed as though it had reset its traps and was to lay in waiting for its next victims…

"How far is Elmshir?" Maxum asked Handoe.

"About twenty miles," Handoe replied. "We

could make it in a day. But we're not going there just yet."

"Oh, we're not," Maxum asked, cocking up an eyebrow. "Where *are* we going, then?"

"Cranch Hollow Warren," Handoe replied, his eyes narrowed and glinted. "Or what's left of it."

Handoe said nothing more. He started running toward the West. Maxum and Sandstorm glanced at each other, shrugged, and then sprinted to catch up.

CHAPTER FOURTEEN

-A CHANGE IN PLAN-

It took *The Mudskipper* a full day to go from Drallics, Green Dragon Territory, to the Vulcria Islands. Once there, the boat spent three more days chugging from port-to-port loading and unloading various cargoes. Close to a thousand islands made up the Vulcrian chain. The largest island was about half the size of Green Dragon Territory, which was pretty good sized. The smallest islands (if, indeed, they could be called such) were mere sandbars with gray, flat bread shaped rocks poking out from them.

Moira had gotten used to the loud hissing sounds the water made as it lifted out and splashed around with the rhythmic slaps of the paddle wheel as its blades rotated back under the surface. Other than watching Captain Ako

Warriors of Dragonsrod

order River Rat and his crew-mates around, there wasn't much to do. Moira's nurses looked dreadful with sea-sickness. It seemed they took turns racing from the crew quarters to the deck and vomited out the food, they had just eaten, over the side. The crew found this to be very amusing. Whenever one of the nurses would sprint to the deck to throw up, she would be chided mercilessly;

— "There she goes again!" —

— "If she's a white dragon, she's looking awfully green to me!" —

— "I know how ya feel, I can't keep River Rat's cookin' down, meself!" —

In an ironic twist, Moira acted as the nurse. She looked after her aides and made them lie down. She didn't understand how they could be so ill, the water was calm and glassy. Moira had no problems at all with sickness. She would wander around the deck and gaze out at the sea or stare at the rocky, Vulcrian shoreline as *The Mudskipper* slid toward yet another port town.

The crew off-loaded cargo and would stow more on, while Captain Ako stood and directed where things were to go in the cargo hold.

Captain Ako told Moira and her nurses they were to remain in the crew cabin, where they would be safe — and out of the way. Time oozed by for Moira. She tried to read a book that she packed along. All the thumping, banging, padding of feet, and swearing she was hearing, had completely destroyed her concentration. She slammed the book closed. With nothing else to do, she lay on her cot and tried to block out the barrage of cuss words that had been assaulting her ears. It was too warm in here. She felt that she now had an idea what a loaf of bread might feel like as it was being baked.

She thought about investigating the boiler room. Not a good idea! Her nurses refused to let her leave the room — rightfully so. If Captain Ako, who was gracious enough to let them ride on his boat, eat their food and take up their space were to see her poking around in such a sensitive area, he'd throw them off with no hesitation, make them swim back to Dragonsrod. She didn't like it, but all she could do was sit and wait... and wait... and wait... .

Moira and her nurses were jolted awake as they felt the boat jerk forward. River Rat poked his head through the doorway.

"Awfully sorry that took so long," he said, smiling. "We're underway. The captain wants you to stay here just a little bit longer, until we get out to sea."

"Yeah, sure," Moira growled, she shot River Rat a sharp glare.

"Are you alright, ma'am?" River Rat asked.

"Just *bored,* there's nothing to do!" Moira snapped.

River Rat flashed a tight-lipped grin.

"I am sorry, ma'am," he said. "Captain's orders — just a little bit longer."

He was back on deck before she could say anything in protest.

"Okay, ma'am," River Rat said, politely. "Captain said you can come out now."

"It's about time," she snarled.

She jumped from her cot and looked at her nurses. "Let's get some fresh air. I think we could all use some."

The nurses reluctantly followed her to the doorway. She blinked her eyes as the bright sunlight hit her face. Her nurses poked their heads out the doorway but would go no farther.

Moira looked around at the little waves and breakers as they lapped against the boat's hull. She stepped on to the deck. Her eyes darted from the waves to the looming, triangular mountain, behind them, that was one of the Vulcrian Islands.

Moira walked to the pilot-house where Captain Ako stood at the helm.

"Ar, me lady!" he said with a pointy toothed grin.

"How long will it be before we reach the main-land?" Moira asked.

"About a day — day and a half," he said.

"A day and a half?" she gasped.

"My apologies, me lady, but this isn't a luxury vessel —"

"I apologize, Captain," Moira said politely, "I'm not sure how much more of this my poor nurses can take."

She looked over her left shoulder and saw they had vanished back in to the crew cabin.

Captain Ako burst out laughing. "S' quite alright, me lady. The sea's not fer everybody."

A full moon lit up the inky black sky and its reflection shimmered over the calm ocean

Warriors of Dragonsrod

surface. *The Mudskipper* seemed to be making good time. The paddle wheel boat was moving westward toward a mass of land that loomed over the horizon. Moira couldn't sleep. She was restless and needed a breath of fresh air. Her nurses were feeling queasy again and elected to stay in the cabin. She stepped on to the deck and took in a deep breath of the cool, salty air.

"Ar, me lady," Captain Ako said as she passed by the pilot-house.

"Good evening, Captain," she returned.

"Careful where ya walk around, up front, don't want ya fallin' overboard."

"Thank you for your concern, sir, but I can see very well in the dark."

Captain Ako tipped his hat to her as she walked toward the bow. Moira saw River Rat sitting near the bow with his back to her. She could see that he was twittling a piece of rope, rather absent-mindedly, through his fingers. He was staring out into the night. Moira sat next to him.

"Can't sleep, ma'am?" he said, not looking at her.

"No," she returned, "I had a bad dream."

River Rat's red eyes slid up to her face. "Bad dreams, eh?"

"Yes," she said quietly. "I'm very concerned about my family."

He nodded his head a couple of times. "Are they well?"

"I hope so. It's a long story, I really shouldn't get too deep into it."

"Understandable, ma'am."

Moira looked down at River Rat, who was again staring out into the distance. "Shouldn't you be asleep with the rest of your crew-mates?"

"I can't," he sighed. "I have also been having bad dreams."

"Oh," Moira mouthed, nodding her head.

"Do you miss your home?"

"Very much. I've only been away for just a few days, but it feels like a thousand years."

"I haven't been to my home since before the war."

A short pause followed and then River Rat spoke again; "We, zaltee, allied ourselves to the griffons when they attacked Dragonsrod. We were eager to prove our worth to them. The griffons gave us some land to settle on and we were grateful to them for it."

"Your people were nomadic before that?" she asked.

"Well… yes. We felt we owed them a debt of gratitude. We signed on by the thousands. As time went on, I had been in many battles and saw a lot of ugly stuff committed by both sides. I was tired of war, I was getting out of the army and going home in just a few days. Then it happened. The dragons and their allies attacked and surrounded us. A siege ensued, we used up everything, ammunition, food, hope. We surrendered, expecting fair treatment. There was a black dragon in charge of the unit that captured us. He was as mean as his troops. They belittled us, called us all the derogatory names they could think of, threatened us and the like," River Rat's eyes narrowed as he spoke through clenched teeth. "The black dragon leader ordered us lined up shoulder-to-shoulder. We were going to die that day. Right at the moment his troops leveled their crossbows at us… A white dragon officer appeared. The two started arguing and shortly after that, they stormed away from each other," River Rat's face lifted into a smile and his tone of voice changed. "We were being marched to the rear as prisoners

-of-war."

"That still sounds awful!" Moira gasped, giving him a sympathetic stare.

"Not really," he countered. "We were happy to be alive. It took a little while, but, some of us applied for and were given jobs — mainly menial things no one else would do. But, it was something to do and it got us away from the prison camp. Trust me, prison life is *extremely* boring."

River Rat was about to speak again, but Moira beat him to it; "So is that how you ended up on this boat?"

"Pretty much," he said, nodding his head.

Another pause followed.

He cast his eyes up to hers.

"Your husband was the officer, who saved us. I got to know him, after the war, that's another long story for another time. So, to answer your question from the wharf, yes I was your contact."

Moira gasped. Goldeye had told her a lot about himself, and about some of his war-time experiences, but not about this. River Rat seemed to be studying the shocked expression on her face. He was about to speak when they were engulfed in a bright, white light followed by a deafening *BOOM!* The force hurled them into the darkness as though they had been slapped off the deck by a giant, invisible hand.

Moira let out a loud gasp as she thrust her head up from under the chilly water. Stunned from what had just happened, she took a few moments to recollect her senses. She was a very good swimmer, so it was easy for her to keep her head above water. She shifted her body as she looked around, trying to figure out where she was. Her eyes rested on the twisted, burning wreckage that, only a moment before, was *The Mudskipper*. She gazed, horror-struck, at the glowing flames and the billowing, orange-yellow smoke as it plumed up into the night sky.

Moira screamed out for her nurses and met with no reply. She called for River Rat, meeting the same results. Only the low, grumbling roar and hiss of the inferno answered her cries. She couldn't stay here much longer. Bigger and meaner things than sharks lurked in these waters and would soon be here to investigate the scene.

She shifted her body away from the fireball

and squinted into the inky, black that surrounded her. Her eyes fell on the silhouetted, triangular humps of land that they were steaming toward. The land was several miles distant, but it was her only option. She cast one final, mournful gaze at the dying boat for any possible glimpse of survivors. Nothing. She proceeded to swim for those black lumps of land and with any luck, she would be there by dawn.

Councilor Zare's mansion; Kublisa,
Goldeye angrily paced back-and-forth in front of the check point leading to Zare's castle-like mansion. The black dragon guards stood statue-like behind him, while the nervous Walker watched. Goldeye's face scrunched and his nostrils flared as he reached into his tunic and pulled out a timepiece. He snorted and then shoved it back under his shirt.

"It's 5:15!" he shouted at the flinching Walker. "You said he'd be here by 4:30! Where is he?"

"I-I don't know, sir," Walker wheezed, sweating profusely. "Councilor Zare does not tell me of his daily itinerary!"

Goldeye studied the trembling adjutant. He took note of Walker's medal-free jacket.

Definitely a low rung on the ladder.

"No," Goldeye said quietly. "I guess he wouldn't."

"There he is!" exclaimed Walker, pointing a finger at a four tyrocc drawn coach that just rounded a corner and was on the straight-away in front of the checkpoint.

Goldeye looked at the cross-bar beside the checkpoint station. A guard placed his hands on the stone weights to lift up the bar.

"Leave it down!" Goldeye ordered, holding his left hand at the guard.

"But sir," the guard stammered, his bulging eyes glued to the coach as it drew closer.

"Leave-it-down!" Goldeye demanded.

The guard stepped away from the cross-bar and resumed his post. The coach driver (a young male black dragon) pulled up on the reins bringing the coach to an abrupt halt just a few feet from the cross-bar.

"What's going on out there?" Zare's voice rang from inside the coach.

The driver sprang from his bench and poked his head inside the coach's open windowed door. Goldeye's frown drooped even further as he listened to the muffled and inaudible voices coming from the coach. The driver popped open the door and stood at attention. Goldeye's scowl lifted into a surprised stare as Robsko's oldest son, Garth, emerged from the coach, followed by Zare.

"Garth," Goldeye said, "What are you doing here?"

Garth was a mirror image of his father in a younger day. He bowed to Goldeye. "My father asked me to survey the work being done on the defenses in Black Dragon Territory."

"And I approved," Zare said, flashing a strained smile.

"Very well," Goldeye said, his eyes sliding from Garth to Zare. "Garth, Walker, thank you," Garth and Walker bowed and went their separate ways. "Councilor Zare, walk with me."

The two walked side-by-side, but did not look at each other. The air around them was tense, teetering on hostile. It was no secret that these two loathed each other, both personally and politically. So much so that they wouldn't hesitate to draw their swords and fight it out — right here, right now! Not today. Civility was the course of action, not violence.

"I hope your *business* at the border has been dealt with," Goldeye asked.

"It has, thank you," Zare said.

"I called an emergency session," Goldeye snarled. "Everyone else made it but you. You didn't send any of your senior staff. All you sent was an aide, who looked as though he should still be at the academy!"

They stopped and faced each other.

"My *Senior Staff,* as you call them, were with me at the border." Zare replied with a casual tone of voice.

"Don't blow this off!" Goldeye spat, his brow as low over his eyes as it could sink. "This is a *serious* breach of protocol — worthy of an investigation!"

Zare's face scrunched up, an angry glint in his eyes, his jaw muscles tightened. "I assure you—"

"I assure you, councilor," Goldeye interrupted, "If this happens again, I will *personally* launch an investigation into what kept you and I will check into everything. Am I understood?"

Zare flashed another uneven, toothy smile that appeared to be as phony as his reason for missing the meeting. "Quite."

"Take no action against Walker or your guards," Goldeye ordered, still visualizing daggers piercing into Zare's heart — if he had one. "They were acting under my orders. *Do not* let this happen again, councilor… Good night!"

Zare gave a half-hearted bow as Goldeye turned and stormed away from him. He stood back to his full height, launching his own volley of arrows and daggers, through his eyes, at the back of Council-Leader's head.

"You are not going to interfere with my plans," he hissed to himself. "You don't know it yet, but your days are numbered, you old *son-of-a-berk!*"

Zare stormed back to the checkpoint, his fists clenched, his nostrils flared. The gods help whoever gets on his bad side today!

CHAPTER FIFTEEN

-THE RESISTANCE FIGHTER-

Cranch Hollow Warren, western Black Dragon Territory,

Handoe, Maxum and Sandstorm were still digesting what the Mystics told them. Especially Handoe. His past seemed to creep up on him and throw itself up in his face like a wall that had just sprung up from the ground. He kept quiet for long periods of time, occasionally, he would mutter the names of Fras and Fray, but little else.

Before long, the trio emerged from the tall and spiny scrub brush on to a road that looked as though it hadn't been used in years. Grass grew down the middle of the path, while broad-leafed plants sprawled and stretched across the dirt trails. Handoe still led the way as they rounded a curve in the road that flowed into a sprawling ruination. He froze in his tracks, Maxum and Sandstorm, again, nearly ran him over. The two cats were about to verbally tear into him, for this was the second time he had stopped abruptly, nearly causing a pile-up. Handoe's eyes practically bulged out of his skull and his ears dropped against his neck and shoulders.

"Where are we?" Maxum asked.

"I'm-I'm home," Handoe weakly replied. "This is Cranch Hollow Warren."

The town looked like the ruins of an ancient city from a long since fallen civilization. Paths, that were once straight roads, crisscrossed each other at evenly spaced intervals and were cracked and broken with tall grass and stiff, yellow plants sprouting up here and there. Lots, where buildings once stood, were now overgrown with shrubbery, stunted trees and tall grass. Ghostly remains of building foundations peeked up like forgotten tombstones from the undergrowth. A few mound shaped buildings still stood, but were heavily overgrown, the window spaces and doorways of these structures looked like cave entrances, dark and forbidding, and gave the impression they would collapse at any moment.

No sounds of birds chirping, no insects buzzing or hissing, not even the whispering of the wind through the trees could be heard. Just a heavy, thick, eerie silence.

"What happened here?" Maxum asked.

He and Sandstorm seemed completely taken aback by the destruction of this place.

"We're at a place of death," Handoe said. "A battle was fought here."

The trio kept their senses on full alert as their eyes slid from one wreck and ruin to another.

"This was the furthest advance south the Griffon spearhead thrust into this territory," Handoe told them.

They cautiously stalked down a street that led to what was left of the town square.

"What happened here?" Maxum asked again, with an irritated tone to his voice.

"The griffons surrounded us," Handoe replied, his eyes flashed as he relived the memories of that terrible day. "They sent their *vermin* allies, the zaltee and goblins, to finish us off."

"Didn't the dragons send two armies to stop them?" Sandstorm inquired.

"Yes," Handoe answered. "The griffons scattered them like shooing flies from food. Before we knew what was going on, the enemy encircled us. We were trapped! Our puny defense force couldn't protect hundreds of civilians. We had to get them out of here, or this would be a bigger massacre than what it was."

"What did you do?" Sandstorm asked.

"The people built a network of tunnels for just such an instance or for some other emergency," Handoe said. "We had just got the last of the civilians out when the goblins and zaltee attacked. We were outnumbered twenty-twenty-five to one, but we had to give our people enough time to escape."

"How many of you were there?" questioned Maxum.

"Nowhere near enough," Handoe grunted. "Maybe two hundred and fifty. I was one of five officers put in charge of the defenses."

"Which were — what?" Maxum pressed on.

Handoe slid a sideways look to Maxum.

"Trenches, abates, spikes, bows-and-arrows, crossbows, everything we had," he said. "Captains Leaf and Rhil took the left flank, I took the right flank. *Colonels Fras and Fray*, took up the center."

Handoe did not hide his bitterness when mentioning the colonels' names. The three slowly walked down the remnants of the overgrown town square. Sandstorm's eyes fell to the right on the splayed skeletal remains of three goblins…

"It didn't take them long to overrun us," Handoe continued. "The fighting was hand-to-hand and soon became a running battle. Very few — if any of us escaped without some sort of injury. I was stabbed under the left arm and had two ribs broken."

"What happened to Fras and Fray?" Sandstorm asked.

Handoe tensed again, but quickly relaxed as he looked at his friend.

"That was the question," he said. "I didn't see them until after the battle was over. Neither appeared to be injured. Neither appeared to have even been in the fight at all."

"How many of you survived?" Maxum asked, his eyes were fixed on the mummified remains of a large animal laid out across the southeastern corner of the square.

"Maybe a third," Handoe muttered, "maybe a little less," he tensed up and his eyes flashed again. "I've hated goblins and zaltee ever since…"

Handoe's ears shot up, all three stopped, rooted to the spot. Their fur bristled as they felt vibrations in their foot pads of something large that was moving toward them.

"We can't stay here," Maxum said, his ears cocked toward the thumps and his tail swished nervously.

The trio cranked their heads every-which-way looking around at the ruined structures for suitable cover. The vibrations pulsed heavier.

"Over there!" Handoe cried out, pointing to a mound on the left side of the square.

The three sprinted for the mound's cave-like entrance and dove inside at the same time as a large creature stepped on to the square. Inside, the dilapidated mound was hollow, dark and looked to be losing the on-going battle with time and the elements. Rays of silvery sunlight poked through windows, the doorway and holes and cracks in the building's cavernous roof. The ground level was littered with debris from the building's second floor, which had completely collapsed on to it.

Handoe and Sandstorm rolled behind a wooden section of the floor that stuck up, looking like a picket fence in bad need of repair. Maxum slipped and fell and lay sprawled out on the floor for several moments. Two large, sandy colored feet, with three toes on each, ending with vicious, hooking claws stood just outside the mound's entrance. Maxum groaned loudly before slowly rising to his feet.

"Oh, ouch," he moaned rubbing his chin, his eyes were cloudy and unfocused.

The thing outside backed away from the doorway. Handoe and Sandstorm could see through the curtain of settling, gritty dust the shadow of the reptilian beast as it lowered itself to the entrance.

"Hide!" Handoe strained as he and Sandstorm pointed and gestured to the entrance.

Maxum recovered himself quickly. He darted to the right side of the doorway and crouched down, throwing the hood of his traveling cloak over his face. A large, oval-shaped head with lime-green scales and a red, triangular shaped crest over an eagle-like, amber eye, slowly rested on the ground just outside the doorway. The creature's mouth was closed, but pointy teeth protruded down from its upper jaw. The beast's pupil expanded from a tiny, black dot to a large ball with an amber lining.

Nobody dared move, let alone breathe. The creature moved its head closer to the entrance, poking its eye into the doorway. Its pupil bounced and darted back-and-forth trying to catch any kind of movement. The creature lifted its head from the doorway.

Maxum was still crouched down and resembled something between a dusty, moss-covered rock and a bag of meal. He lifted his hood from his eyes and glanced outside. He could see the creature had returned to its full height. He shot a glare to Handoe and Sandstorm, still hiding behind the floor wreckage.

"It's still out there!" he whispered, pointing to it. "It's moving again."

The creature had repositioned itself, stood in

the square, and faced the mound. Maxum sprinted from the wall and dove next to Handoe and Sandstorm. The creature stuffed its snout into the doorway, its almond shaped nostrils flared in-and-out. The sniffing and snuffling noises, it made, resonated like a bell inside the hollow structure.

Once again, the trio started looking for an avenue of escape. Only one window hole was on the ground level. It would do more to get them killed if they tried to get out through there. This route of desperation was directly to the left of the monstrous, tooth-filled mouth that blocked the doorway. Two more holes were perched above the entrance on what used to be second floor. Unless Handoe, Maxum and Sandstorm magically sprouted wings and learned to fly, they weren't getting up there. They were trapped. This thing, blocking the doorway with its snout, looked perfectly capable of bringing the rickety structure down on top of them if it got excited. Now was *not* the time to be doing anything stupid. All they could do was sit where they were and make like pieces of wreckage.

Faint, rhythmic taping sounds like wood-on-wood could be heard from somewhere outside. The creature pulled away from the entrance causing a part of it to collapse throwing up a brown, gritty dust cloud. The tapping continued, the creature was totally attracted to the sounds. It turned toward the noises and slapped its tail against the mound causing another section of the wall to fall down. Creaking and groaning sounds, from the weakening structure, echoed like thunder.

"To state the obvious," Sandstorm cried, "I think we had better get out of here."

"No argument here," Maxum replied.

The three rushed to the crumbling opening and hurtled over the debris pile out on to the square. Not knowing if the creature was still around here, they sought the cover of a neighboring ruin.

The beast had disappeared behind a copse of Dogwood trees and did not return to the square. A warm wind blew and whistled through the ruins and hissed through the tree tops, thus disturbing the crushing silence. Handoe, Sandstorm and Maxum lifted their noses and took in deep sniffs. The danger was gone. This did nothing to lighten Maxum's mood. He shook the chocolate colored dust from his head and cloak and shot a stern gaze at Handoe.

"What are we doing here?" Maxum snarled.

"I need something," Handoe returned with the most nonchalant tone of voice.

"What?"

Handoe didn't answer at first. He and Sandstorm sat on opposite sides of what used to be the doorway of a now open-air, igloo-like ruin. The rabbit's silence only aggravated Maxum even more.

"Start talking!" Maxum yelled, pointing a finger at Handoe. "What are we here for?"

Sandstorm apparently was wondering the same thing. "What *are* we here for?"

"A crest," Handoe said.

"A crest?" Maxum cocked up his brow. "Like a shield — coat of arms — flag — what?"

Handoe stood up and paced slowly. His face scrunched up, he was apparently deep in thought.

"I'm looking for a breast plate," he finally said, keeping his voice calm. "It has a badge on the left side near the shoulder."

"Didn't you have it on?" Sandstorm asked, sliding a look at Handoe.

"Yes and no," Handoe replied.

Maxum snorted, while shooting the rabbit a poisonous glare. "What the *spleck* does that mean?"

Handoe sighed and then answered the testy puma; "When I was stabbed, the blade of the spear cut the shoulder-strap under my left arm clean through. My breast-plate was a hindrance, not a help, so I got rid of it."

Maxum's eyes shifted around the ruins, the scowl on his face only seemed droop further. "We could be here forever! There's so much junk and debris laying about — it could be *anywhere!*"

Sandstorm opened his mouth to speak, but was tapped on his right shoulder by the sharp blade of a sword, which quickly moved to his neck.

"No one move," ordered a black dragon female as she emerged from behind the ruined wall Sandstorm sat against. "Or I spill the snow leopard's blood!"

Handoe stopped pacing. Sandstorm stayed perfectly still. Maxum's brow migrated back toward his nose as he sneered at the dragon.

"Who are you?" he growled.

"I ask the questions!" she shot back, flashing a pale, yellow eyed glare at Maxum.

The black dragon female wore the characteristic body armor of her people; dull, black colored chest and shoulder plates over a chain mail shirt. She kept the sword firmly against Sandstorm's neck. She looked as though she knew how to use the weapon, best not to test her skills —not yet anyway. The trio slowly rose their hands.

"It's obvious the snow leopard, here, doesn't have the egg anymore," she said, her eyes coursing over the other two, who still sported their traveling cloaks. "So, which of you has it?"

"What's it to you?" Maxum spat, matching her icy glare with one of his own.

"You *fur-balls* have no idea what you're holding on to," she snapped, nearly pushing Sandstorm over with her sword.

"We know more than you think," Handoe said, slowly sinking next to Maxum.

"WHO HAS IT?" she shouted.

"I do," Maxum growled. "You want it, you'll have to fight me for it."

Something seemed familiar about this dragon, her eyes, her voice, her features. Sandstorm raised his eyes to hers, his eye brows cocked up; "I know you now," he was careful not to move around too much with the sword blade still stuck at his neck. "You're the waitress… Jessa!"

It clicked with Handoe and Maxum as soon as he said it.

"You're the resistance fighter?" Handoe asked.

"Very good, *fur-ball,* she snarled, lifting the sword from Sandstorm's neck. "Get up! We're getting out of here—"

"No one is going anywhere!" came a voice from behind the ruin.

Handoe's fur bristled, he stood up and faced the back wall as several rabbits, all wearing chrome-like chest plates and helmets that gleamed in the sunlight, climbed over the wall and into the ruin. The rabbits all carried crossbow repeaters and had swords sheathed at their sides. Several of them ran out into the square to secure the scene.

"Put it down, *scaly!*" said a brown furred rabbit with a long diagonal scar across his face from his left eye, which was white and dead looking, to the edge of his nose. "Or you're gonna know what it feels like to be perforated!"

Jessa lowered her sword.

The brown rabbit turned to Handoe and Maxum. His chest plate was scuffed and scratched and had some deep grooves sliced into it. His helmet had two diamond shapes on it — none of the others did. This must be the patrol's commander.

"Handoe?" he said, his mean expression lifted into a smile of recognition.

"Hello, Leaf," Handoe said, smiling, "It's been a while."

Leaf's smile faded into a sorrowful frown and a pained expression crossed his battle-scarred face.

"Oh, Handoe," he groaned, "It's good to see you and all, but, since I found you in *these* rabbit lands, I got to take you in."

"I know, Leaf," Handoe said, still smiling. "That's why I came back. I have to confront those two."

Maxum, Sandstorm and the now disarmed Jessa, filed out of the ruin. Handoe walked along side Leaf. They moved southward out of the square and into the overgrown ruins and wreckage and out into the open.

"Be warned, my friend," Leaf cautioned, seeming to know of whom Handoe was speaking. "Fras and Fray are more powerful and dangerous than you realize. They have Councilor Zare's backing. There's a reward out for you. They may have you killed the moment you walk through the gates of Elmshir."

"I know," Handoe said, unmoved. "I should have done this along time ago."

CHAPTER SIXTEEN

-A HOUSE DIVIDED-

Grand Council Chamber, Kublisa.

The Council Chamber buzzed with activity. Voices of the delegates and their entourages echoed off the chamber's cavernous walls. The chatter slowly died away as Robsko and Goldeye stepped up to the podium. The old white dragon studied the faces of his counterparts. Some looked worried. Some tried to conceal their doleful expressions with impassive looks and attempted neutral faces. Yet their eyes told a very different story. Fear and worry robbed the twinkle out of them. The bags and dark circles around their eyes and the pale-faced complexions suggested they haven't slept much over the last few days.

If anyone needed to be worried, it was the council-leader himself. A call for mobilization was a call for war. Who was the enemy? Where were they? The Dragonsrod presses were already roasting Goldeye over the hot coals and were criticizing him mercilessly for the decision to mobilize calling it *'Unfounded!' 'A rash judgment!' 'An unpopular move by an unpopular leader!'* Some even called for him to step down and let a younger, more sound-of-mind dragon take over.

Only the black dragons wore any looks of confidence on their faces. Goldeye found this reassuring, yet somewhat puzzling at the same time. The old dragon was already suspicious of Zare over his most recent actions — or lack-there-of.

"This meeting is now in session!" Robsko said, pounding a new stone gavel on the podium. "Council-Leader Goldeye has the floor!"

"Councilors and staffs," he wheezed. "I sent you to your home provinces to muster support from your people… I can tell by strained looks on some of your faces that it didn't go over too well."

"My people just don't see the emergency," Tabric said.

Zhangi shot up out of his seat like someone had just stuck him in the backside with a needle.

"COWARDS!" he shouted, facing the red dragon councilor. "YOUR WHOLE LOT!"

Robsko, Goldeye and Jossic launched themselves at Tabric and Zhangi, who had come at each other and were throwing punches. The red and gold staffs spilled onto the floor and joined the melee. Blue, White and Orange security troops dressed in blue shirts and iron gray helmets, chest and shoulder armor, stormed into the chamber and entered the frackus. Fists flew, head butts dealt, insults hurled, arms were twisted, noses bloodied and eyes were blackened.

Order had been restored. The security troops stood facing the delegations, holding club-like batons and throwing menacing glares into the stunned and angry representatives. Goldeye was furious. His left cheek was puffy and bruising where someone's fist had landed across it. Medics moved around treating the injured. Sheema was surrounded by her entourage. They all leaned toward her apparently in deep conversation. Deela's black eyes were so wide they practically bulged from her skull. Whatever color she had in her face was long gone. Zare sat back in his chair, clasped his hands over his belly and looked on with a crooked, almost malevolent smile. He was *loving* this! What he loved even more was watching Goldeye struggle. The punch across the old fool's chops was a nice added touch. He wished he was the one who threw it.

Goldeye and Robsko returned to the podium.

"This behavior is shocking!" Goldeye ranted. "We are in a state-of-emergency don't you realize that?"

The council-leader's temper had boiled over and he was about to let it flood over his councilors. "If this barbarism happens again, arrests will be made and those delegations *will be* sent home for the remainder of the season!"

A deafening silence fell over the chamber as Goldeye continued to speak; "The security troops will be staying here for the rest of the season. I know this has been difficult — and judging by the news prints, not very popular," Goldeye's gaze slowly moved over the faces of the delegations. "But we are *not* in a popularity contest here. This could be war. Now, I asked about mustering troops. Who — if any — can send help to the border?"

Jossic stood. "The Blue dragons are sending five infantry regiments, one cavalry regiment and an artillery battery. They should be there in about two days."

Zhangi stood. His right eye was swelling shut and he spoke in a low, croaky voice. "We can only send one regiment at this time."

Deela stood. She still looked deeply shaken by the chaos that erupted earlier. "My people are a sea-faring people," her voice was soft and nervous. "We have a tiny standing army, barely strong enough to defend our own territory, let alone defending a neighboring border. But we have a strong navy. It will be put on alert."

Deela returned to her seat. Tabric stood with a bruising bulge on the left side of his mouth and a cut under his right eye. "We shall continue to talk to our people... But I guarantee nothing."

Sheema stood. "We, too, need more time."

"And you, Council-Leader," Zare said, standing up. "What are you, the white dragons, sending?"

Goldeye turned to Zare. "The white dragons are sending three infantry regiments and one artillery battery."

Well, it was a start. But would it be enough? It wouldn't be if the vordral chose to attack now. Maybe that's what he needed. It was a terrible thing to wish for, but his people were badly divided. An attack by an outside force would unite the people. It happened when the griffons invaded. But could Dragonsrod endure another war? It barely survived the last one and many of its wounds were still open.

Goldeye sat alone in his office. His desk had been overrun with files, paperwork and reports and dispatches. He ignored it. Light from a small lamp on the left corner of his desk shimmered against the growing darkness. He sat back in his chair reading from *Ancient military campaigns of the Dragonsrod.* He read and reread the section about *Gortha the Great* and his battles against the vordral.

An increasingly haggard looking Gisko entered the office with a slip of paper in his right hand. "Sir, this came from Ambassador Romar."

"What does it say?"

"The griffons-griffons have sent a recognizance-in-force into the w-wastes to track the vordral and see where they are going," the heavy-lidded Gisko stopped for a moment and let out a gaping yawn and then kept reading. "Ambassador Romar suggests we be ready for a vordral attack."

Goldeye nodded and closed the book he was reading. He looked at Gisko, who gave the impression he was about to fall over, his eyes were red, baggy and dark.

"When did you sleep last?" Goldeye asked.

"I don't remember, sir."

They both yawned. Goldeye sighed and then cast his eyes to Gisko. "Send this message to the other councilors. Then go home and get some sleep."

"Yes, sir."

Sleep. Good idea. The old dragon's brain had turned to mush. He wasn't doing himself any favors by depriving his body of what it was screaming for right now. He rose from his desk, extinguished the lamp and went home.

CHAPTER SEVENTEEN

-WHERE TO NOW?-

Moira emerged from the pounding surf, like a crocodile, on to the sandy beach. Exhausted, she crawled onto the dunes and sat down. Her gown was soaking wet and clung to her body giving the impression that she was in a severe slough. She was cold and in shock. She tucked her legs up to her body and wrapped her hands around her knees and curled her tail over her feet.

She wanted to cry, but the tears wouldn't come. She never felt more alone than she did now. Moira yearned for Goldeye's warm embrace. She wanted to be holding her child.

She wanted to be home. She could think of a hundred other places to be than here. Question was, where is here? Her eyes scanned the watery horizon and locked on the thick, black plumes of smoke trailing up into the moody, purple-gray clouds. The wreck of *The Mudskipper*, apparently, was still afloat.

It seemed she was the only survivor of the seven crew and three passengers on board. She had an eventful swim, one she very nearly didn't survive. Sharks had brushed against her, ripped her gown and scraped her skin. She had to out-swim and outwit a big mosasaur. She slapped it with her tail, kicked at it when it got a little too close, including once in the beast's right eye. Finally, the creature decided Moira wasn't worth the trouble and went off looking for easier prey.

She shivered and slowly rocked back-and-forth. Her eyes landed on something in the water. It was swimming toward shore. It appeared to be struggling against the heavy surf as wave after wave scooped it up and swallowed it and then released it only to be taken in by the following wave. The mass stuck up a pointy nose out of the crashing water and it looked to be gasping for air. Moira stood up and walked toward the angry waves. She recognized the pointy nose as belonging to River Rat. He was pulling the limp, seemingly lifeless, Captain Ako with his right arm and swiping his left arm against the water in an attempt to reach shore.

Moira rushed into the surf and pulled River Rat and Captain Ako to the dunes. The zaltee collapsed spread-eagle on the sand, his chest inflated and deflated in a heavy, rapid succession. Moira gently lay Captain Ako next to him. The orange dragon was alive, but with terrible burns on his face and neck and much of his jacket.

"What happened?" Moira asked. "I mean, how did the boat—"

"—blow up?" River Rat gasped. "Boiler explosion. It's the only thing on the boat that could've exploded."

Captain Ako groaned. He was laying between Moira and River Rat, neither really knew what to do. River Rat sat up and looked sympathetically down at him.

"He was lucky," he began.

"How so?" Moira asked.

"The pilot house must've partially shielded him from the blast. When I found him, he was floating face-up and unconscious."

"Do you know where we are?"

River Rat shrugged. "I don't know. Silver Dragon Territory, maybe. This shore line looks a bit familiar to me."

The wind was picking up to a cold and steady gust throwing sand particles and sea-spray in their faces. Dark gray to purple-gray clouds floated over them as if preparing to attack.

"This is going to be a bad one," River Rat cried, casting his eyes skyward.

"We need to move inland," Moira said, standing up.

She studied the landscape, its rolling, grass covered, sandy hills looked as though they lapped into a barrier of pine trees, a couple miles distant. Waves crashed against the shore with ever-growing ferocity and seemed to be creeping in closer and closer.

"The sea's angry," River Rat said, gazing out at the pounding surf. "She's angry that she didn't get us all." He stood up and threw a fist at the ocean. "We cheated you *again!*"

Moira was not one for tempting fate.

"Let's grab the captain and go!" she demanded as they bent down and gently picked him up by his arms.

The storm was quickly upon them assaulting and lashing them with everything it had. The gale slapped their faces, threw sand in their eyes, mouths and noses only to be washed away by a driving horizontal, sheet-like rain that soaked and chilled them to the bones. Thunder boomed and crashed across the infuriated sky. Lightning flashed and streaked, hitting near the trio as they fled. A couple of times, they had to dive for cover as white, hot bolts of electricity sizzled and shot to the ground just a few feet away.

"I don't think it was overly smart of you to have taunted the ocean like that!" Moira yelled, her brow furrowed, firing an angry glare at River Rat.

The pine trees weathered this storm just as they had done with storms throughout the years. The wind howled through the tree-tops causing the trees to sway and creak and groan. The salty smell in the chilly air was replaced by that of pine needles and must. The ground in here was dry the trees grew so close together little to no precipitation and not much light reached the soil. It only made their moving around all the more difficult.

They fell to the ground in front of a large tree trunk. Captain Ako groaned, due to his many burns, as he sat down. Moira wiped the sandy sledge out of her eyes, nose and mouth. River Rat shook himself dry.

The realization of what happened seemed to hit Captain Ako hard. He slumped against a nearby tree.

"Gone," he moaned, his head sinking to his chest. "Seventeen years... Gone!"

Moira looked with sad eyes at the captain. River Rat piled up dead pine needles and branches into a mound. He felt around in his pants pockets.

"A-ha!" he exclaimed as he pulled out a couple of waxed stick matches.

He swiped one against his shirt again and again until it finally hissed to life. He placed it in to the debris pile and gently blew on it. Moments later smoke, then an orange-yellow flame blinked and shimmered and rapidly spread over the kindling.

"Wow," he said. "This stuff is really dry."

Moira stood up, her head swiveled as she peered into the pitch black darkness.

"See anything?" River Rat asked.

"No," she replied, "the trees are too close together."

The flickering orange glow bathed River Rat's face and illuminated his red eyes as they moved to Captain Ako. "Captain, come and sit with us near the fire."

No response.

"He'll be alright," River Rat assured Moira, who sat across from him.

A thunder clap rolled through the sky like a ball on a wooden floor.

"I'm sorry for the loss of your crew-mates," she said. "Did you know them long?"

River Rat was quiet for a moment. He drew in a deep, sad sigh and cast his eyes at her. "About four years. How long did you know your nurses?"

"Not that long."

A white flash of lightning blazed through the woods followed by a long rumble of thunder.

"Where to now?" Moira asked.

He shrugged his shoulders. "I don't know.

Maybe we should keep moving inland. Try to find some civilization and find out where we are. Then move south after that."

Captain Ako was snoring softly behind them.

"Sleep sounds like a good idea," River Rat said, casting a tired gaze to Moira. "I'll take first watch."

Moira didn't argue. She leaned back against a tree trunk, rested her hands on her chest, and closed her eyes.

CHAPTER EIGHTEEN

-FROM BAD TO WORSE-

Behind Goldeye's stoic, statue-like demeanor, hid a terrified, tortured, scared and yearning dragon that very few knew. He missed Moira so much it hurt. He knew nothing of her whereabouts or that of their egg. He wanted nothing more than to be with his family and hoped and prayed they would be together soon.

Issues of disunity and the threat of an impending attack, that only he seemed to know was coming, ripped and tore at his already shredded soul. He knew Zare was plotting at something, but what? He never did like Zare — found him to be conniving, too untrustworthy, too ambitious. He also knew that whatever Zare's plans were, he stood in the way. That suited him just fine, thank you very much!

Goldeye was convinced that the black dragon councilor was up to no good. If it meant that he had to stand in Councilor Zare's way to keep Dragonsrod in one piece and keep Zare from achieving whatever twisted goal he was striving for, then so-be-it! He'll stand in Councilor Zare's way until the infernal regions, themselves, froze over in ice twenty miles thick in every direction! Other, bigger, problems invaded his thoughts.

Goldeye knew all too well about the animosity between the gold and the red dragons. Physically, they are closely related. Psychologically, they were a universe apart and spreading further by the moment. During the war, griffon legions spilled deep into Gold Dragon Territory. The reds promised to help their cousins. It never arrived. Many gold dragons died as a result. The reds didn't feel threatened and didn't send troops. It was only when the Grand Council ordered the reds to send troops did they act. But the fighting had shifted northward, by then, and into the Buffer Zone. The gold dragons pledged to never forgive their cousins for this act of cowardice and have shown a good deal of disdain for them ever since. The golds have closed their borders to *all* red dragons and the two clans continue to have nothing good to say about the other.

The reds and golds weren't the only ones with border issues. Robsko's green dragons and Zare's black dragons were still fussing over the Sandrega River Valley. It seemed logical to just make the border right down the middle of the river as it cut its way west. Neither was satisfied with this setup. What was agreed to by both clans, was that all of it was owned by their side and none of it belonged to the other. At least now they were working together on the eastern defenses.

The eastern defenses — three infantry regiments and an artillery battery were going there today. These are units from the famed *Manticore Legion.* During the war, a division of white dragons was said to have fought with all the ferocity of a Manticore — the name stuck. Goldeye served in this division. In fact, one of the regiments leaving today, the Third, was the first regiment he was assigned to. He was a junior officer at the time, but rose quickly through the ranks and took command of the *Third Foot Infantry*. By the middle of the war, he commanded the vaunted division. Soon, he would be the leader of the army the *Manticore Legion* belonged to.

These were his boys leaving. Next to Moira, Gisko and Bard, the *Manticore Legion* was his extended family. It pained the old dragon to send these regiments away — he didn't want to do it. But they were soldiers, and so was he. He called this brigade to duty, they obeyed. Goldeye was going to wear his chest and shoulder armor today as a show of unity and respect for his old unit. He just hoped his tan colored, battle scarred hardware still fit him, for it had been a few years since he last wore it and he had put on a few pounds since then.

Thousands lined Kublisa's main street to watch the four regiments as they marched out of the capital. Dragons and mammals alike cheered, waved their hands or waved small flags, threw flowers and confetti at the soldiers as they walked by. All the councilors and their entourages stood on the steps of the Grand Council Building. The gold dragon regiment was the first to march. Goldeye wasn't the only one to don the old duds, Zhangi wore his battle armor, which gleamed gold in the afternoon sunlight. He, Goldeye, Robsko, Jossic and Zare threw up stiff solutes. Sheema, Tabric and Deela placed their hands over their hearts.

After the long lines of the gold dragon regiment passed, came the battery of tower-like trebuchets and the wagons containing the projectiles they fired. These devices-of-war were pulled by teams of eight tyroccs. White dragon riders sat on the first two of each team, keeping them in motion and under control. Then came the moment Goldeye was waiting for, the first of the three regiments from the famed *Manticore Legion*. His eyes misted at the sight of a large, black banner with the gold painted face of a manticore with the number three in its wide open, tooth filled mouth. This was the standard for the regiments in this brigade, each one having its regiment number inside the mouth of the manticore. The stamping feet of the soldiers and the clanking of their armor mingled with the thunderous roar from the crowd seeing them off.

Goldeye stood at attention, his armor fit just

as good now as it had when he was young. His eyes were glued to the Third as it snaked by the councilors. A tightness gripped his gut, a feeling he hadn't had since the war. He wanted to lead these troops, personally into the battle, he was sure was coming. His pride soared as the banners flapped and soldiers from the *Third, Seventeenth,* and *Thirty fifth Foot Regiments* marched on. The brigade's supply wagons closed out the parade.

Goldeye was is his office chatting with Robsko and Jossic. The three held goblets of cara-berry whiskey, a potent, ruby-red mead that was best sipped to avoid instant intoxication. Jossic was in the middle of an old war story when Gisko entered, he carried a slip of paper in his left hand and a troubled look on his face. An instant silence fell over the room as all three councilors turned and looked at Gisko.
"What is it?" Goldeye asked him.
"This came in sir," Gisko said as he handed Goldeye the paper. "I-Its about Moira."
Robsko and Jossic exchanged concerned glances then turned to Goldeye, now standing, with his eyes fixed firmly on Gisko.

"What does it say?" he asked his aide.

"The boat, Moira was on, had an... accident." Gisko said, reading from the paper.

The color drained from everyone's faces, their eyes bulged and their jaws hung open.

Gisko read on; "A silver dragon corvette found the wreck of a paddle boat they believe to be *The Muddskipper*. They said the boat looked to have... exploded. Four bodies, so far, have been recovered. Moira was not among those found."

Goldeye fell into his chair, staring at his goblet as though it were going to give him an answer besides *'have another drink, you're gonna need it.'* His head sunk toward his chest, looking like a balloon that was slowly leaking air.

"...Silver dragons are continuing to search the area. They'll let us know if they find anything else." Gisko finished, dropping the paper on Goldeye's desk.

How can this be happening? Why was it happening so fast? Just a short time ago, everything seemed to be perfect in the universe. He was going to be father for the first time. He had a wonderful, loving, supportive wife he enjoyed coming home to every night. The country, he was the council-leader of, seemed to be on the verge of greatness and prosperity. Now? His wife *and* unborn child are missing. The country was on the verge of ripping itself apart. An enemy threat, that seemed to pop up out of the blue, and nobody outside his inner-most circle seemed to see coming, was massing on Dragonsrod's eastern border. All the old dragon wanted was peace. It seemed he will get war in return.

Councilor Zare's mansion, Kublisa.
Zare slowly paced back-and-forth in the middle of a large room on the ground level of his castle-like mansion. His entourage grouped in a semi-circle behind him. Zare's head was dipped toward his chest, his face scrunched up in thought, his hands clasped behind his back. He held a slip of paper in his right hand.

He stopped pacing and faced his staffers, only adding to the already suffocating tension and mounting nerves as he slapped them with icy glares. He wasn't happy about something. Zare's belittling gaze fell on a white bearded general officer, who wore as many medals, sashes and badges as he did. Yet this staffer didn't flinch every time Zare breathed in his direction. He was either too old, or too weathered to care. Zare's eyes bore down on him.

"This report is true?" Zare asked the elderly staffer.

"Yes, sir. The griffons sent a recognizance-in-force to the wastes to find the vordral. They found nothing until they tried returning home."

Zare impatiently nodded.

"Yes, yes, I read the report!" he smiled. "The vordral beat them back into their empire."

"The vordral are more restless now than ever," the old staffer warned. "Their *High Ruler*, Loothar, is growing impatient. He wants to know when you plan to act?"

Zare's eyes narrowed to slits. "They'll wait until *I* give the order! No other time!"

An armor-clad black dragon soldier entered the room, seeming to take care not to be noticed by Zare. He stopped behind Walker, tapped him on the shoulder, and handed him two pieces of paper. Wasting no time, Walker took the papers and skirted around the entourage, until he stood in front of Zare.

"Begging your pardon, sir!" Walker threw up a stiff solute. "These were just handed to me."

Zare yanked the papers out of Walker's hands, the young dragon shrunk from his view back behind the rest of the entourage. Probably a good thing too. His eyes slid down the first paper, then the second, a frown stretched over his face. He calmly stuffed the papers into a coat pocket and turned to his staffers.

"Well," he said, his eyes coursing over the nervous, pasty faces of his subordinates. "I received some interesting news. Some of it is good. Some of it isn't."

The tension in the room just blasted into the stratosphere again.

"Graff?" Zare called in a calm voice.

"Yes, sir," returned Graff, a younger dragon with a couple of medals on his jacket and silver epaulets on his shoulders, stepped forward.

Zare faced him.

"Your intelligence network has been good — until now."

"Sir?"

Zare's eyes narrowed, Graff started to tremble. Everyone else seemed to sense something was coming. Zare fired his right hand to Graff's throat. The young dragon instinctively wrapped his hands around Zare's arm.

"Your intelligence network has let us both down," Zare hissed, tightening his grip around Graff's throat.

The young dragon's knees quivered and he sunk to the floor, still clasping on to Zare's arm.

"I-I don't understand, s-sir," wheezed Graff.

"Don't you now?" Zare spoke in a very calm voice. "It appears that the council-leader's wife survived the explosion, from the bomb your agent set on that boat. Her body was not found in the wreckage."

Graff started to gasp and gag and looked as though he was going to pass out. Zare released his grip. Graff collapsed to his hands and knees, he coughed and gagged and shivered.

"Get up!" Zare ordered. "You're too valuable right now. Well? What's your explanation for this?"

Graff shakily got to his feet. Zare resumed pacing.

"I-I told my agent to sabotage the boiler," Graff explained, fear heavy in his voice now. "He vanished after that. He-He may have been killed in the explosion. A storm blew in the following morning. He hasn't been heard from since!"

"I see," Zare said. "Accidents do happen, from time-to-time," he pointed a finger at Graff's nose, barely touching it, the most malicious of looks spread over his face. "You had better hope that is what happened."

Graff quaked almost uncontrollably. Zare's eyes coursed his staffers for a moment. "Dismissed — all of you — except you, Graff and you, Walker."

The other dragons either bowed or saluted before beating a hasty retreat from the room. Walker and Graff inched closer until they stood side-by-side. Zare approached Walker first. He studied the youngster for a moment, from his wiry mustache to his thin features and his medal-free black jacket. "Walker, is it?"

"Yes, sir!"

"How would you like to earn a few medals to cover up some of that black?"

"Oh, yes, sir!"

Walker's eyes twinkled and the corners of his mouth lifted into a grin.

Zare's attention shifted to Graff. "Our rabbit friends, at Elmshir, are about to receive some guests — four according to this paper — I think five is more accurate."

A quizzical look crossed over Graff and Walker's faces.

"Five, sir?" asked Graff.

"One of them is carrying Goldeye's egg," Zare said, his attention shifting back to Walker. "That's where you come in."

"Yes, sir!" Walker barked. "Uh... sir?"

Zare held up a hand to silence the youngster. "I'm getting to that! One of my contacts reported that a female black dragon left Borq, shortly after the egg bearers did, and she was going in the same direction as they were. She is a suspected resistance member and I want her arrested and brought to me, along with the egg."

"Yes, sir!"

Zare folded his arms and faced Walker. "Go to Elmshir and bring them to me. Well? What are you standing around for? Get going!"

"Yes, sir!" Walker saluted and rushed out of the room.

Zare fixed his icy glare on Graff, who started trembling again.

"You and your intelligence network are getting a chance at redemption," Zare said.

"Thank you, sir."

"Find Goldeye's wife and take her into custody."

Graff shot Zare a confused look. "For what, sir?"

"Think of something!" Zare shouted, causing Graff to flinch. "Trump up charges! If she resists — *kill her!* Use your imagination and be creative for once! Report back to me when you have her."

"Yes, sir." Graff saluted and quickly exited the room.

CHAPTER NINETEEN

-ELMSHIR-

Leaf's company snaked down a long and narrow dirt path that meandered through the thick and prickly underbrush. He sent a third of his company ahead to make sure the road was clear of any unwelcome visitors. The low pitched whoops and roars of the wildlife blended with the squawks, chirps and hisses of birds and crickets that serenaded them from all around.

If Handoe was a prisoner, it didn't seem like it. He strolled with his arms swaying at his sides. Leaf trod beside him, while Maxum and Sandstorm followed close behind. Jessa paid them no attention, she walked just ahead of the rest of Leaf's troops, gazing out into the gnarled tangle of trees.

"In a way, we owe the wildlife, here, a debt of gratitude," Leaf said.

"Yeah," Handoe added. "Like that carcharodontosin we ran in to earlier."

"How so?" Maxum asked.

"Stories abound," Leaf said, glancing back at Maxum and Sandstorm, "the goblins tried to reach Cranch Hollow Warren, first, to destroy it."

"Sent an *entire* army," Handoe put in.

"Yep," Leaf smiled. "These goblins were attacked by a horde of scorpions."

"The goblins were driving on us from the East and North," Handoe added.

Maxum and Sandstorm's attentions shifted to each rabbit as he spoke in turn.

"Scorpions found them first," Leaf continued, "*annihilated* them. Both wings!"

"Some of the bigger creatures paid the griffons and zaltee a few visits," Handoe spoke. "Scattered them like the leaves in the wind."

"That explains why the griffons drove west and attacked Kublisa," Sandstorm said.

"Yes," Handoe replied.

Two soldiers from the advance guard approached Leaf and Handoe. "Sir," spoke one, of them, saluting, "We're there. Just around the bend and over the next hill, and we'll be in Elmshir."

Cranch Hollow Warren, even in its finest days, couldn't hold a candle to the opulence that was Elmshir Warren. It had the same mound-like buildings, but many more of them, and some were much taller and better built. Some of these mound-pillar-like structures were as tall as ten stories. The streets were clean, the trees and lawns neatly pruned and manicured.

Leaf had restraints on Handoe before they walked over the hill leading into town.

"We need to make this look good," Leaf's facial expression showed he wanted nothing to do with this.

"Let's do it," Handoe replied.

"What about us?" Sandstorm asked, his gaze falling on Leaf.

"To my knowledge," Leaf said, "you'll be treated as guests," his attention shifted to Jessa. "All of you."

She nodded her head once.

Maxum was getting the same repressive and tense feelings about Elmshir that Borq had, minus those grotesque statues of Zare. A group of rabbits, all wearing breast-plates, all armed with repeating crossbows except the lead rabbit, who was unarmed, approached Leaf's column, now standing at the town entrance.

The unarmed rabbit stepped in front of Leaf. He was tall and gray furred. He had circular, wire framed glasses parked on his nose and wore a haughty, pompous expression on his scowling face. He wore a blue jacket with all the usual showings of importance, medals, sashes, badges and the like. He shot a contemptuous glare at Handoe before shifting to Leaf.

"Where did you find him?"

Leaf threw up a stiff solute before answering. "Cranch Hollow Warren, sir."

The gray rabbit's attention slid back to Handoe.

"Handoe Wextal," he said in a low voice that oozed contempt. "You were warned to stay away from the rabbit warrens—"

"I came here on my own accord, Jaylem," Handoe interrupted.

The gray rabbit, named Jaylem, swung a hand

across Handoe's face. Sandstorm scrunched up his face, flashed his fangs and moved toward Jaylem. Both Maxum and Leaf held him back.

"Remember where you are, snow leopard," Jaylem boomed, throwing a particularly affronted glare at Sandstorm. " This is Rabbit Territory and you *are* subject to our laws!"

"Only because we let you," Jessa snarled, her eyes boring down on his.

Jaylem seemed unimpressed. He casually strolled to her and lifted his arrogant, black eyes to her face.

"And you are?"

"Jessa."

"What is a *black dragon female* doing with this lot?"

Jessa's eyes narrowed and the corners of her mouth dripped into a frown. She looked as though she wanted to turn Jaylem into a bloody pile of goo. *"That* is none of your business!"

Jaylem acted like he didn't hear what she said and walked back to Handoe. "Handoe Wextal, you are under arrest for violating your banishment, by the authority given to me by *Their Lordships, Fraz and Fray,"* Jaylem looked to the other three. "You are to consider yourselves

Guests of the State."

Jaylem balled up his right hand and lifted it over his left shoulder, coiling it to slap Handoe again. Handoe's eyes glinted; "You slap me again, Jaylem, and that will be the last thing you ever do."

Jaylem looked to Leaf, who kept his eyes fixed ahead and stayed silent. He lowered his hand, pointed a finger at Handoe, while looking over his left shoulder to his troops. "Take him!"

The *State's* accommodations were small and bland, and five stories up in a seven story building. Maxum and Sandstorm sat on small, wooden chairs (the only other furniture in the room were two narrow beds under a rectangular window.) They said nothing to each other. Both seemed deep in thought. Maxum shed his traveling cloak and the pouch and set them on his bed. Jessa was in a room next door.

A knock at their door prompted them to stand and face it.

"It's open," Maxum announced.

Leaf entered. He wore a gleaming, new looking, chrome colored, chest plate.

"Gentle-beings," he greeted, the door slammed shut behind him. "I've been selected to represent Handoe."

"What do you mean, represent him?" Sandstorm inquired.

"Handoe had to be tried first," Leaf said, meeting Sandstorm's gaze.

"Have you done this sort of thing before?" Sandstorm asked.

"Yes."

"What are his chances?"

Leaf's slashed face fell into a frown. A worried look crossed Sandstorm's face.

"That's another reason why I'm here." Leaf told them.

Maxum placed his chair next to Leaf, who sat down. Maxum sat at the foot of his bed, carefully putting himself between Leaf and the incubator. The rabbit shifted his black, living eye and white, dead eye to Maxum. "Relax. Handoe told me about the egg. It's safe."

"Sorry," Maxum returned, yet he didn't lower his guard much.

"Handoe told me you were at Cranch Hollow looking for his crest," Leaf spoke.

"He told me about it, yes," Maxum said.

"We didn't get very far," Sandstorm added. "We ran into you guys a short time later."

Leaf nodded.

"Handoe didn't mention anything as to why it was so important," Sandstorm stated.

"Well," Leaf replied, "it could be very helpful — especially with what he is being charged—"

"Which is, what?" Sandstorm interjected, irritation clear in his voice, his eyes glinted and narrowed.

Leaf drew in a deep breath and slowly let it out, "Cowardice."

Sandstorm and Maxum burst out laughing, while Leaf sighed again.

"I've known Handoe for six years," Sandstorm chortled. "We've been in more scrapes and scuffs and fights and brought in some of the worst criminal gutter slime to pollute Dragonsrod. Handoe is no coward!"

Maxum shifted his attention from Sandstorm to Leaf.

"I know," Leaf said. "I, too, have fought along-side Handoe on many occasions. It is ridiculous to think of him as a coward. That's what I now have to prove."

"When you approached us," Maxum asked,

"you wore a different chest plate. It was scratched, grooved and dented up. Is it like a battle record?"

"Yes," Leaf nodded.

Sandstorm sat back in his chair, his eyes on Leaf, seeming to be studying him carefully.

"We weren't at Cranch Hollow the night it fell, you were," he said. "If you don't have the crest, where do we go to find it?"

"I *don't* have it," Leaf admitted. "Yes, it could be anywhere. That's where you two come in."

"Great," Sandstorm grunted, standing up and started a slow, back-and-forth pacing.

Maxum shot him a stern glance before returning his attention to Leaf. "Where would you suggest we start looking for it?"

Leaf leaned forward on the chair. He rested his elbows on his knees and stroked his chin with his thumb and index finger. He scrunched up his face with a thoughtful expression. "Try the old barracks on the northern end of the ruins."

Sandstorm stopped pacing and looked down at Leaf. "What would it look like?"

"It was L-shaped. Compared to the standard mound-like structures in Cranch Hollow, it...

should be easy enough to find."

"Are you coming with us?" Sandstorm asked.

"No," Leaf muttered. "I have to stay here and prepare Handoe's defense — talk to witnesses, do research, do more paperwork and the like."

"What chance does Handoe have if we don't find this breast-plate?" Maxum asked.

Leaf let out an uncontrollable chuckle. "With Fras and Fray on the judges panel, little to none!"

A short silence followed before Leaf spoke again; "As you are aware, this won't be easy to find. You may have a lot of sifting and sorting to do. You are not prisoners here. You may come and go as you wish. Be warned, Fras and Fray are unpredictable at best, down-right cruel at worst. They probably won't stop you from leaving. You may encounter some resistance on your return trip, which means you may have to resort to some creative measures to get back into the city. I would suggest you get going as soon as possible."

"Understood," Maxum acknowledged as he and Sandstorm nodded.

"Time is short, gentle-beings," Leaf warned, a

look of the deadliest seriousness in his eyes. "Handoe is doomed if you don't find his crest. I need physical proof to back up his story. I will leave you to conduct your search, best of luck, you're going to need it."

"To us all," Sandstorm finished.

CHAPTER TWENTY

-THE THINGS THAT AREN'T AS THEY SEEM-

Moira was jolted awake by River Rat.

"Someone's coming," he said, pointing beyond the trees.

"Well, who is it?" she asked, still half asleep.

Captain Ako also woke up and grumbled something inaudible.

"I was hoping you could tell me," River Rat said to Moira. "You're the one with the height advantage."

Moira stood up and looked in the direction River Rat was pointing. She saw shadowy figures off about one hundred yards distant. They wore dull, charcoal black chest and shoulder armor and helmets. She could see about a dozen of them. They were moving in a column in a southerly direction.

"It's all right," she cried, cracking a wide smile and looking down to River Rat. "It's a group of black dragon soldiers! We're saved!"

River Rat shuddered. "This isn't Black Dragon Territory. What are they doing here?"

"What does it matter?" asked Moira, taken aback by River Rat's sudden caution.

"Black Dragon Territory is land-locked," he countered. "Something's not right here."

"What's goin' on here?" Captain Ako barked, looking highly agitated.

"I say we go and talk to them," Moira said, her gaze shifted from River Rat to Captain Ako. "There's a black dragon patrol out there. My husband probably sent them to find us — we're saved!"

"Agreed," Captain Ako flashed a pointy toothed grin.

River Rat threw his hands around Moira's right wrist and gazed imploringly into her eyes.

"Ma'am, please," he pleaded, shaking his head. "Something *isn't* right about this!"

He stood a better chance of arguing with the

surrounding trees. Moira yanked her hand away from his.

"I'm going!" she snapped.

"We're goin' too, sailor!" Captain Ako ordered, looking sternly at him.

River Rat's head dipped toward his chest, his shoulders sunk as he blew out a dejected sigh. "Yes, sir."

Moira, Captain Ako and a very reluctant River Rat, emerged from the tall and dense wood onto a flat, open meadow toward the squad of soldiers.

"Hello!" Moira called, smiling broadly, holding up her arms. "Hello, we're safe!"

The soldiers exchanged glances with each other before craning their necks to the trio. They wasted little time moving in on the three and quickly surrounded them.

"Who are you?" barked a soldier with one red line on each shoulder plate (a lieutenant's rank.) "What are you doing here?"

Moira was stunned by the lieutenant's harsh tone of voice. This wasn't how a rescuer talked to the rescued. "I'm Council-Leader Goldeye's wife, Moira!"

Warriors of Dragonsrod

The soldiers threw a new round of confused looks at each other.

"Are you now?" the lieutenant growled, his eyes flashed and his alligator-like face lifted into an evil grin.

"I'm Captain Ako and this is my—"

"Fine, fine!" snarled the lieutenant, holding up a hand to silence the captain.

Uh-oh. Something seemed not quite right about this lot they threw themselves to.

"You are a search party, aren't you?" Moira asked, a bewildered look stretched over her face.

The soldiers exploded with a round of deep belly laughs.

"No, lady," chortled the lieutenant, "We're not a search party. But you are coming with us. The three of you are under arrest."

"What for?" shouted River Rat.

"Silence, Zaltee!" the lieutenant shouted back.

He pivoted on his feet and swung his tail, slamming it into River Rat knocking him to the ground.

"Well, really!" yelled Moira incredulously.

Captain Ako stepped toward the lieutenant. His soldiers leveled their crossbows at them. The lieutenant drew his sword and pointed it at

Ako's throat. "Stand down, you!"

"What are we being arrested for?" Moira said to the lieutenant.

"Sabotage."

"Sabotage?" barked Captain Ako.

"Yes," countered the lieutenant icily, who seemed to be enjoying this. "The Silvers found the wreck of a boat and said it looked like it had been deliberately destroyed."

"My scaly tail it was deliberate!" barked Captain Ako.

River Rat grunted as he slowly stood up.

Moira cast him a regretful gaze.

"You should've listened to me," he hissed, glaring back at her.

"The zaltee speaks again, kill him," the lieutenant barked, his cold stare firmly set on Moira. "You are under arrest — now move it!"

Elmshir

Leaf sat behind a small table in a dimly lit room that looked more like a broom closet than an office. Text books on the rabbit legal system were stacked behind him. A small gas lamp softly hissed on the right corner of the table bathing the room in a dull, silvery-yellow glow.

He was reading through statements he had taken and was flipping through a couple different law books that had relevance to this case.

Two tall, dark furred rabbits walked into Leaf's "office" and stood in front of his table. They were identical in appearance from the blue, long tailed coats and white, frilled shirts to their ears lying down behind their heads. They both had a haughty, arrogant strut and an even more pompous sneer on their faces. These were Fras and Fray. The only difference was Fray wore a circular monocle over his left eye.

Leaf stood up, but not at attention.

"I'm very busy," he growled, "What do you want?"

"Is that any way to speak to your older brothers?" Fras asked.

"Not to mention superiors?" Fray added.

Leaf returned to his seat, casting a dark gaze at the two.

"In public, no," he snarled. "In private, *yes!*"

A sharp silence followed.

"What is it, you want?" Leaf asked again, keeping his attention fixed on his research.

Fras and Fray glanced at each other then

down to Leaf.

"We have come to inform you that *new* charges of smuggling are being filed against the accused," Fras said, an evil grin stretched over his and Fray's faces.

"What?" Leaf shouted practically jumping out of his seat. "Smuggling what?"

"Well," began Fray. "We have been informed that one of the accomplices of the accused is carrying stolen property. And one of the accomplices is a fugitive."

"What are you talking about?" Leaf said loudly. "Stolen property? Who's a fugitive?"

Fras and Fray's smiles split even wider. Their eyes glinted against the dull gas light.

"Council-Leader Goldeye's surviving egg is missing," Fray reported. "It is believed that either the accused or the puma is carrying the egg."

"Plus the puma is a wanted criminal," Fras put in.

Leaf regained his composer and returned to his seat. "Wanted for what?"

"Murder of a black dragon soldier," Fray said.

"Thank you for this, information," Leaf sneered. "Just because one of them is carrying the council-leader's egg, doesn't make them smugglers."

"Doesn't it now?" Fras inquired.

"No," Leaf countered. "Suppose the council-leader asked them to take it to safety? His entire clutch was destroyed by *still unknown attackers*. Only the one egg survived. I would like to know what you two would have done differently if it were you."

A brief silence followed.

"Oh, I simply *love* this!" chirped Fray, looking at his twin, Fras . "We have a smuggler whose a coward and a fugitive—"

Leaf shot out of his chair. His facial expression was so dark, it practically changed his brown fur to black. He pointed a finger at Fray whose smile quickly vanished. "You may have an easier time convicting him of smuggling than of cowardice. There are four of us who know what really happened the night Cranch Hollow fell."

Fras and Fray seemed ready for this. They didn't look moved.

"That's why it must remain a secret, dear brother of ours," Fray said, his eyes now twinkling in an evil sort of way.

"Yes the accused was the scapegoat," Fras said, taking up from Fray. "But it was for the betterment of the survivors of our warren."

It was Leaf's turn to be unmoved.

"And just where are the survivors from that night?" Leaf snapped. "I can't get anyone to talk to me, especially from Handoe's unit. What did you do, order them not to talk — threaten them? Bribe them?"

Fras and Fray said nothing, but kept their haughty expressions.

"I'm ashamed to call you my brothers," Leaf spat.

"Be fortunate that we don't feel the same way," Fray said, he and Leaf exchanged glares, "because if we did, it would be unfortunate for you. You know too much, as does the accused. He *will* be silenced."

"And you will as well if you are not careful," warned Fras.

Leaf pointed to the door. "You're wasting my time."

The twins looked at each other for a moment and then flipped another arrogant gaze at Leaf.

"Well," Fray said. "Back to work, then."

"Yes," Fras added, "hop to it."

The two turned to the door and exited, deep in conversation. Leaf sunk into his seat again, keeping an ear focused on the fading sounds of his older brothers' voices until he could no longer hear them. He leaned back and grabbed the top book from a stack behind him. He pulled some folded papers out from under the book's bottom cover and sprawled them on the table. With a pencil, he scribbled the words *'Cranch Hollow: The truth…'*

CHAPTER TWENTY-ONE

-THE TRAVELS OF GENERAL ZMOGE-

Councilor Zare's mansion, Kublisa

Zare was jubilant. He laid in his king-sized bed, smoking a long, green cigar. The bed chamber was dark except for a dim, orange-yellow glow of the streetlights penetrating through the curtains. All was going according to plan. He received the message of the capture of Council-Leader Goldeye's wife. Those carrying the egg were also in custody. His soldiers arrived in Silver Dragon Territory to a thunderous welcome, from what the news prints said. His troops were to train the Silvers in case war should visit their borders — which it will.

He drew in a deep drag from his cigar and

blew out a large cumulus cloud of peppery, sweet smoke. What to do with his "hostages?" He can't let them go. They could blow the lid off of this scheme. He can't kill them either, not yet. Soon it won't matter. Things are going to be very different here. Two obstacles remained, soon, they too, will be dealt with...

"You disappoint me, councilor," came a low pitched, smooth voice from the darkness.

Make that three obstacles.

Zare was unmoved by the sudden intrusion on his privacy.

"I was expecting you," he said to the unseen being. "Well c'mon, show yourself!"

"As you wish."

A shadowy, muscular figure with an ape-like upper body, long arms and goat-like legs and hooves, moved silently from the darkness and stood against the window. He opened his glowing, red eyes and sprouted long, curving ram-like horns from his head. "Better?"

Zare chuckled as he stood from his bed. He discharged another large, super cell-like cloud formation of cigar smoke, which scattered into wisps as he walked through it toward the creature.

"You're moving too slow, councilor," the being criticized.

"No," Zare quickly countered, facing the creature and pointing at it. "You're too impatient! I told you to wait before attacking the griffons—"

"The griffons are no bother to us," the creature said, almost laughing.

"Don't underestimate them," Zare warned as he started pacing.

The creature chuckled again. "They fall back at the mere sight of us. The griffons haven't yet realized the goblins have betrayed them, and are allied to us now."

"HMPH!" Zare snorted.

He hated goblins. They were conniving and cowardly and only found courage when they held an advantage in numbers, or size, or had bigger friends with them. Totally untrustworthy filth. He remembered once seeing a dozen gold dragons kill off half a goblin legion and frighten away the other half just by their size.

"You are being lured in, Loothar," Zare said, shooting an icy gaze at the creature. "The griffons *will* counter-attack. You had best be ready when they do."

"When are you going to act?" Loothar asked.

"Very soon. I'm waiting on one last piece to put itself into motion."

"Does this Councilor Deela suspect that you have taken over her country?"

Zare grunted. "No. She is convinced that my troops are training her pathetic lot in case war comes."

"Hmm," Loothar growled. "What of Councilors Goldeye and Robsko?"

"They are too suspicious of me. I can't move against them both at once without being exposed."

"You do have a problem."

"As I said, I have a piece that is about to move, which will be another few days."

Loothar's eyes followed Zare as he paced.

"Inform me when you have moved!"

"Yes. Yes, I WILL!" Zare shouted at a dark and empty room. "I hate it when he does that!"

Orzolla Pass, White Dragon Territory near Red Dragon border.

The landscape in this area was the polar opposite from the trouble-spot wastes in the East. Here, large snow capped, craggy mountains shot up thousands of feet into the atmosphere, while coniferous forests carpeted the valley floors, looming over roads, rivers and paths.

General Zmoge casually rode his tyrocc down a dusty, bandy road toward the Red dragon border. He knew bandits hid out in these valleys. He wasn't really concerned. If anyone was stupid enough to jump out from the trees and try to take his mount, his armor and his weaponry, they would be sorry…

Three large red dragons charged out from the pines and stood in front of him. One held a cross bow aimed at Zmoge's head. Another grasped the tyrocc's reins with one clawed hand and held his sword in the other. The third one casually held his sword with the blade pointing down, apparently thinking that this would be an easy target.

"Get off the beast and give us everything you have," he demanded in a deep voice.

Zmoge's eyes narrowed and his alligator-like face lifted into a crooked smile.

"I don't think so," he hissed.

Zmoge's tyrocc launched itself up on its hind feet throwing the reins out of the second

Warriors of Dragonsrod

dragon's grasp. Zmoge reached for his sword. The dragon with the cross bow fired — Zmoge blocked the bolt away with a slash of his sword and charged his mount at that dragon. As the tyrocc trampled the cross bow shooter, Zmoge sprung from the saddle, bounded once from the ground, and decapitated the rein grabber with one swipe of his sword before landing gracefully in front of the stunned ring-leader. He flicked the blood off of his sword before sheathing it.

The surviving bandit's eyes bulged from their sockets and his mouth hung open. He threw his sword to the ground and sprinted down the road shouting, "Mercy, mercy — have mercy!"

"Oh, no," Zmoge hissed. "You were going to show me no mercy, so I shall show you none."

He picked up the terrified criminal's sword and raced after him with it, cutting him down moments later. Zmoge climbed back on his mount and proceeded down the dusty road as though nothing had happened. Too bad, really, that was the kind of rabble he needed. But this lot left him no choice. He couldn't afford to let this happen again. After all, he was supposed to be recruiting these low-lives, not single handedly wiping them out. He pulled on his tyrocc's reins and steered the beast back to scene of the slaughter.

He needed to show these dregs that he meant business. He figured this element either knew each other, or knew of each other and if they saw these weapons dangling from his tyrocc's neck, they would be wise to hear what he had to say.

Zmoge rode his tyrocc several miles into Red Dragon Territory before stopping in front of a thatched roofed, cream colored, T-shaped building. The swords he took from the bandits clanked together around his mount's neck. A muscular red dragon wearing a brown vest over a tight, white shirt and a bar tender's apron around his waist stepped out of the building. His attention immediately fell on to Zmoge, who was crawling down from his mount.

"G' morning," greeted the red dragon.

Zmoge nodded.

The red dragon's eyes slid to the cutlery hanging from the tyrocc's neck.

"I recognize those swords," his voice was casual.

"Do you now?" Zmoge cocked up an eyebrow.

"Yes. How did you take them from Bragg and his brothers?"

Zmoge's face lifted into a twisted grin. "Let's just say they didn't give them to me."

The red dragon nodded.

"Can't say I'm sorry," he said. "Bragg lived up to his name. In fact, he lived up to it all too well."

Zmoge remained silent.

"He had it coming, if you ask me," the red dragon added.

Zmoge's eyes absorbed the landscape around the tavern. They moved from the mountains and dense forest that surrounded him, to the open and picturesque view of the rolling hills and deep cut valleys that made up much of Red Dragon Territory.

"What kind of clientele do you get around here?" Zmoge asked, still looking around at the breathtaking scenery.

The red dragon shrugged. "All kinds, really. Travelers, bounty hunters, soldiers and most likely the criminal element, just to name a few."

Zmoge's eyes zipped back to the red dragon. "Of course you don't ask them about their business?"

The red dragon flashed a smile. "That's one reason why I'm still alive."

"What's the busiest time of the day, here?"

The red dragon scrunched up his face in thought as he gazed skyward. "After dusk, usually."

Zmoge nodded again. "Do you have lodging here?"

"Yeah, sure."

The red dragon stepped back and opened the door and waved his left hand inward, his smile seemed to grow wider. "If you will accompany me, I will check you in to one of our rooms."

"That would be acceptable, thank you," Zmoge replied, stepping by the red dragon and into the tavern. "I want to get a look at who habits this place."

Zmoge leaned back in his chair, folded his arms, and placed his feet on his table, ale slopped out of a tankard that was an arm's reach away. He sat in a dark corner and watched the patrons as they came into the tavern. He studied each one putting them through a mental process of elimination, the qualifications, of which, were known only to him. Some came in and ate a meal and then left. Others ordered drinks and didn't stop until they were intoxicated lumps slumped over their tables, or at the bar, or sprawled out on the floor. This sort won't do. They were either too tame, or too out-of-control with their vices to be of any use to him. It was still early, however, he was patient — he would wait.

The number of customers grew with the gathering gloom of night and soon the tavern was standing room only. The lights were dim and smoke from cigars and pipes crept and swirled around the place like a thick, bitter smelling fog. Chatter and laughter from dozens of conversations thundered around the walls of the bar. Dragons from every clan intermingled with bears, zaltee, raccoons and various other beings. Zmoge hadn't moved other than to take occasional drinks from his tankard of ale. His eyes were set on a group of nervous looking gazelles seated across the bar from him and next to the door. He wasn't the only one watching them. His gaze slid to the table, in front of his, where four thick-maned lions sat. They were huddled close together and apparently in conversation. Every-now-and-then, one would cast a malicious glance at the gazelles and then back in to the huddle.

Zmoge kept watching, whatever they had in mind was not going to bode well for the gazelles if they got caught. The gazelles seemed to think something was amiss. They all stood up and with a forced calm, exited the tavern. The lions followed moments later.

Zmoge was going to follow them. At the same instant that the last lion walked out the door, five cannidenes filtered in and sat at the table recently vacated by the lions. His eyes ran all over these dog-like creatures, from their stalky bodies to their black, bulbous noses. They looked tough and wore heavy, leather bands on their forearms that were scratched — and had burn marks on them — *myter handlers!* Myters were not for the wimpy or the faint-of-heart.

Zmoge's eyes twinkled. A crooked smile split across his face. This was the right group he needed for his — Zare's — plan to work. He stood up and walked to their table and bought them a round of drinks… time to do some business.

Zmoge had been here at the tavern for days.

The meetings with the cannidene myter handlers went well. The handlers expressed interest in what he had to say. He spoke to many patrons, who in turn, said they would keep their eyes open. The fat monitor lizard, Jinks, strolled into the tavern. His tongue flicked in an excited fashion. His eyes twinkled and his face cracked open with a strangely contorted smile. He invited himself to sit at Zmoge's table.

"I have information," Jinks said, his smile widened.

"What kind of information?" Zmoge asked, his dead looking eyes running all over Jinks's face.

Jinks rested his elbows on the table and clasped his long, clawed fingers together. "Let's talk business first."

Zmoge burst out laughing. The smile slid off of Jinks's face.

"What makes you think I will do business with you?" Zmoge asked.

"Well, I-I-uh know where the egg is," Jinks stammered.

"So?"

Jinks swished his tail stiffly. He flicked his tongue at a faster pace. Beads of sweat glistened on his head.

"Tell me, lizard, where the egg is and I will consider how much it is worth," Zmoge hissed.

"They are at Elmshir Warren," Jinks blurted, irritation clear in his tone of voice.

"Elmshir is a good distance from here," Zmoge stated. "The rabbits in charge are loyal to Zare. If the egg bearers have been captured, then my job is done and your information is worthless. BE GONE!"

A flabbergasted gaze splashed over Jinks's face. He looked as though he was scrambling for something — *anything* — to say that would keep Zmoge interested.

"But don't you want to be the one to hand the egg over to your leader?" was all Jinks could bring himself to say.

Zmoge leaned back in his chair and let out another laugh. He was clearly loving the blank, desperate expressions flashing over the lizard's scarred face.

"Perhaps I should go to Elmshir," he said, "just to see what is going on."

Jinks's face lifted into a relieved grin and his marble-like eyes twinkled. "I know a short-cut in which we could be there in three days."

"Three days," Zmoge repeated, his eyes narrowed. "We'll leave at dawn tomorrow. You had better be right."

CHAPTER TWENTY-TWO

-GOLDEYE, THE SUSPICIOUS-

Council-Leader Goldeye's office, Kublisa.

"He's up to something," Goldeye growled, "I'm certain of it!"

"But what?" Robsko looked nonplussed and shrugged his shoulders.

Goldeye flopped down on his chair, causing it to squeak and groan. It had been another grueling and difficult session today. More accusations and innuendos flew about today resulting in more hurt feelings and bruised egos. Goldeye thought he might have to call on the security troops again when Tabric accused Zhangi of conspiracy after the Gold dragon councilor offered to open up trade relations with their once bitter enemies, the griffons. Zhangi did not react well to this and threatened his nearest physical cousin to a duel right there in front of all the delegations. The whole time, Councilor Zare sat back and watched. Everybody else gasped and showed disdain at the heated exchange — except him. Goldeye still had no proof Zare was up to anything and was not about to accuse him of wrong doing. In a fit of frustration, he slammed a fist on his desk top. Robsko sat in front of the desk and seemed to stare out into space. The two sat silent for a few moments until Jossic entered the office clutching a copy of the *Kublisa Times* in his right hand and wearing a worried expression on his face.

"Have either of you seen this?" Jossic asked, holding the paper up.

"What's being said now?" Goldeye replied in a dry tone of voice.

He cast Jossic a tired, somewhat irritated gaze.

"The griffons have declared war on the vordral," Jossic slid his eyes down the paper. "They are preparing for a major offensive."

Goldeye smirked. "The presses are behind on

this one."

"From what I have been hearing," Robsko said, "it's the vordral who are doing all the attacking."

The news did not surprise Goldeye. It should not have surprised anyone else. In fact, Romar all but announced they were going to attack the vordral and warned the dragons to prepare for war. The old dragon's frustrations grew. He was feeling ever-more powerless in the Grand Council Chamber. Just today, he had been defeated in a vote not to send black dragon troops to Silver Dragon Territory. The three sitting in this room said no. The other five didn't see the danger and approved it. Councilor Zare brought up the matter for a vote. Councilor Deela seemed all-too anxious for it. Robsko was especially worried, he now had black dragon troops to the North and to the South. Goldeye and Jossic didn't like it because Zare could now influence Deela's votes and opinions to fit into whatever twisted scheme he had up his sleeve.

"What is he up to?" Goldeye asked, seemingly for the umpteenth time.

Robsko and Jossic remained silent.

"Why the sudden interest in the Silver Dragon Territory? What's there for him to want?" Goldeye snarled.

"Maybe he's trying to cut my people off from the rest of Dragonsrod," Robsko said, a dark expression crossing his face.

"Could he be planning a coups?" Jossic asked.

The gazes of Goldeye and Robsko fell on him.

"No," Goldeye countered. "It wouldn't make sense to attack Robsko and leave me unscathed. I would know it was him and I would be able to expose him. I don't see Zare making such a stupid move."

"Maybe," Jossic responded. "He also may be going for you both at the same time. He has a lot to gain by taking you two out."

The three sat silent for a few moments, each apparently deep in his own thoughts.

A cool wind whispered through the trees and an inky blackness shrouded over the seemingly deserted streets. The street lamps illuminated the sidewalks in a silvery glow. Goldeye walked the labyrinthine streets from his office to his house, alone. Just as he had done every night. Risky? Maybe. He could have Bard escort him.

He could have had an entire regiment of elite troops hand-hold him to his door step every night. No. He walked by himself every night for several reasons. Added security was not necessary, for one. The crime rate in Kublisa is pretty low for another. Plus, no dragon in his right mind would try to attack an old warrior, who was just as good with most kinds of weapons, now, as he ever was. Most importantly, he wanted to show that he wasn't afraid. It seemed at times he was taunting any would-be attacker— try to assault me — you will be sorry.

    Goldeye walked through the city park down a stone path that cut through a bed of emerald green grass. He was nearly home. He always marveled the beautiful scene, a variety of trees sprouting up here-and-there. He was taken by how the reds, yellows and greens of the leaves seemed to grow brighter at night. He loved the sweet, clean smells and the natural calm it seemed to exude. It was just as relaxing as walking around on his balcony at night. Tonight, however, something was different. An uneasy feeling swept over him. His mismatched eyes scoured the tranquil scene for the source of his uneasiness.

The pitch-black figure of Loothar seemed to appear out of nowhere on to the path no more than fifty feet away. Goldeye froze in his tracks. He reached into his tunic and pulled out a dagger. "Stay where you are! I'm armed and I know how to use this!"

Loothar's eyes narrowed.

"I do not wish to harm you," he said in a deliberate, steady tone of voice. "This is the only time I will appear to you in this manner."

"What do you want?" Goldeye asked, lowering the dagger, but not putting it away.

"To talk with you. One leader to another."

Goldeye sheathed his dagger. "Alright."

The two walked closer to one-another until they stood a few feet apart. Loothar was a good head taller than Goldeye, who didn't seem intimidated. The vordral leader glanced around at the colorfully lit skyline of Kublisa.

"I have forgotten how beautiful this city is," Loothar's lips curved up in a slight smile.

"I do hope you came here for something other than idle chit-chat," Goldeye snapped.

Loothar's red eyes settled on Goldeye's face. "I have come to ask you not to get involved in our war with the griffons."

"We have no reason to get involved. Not as of yet," Goldeye assured the other.

"My people are not as war-like as the griffons say."

"The griffons haven't said much of anything at all," Goldeye tried to keep his tone as neutral as possible. "I visited an attack site recently. I saw huge pillars of smoke. The griffon ambassador told me you were attacking your own. Is that true?"

Loothar's black face showed a white toothed grin that looked as if it were painted on. "That was an internal matter. One of the chieftains stepped out of line."

Goldeye narrowed his eyes and his face slipped into a frown. "So you destroyed a village and massacred the populace to send a message to your horde?"

"You do what you must to keep your people in line," Loothar said in a very casual tone of voice.

"Indeed," Goldeye returned.

A tense pause followed. The old dragon decided it was best to calm things down a bit. After all, this was another leader — a leader of a people he knew next to nothing about.

"Why?" he asked in a calm voice. "Why, after three hundred years, would you wait to come out like this?"

"Revenge."

"Revenge?"

"We have fought the griffons off-and-on for nearly a thousand years," bitterness saturated Loothar's smooth voice. "The griffons attacked us, razed our villages to ground, drove us from our hunting grounds. They pushed us into the furthest reaches of our lands. We had to fight back — we have fought back!"

"I see," Goldeye was not impressed.

"You should be thanking us," Loothar growled. "Instead, you are considering fighting us."

"Thank you?" Goldeye gasped, taken aback by this. "What for?"

Loothar's face scrunched into an angry expression. His fists were balled tightly together and he let out a low, guttural growl. Goldeye considered drawing his dagger again, but decided not to when Loothar stepped back and looked to be trying to calm himself down.

"Why should we be thanking you?" Goldeye pressed on, not backing down.

Loothar glared at the old dragon with such a contemptuous look that could have froze the other's blood. "Do you think that it was your leadership that won your war with the griffons?"

"Well," Goldeye replied, cocking up his eyebrows. "Yes."

"The griffons were fighting *us* at the same time as they were battling with you!" Loothar returned matter-of-factly. "We lured them out to fight, forcing them to send armies to chase after us instead of overrunning you. Make no mistake," his eyes narrowed, he pointed at Goldeye. "we weren't doing it to help you!"

"Yet you are paying me this visit to—"

"—Tell Dragonsrod to stay out of this war!"

Goldeye stood, unimpressed by the vordral's request/threat. "Don't give us any reasons to get involved!"

Loothar smiled, his red, glowing eyes and his bright, white teeth gave him a ghostly, almost demonic look. Goldeye sensed that this meeting was nearing its end.

"You were right not to trust Councilor Zare," Loothar said. "He's far too ambitious — watch your back."

With that parting shot, Loothar stepped off the path and in to the trees where he became one with the darkness. Goldeye stood alone once more. His suspicions deepened. His questions broadened. It seemed this vordral is in some kind of partnership with Zare. But partners in what? Zare could be involved in some kind of legitimate dealings with the secretive vordral. This he doubted. Loothar spoke of revenge against the griffons. The old dragon thought about the *Ancient Military Campaigns of the Dragonsrod* book. Could Loothar possibly be seeking vengeance for the defeat they suffered at the hands of Gortha the Great three-hundred years ago? Was this "friendly visit" just that? Or was it a scouting mission to test what kind of a possible threat Goldeye could be?

CHAPTER TWENTY-THREE

-HANDOE'S CREST-

Elmshir

Maxum slowly creaked open the door. He and Sandstorm quietly exited the room and into the hallway. The next door opened and Jessa emerged from the darkness.

"You weren't planning on leaving without me, were you?" she hissed, her eyes pounding on to their faces.

"No, no, not at all," Sandstorm said, though his eyes seemed to say 'yes we were.'

"I heard everything that rabbit said," she whispered loudly. "Cranch Hollow is not a playground. You're going to need all the help you can get."

"Fine," Sandstorm said, giving in to idea she was coming whether or not he liked it. "Grab your things, we'll wait."

"No need," she responded, still in her chest and shoulder armor, her sword dangled at the ready from her torso belt. "Let's go."

Without another word, the three quietly exited the building and headed for Cranch Hollow.

The time seemed to creep by for Handoe. He had little to do except lay or sit on his bunk, pace on the narrow strip of a wood floor between the bunk and the wall. He could look out the barred entrance of his cell at a naked, gray-green wall across the hallway that spanned the entire length of the jail. He tried talking to the guard. No luck. The guard sat behind a small table kitty-corner to Handoe's cell. He always had his nose buried in either a book or a magazine and seemed statue-like at times. He grunted or coughed from time-to-time, showing Handoe that he was still alive.

Handoe was seeing what it was like to be on the other side of the bars. The only thing worse than the boredom was the deathly quiet. To his knowledge, he was the only prisoner in this building. He made no apologies for why he was in this predicament. He knew, sooner or later, he had to confront the wrong-doing Fras and Fray had burdened him with.

He had faith in Leaf's ability to defend him and clear him of these ridiculous charges. He was certain the brothers were planning something to ensure his doom. He knew how devious they were and what they would resort to, to get their way. He had faith in Sandstorm to somehow find his crest and get it down here — discredit Fras and Fray — and get out of town to get the egg to safety.

No, his friends, Leaf and Sandstorm, wouldn't let him down. He knew the cowardice charge had no chance of sticking. But if Fras and Fray *still could* get a guilty verdict… Well… he wasn't going down without a fight. But for now — all he could do was wait.

Cranch Hollow wasn't as far away as it seemed. The trip to Elmshir, a few days earlier, was pretty slow and leisurely. Now, however, time was of the essence. Sandstorm, Maxum and

Jessa quickly cut and scurried though the twisting and winding road back to the ruins. So quick was the return trip — the sun was not yet up. No matter, the three had excellent night vision, Sandstorm and Maxum had keen senses of hearing and smell. All three were light on their feet which made it easy to lose any one, or anything, that might be tailing them.

The moment they reached the southern-most street, Maxum and Sandstorm went one way, while Jessa went another.

"I hope she knows what to look for," Sandstorm said, his eyes followed her as she vanished into the ruins.

"She claims to have heard what Leaf said," Maxum reminded him.

They ran along a narrow, overgrown path that used to be an avenue, through the square, and into the northern section of the ruins. They stopped in front of a tree and shrub covered L-shaped structure that looked to be losing the battle with time and the elements. Part of the building had already collapsed on itself. The rest appeared ready to go at anytime.

Maxum moved to the structure's fallen-in west-wing, while Sandstorm walked to the other side. The rising sun was raising the pall of darkness from the ruins, casting long, ghostly shadows and bathing everything in a pale, blue-gray light. Maxum drew his sword, better to be prepared in case something comes charging out at him. He peeked around some trees and brush that appeared to be growing out of the still standing North wall. He moved to a ground floor window, the glass had long since been broken out.

Maxum cautiously poked his head through the window. His eyes coursed the wreckage which was now overrun by wave-after-wave of grass that stuck up like a strange looking shaggy, green carpet.

"If it's under all of this," he muttered to himself, "we'll never find it."

"Hey, Max," he heard Sandstorm call. "Over here."

Sandstorm found a doorway that gave the impression it was a cave with all the plant life growing around it. The two gazed momentarily at the dark and dank hole, a slight mildew smell wafted out from it. Sandstorm drew his sword, both cats' tails twitched and flicked with a sort of nervous anticipation. They exchanged glances.

Sandstorm bowed and slowly pointed his sword to the doorway. "Age before beauty, sir."

Maxum belched out a derisive grunt and moved through the doorway. Their eyes were black balls soaking up every ounce of light like sponges. Their ears pricked forward and their whiskers stood at full alert. The hallway was largely in tact with bits of rubble, here and there, and roots snaked across the floor and dangled from the ceiling. The two stalked and padded around the obstacles until they reached an intersection leading down two equally black corridors. Maxum peered into the darkness leading to the west wing.

"It's completely caved in."

Sandstorm nodded.

Maxum's eyes slid toward the east wing corridor.

"Well?" Sandstorm asked.

Maxum stepped to one side, bowed, and pointed his sword into the darkness. "Youth before brains."

Sandstorm flashed a wry smile with a 'get lost' expression on his face and then moved down the corridor. They didn't get very far. Their ears shifted to the sounds of running feet and anxious voices.

"What the—?" Maxum said.

"Shh!" Sandstorm cut in, holding a finger to his lips .

The two made like holes in a wall. Apparently Jessa had run into some friends.

— "She ran this way!" —

— "Watch yourselves, she's armed!"—

"Find her and arrest her!!" shouted an authoritative voice. "We need to be at Elmshir by nightfall to collect the fugitives and the egg!"

Maxum and Sandstorm looked at each other. Maxum's free hand instinctively clutched the straps holding the incubator in the pouch against his back. The sounds of clanking armor and padding feet faded into the distance.

"C'mon," Sandstorm said. "Our time has just gotten shorter."

The two walked a few paces until they found a stair way leading up to the second and third floors. Maxum trusted the rickety steps about as far as he could throw the building. They had to go and check out the upper floors. Sandstorm, gingerly stepped off on the second floor, while Maxum crept up the stairs and scanned the remains of the third floor. Nothing. No metal plates, no swords, no dishes. Just tree shoots, shrubs, some spiders and a few snakes and a lot of debris.

Sandstorm and Maxum emerged from the barracks looking crestfallen. Handoe's crest was the proverbial needle in the haystack. *It could be anywhere!*

Elmshir

Leaf walked in to the jail.

"Leave us!" he ordered the guard, who put down his book and exited the jail.

Leaf had a worried look on his scarred face and cast a mournful stare at Handoe.

"What?" Handoe asked.

Leaf sighed.

"There are new charges against you."

Handoe's brow fell over his eyes.

"New charges?"

"Fras and Fray claim you are smuggling the council-leader's egg out of the country."

Handoe burst out laughing. Leaf remained stone-faced.

"Those idiots will stop at nothing to make sure I'm put away!" Handoe chortled.

"Those *idiots* are also two of the five presiding

judges here," Leaf countered.

Handoe stopped laughing. "Send a wire to Council-Leader Goldeye."

"I have," Leaf said. "No reply as of yet."

A brief silence followed.

"Your friends left for Cranch Hollow during the night," Leaf reported. "In fact, they left their quarters moments before a security detail arrived there to arrest them."

"Good," Handoe barked. "If anybody can find my crest, it'll be Sandstorm."

Cranch Hollow ruins

Sandstorm and Maxum stood in front of a long, snaking, shallow depression, just to the north of the barracks ruin. This depression was once a defensive trench that ran behind the grass and moss covered remains of a wood and earth defensive wall. Sandstorm's eyes sunk to his feet to two leg bones and a skeletal foot, most likely belonging to a goblin.

"This trench could go on for miles," Maxum said, looking to his left.

"Didn't Handoe say he was on the right flank?" Sandstorm asked, his eyes fixed on the leg bones.

"He did."

The two stepped in to the overgrown trench, scanning every inch as they moved. Sometimes, they would pad their feet against something metallic.

"Watch your step," Maxum warned, "you may stab yourself with an old arrow head, or a rusty sword if you are not careful."

Good advice.

Maxum and Sandstorm poked the ground with their sword tips. Other than a couple of rusted cans and swords, an arrow head or two they found nothing that would be of any help to clearing Handoe's good name. Sandstorm's frustrations grew, his face slid into an angry scowl, his ears sunk closer to his head.

Maxum and Sandstorm moved away from the trenches and the barracks and toward the ruined town. This search was not getting any easier, it was like trying to catch sunlight with one's furred hands. Jessa emerged from a wrecked mound holding a partially rusted, beat-up piece of metal, resembling a chest-plate.

"Here," she said, throwing the plate at Sandstorm's feet. "Is this what you're looking for?"

Sandstorm's face and ears pricked up as he scooped up the armor and studied it. This plate had deep scratches and grooves cut across it from swords and other blades. A large dent, the size of an orange, from what was probably a hammer blow, sat just under a diamond shaped indent where a crest had once been. The right shoulder strap was completely rotted away and the left strap looked to have been cut in two. Whoever wore this plate, did not escape injury.

Jessa's eyes fell on Sandstorm. "Does this belong to your friend?"

"Without the crest, there's no way to be sure." he said.

"Where did you find it?" Maxum asked.

Jessa pointed to the ruin she had just stepped out from. "I saw another plate, similar to that one in the same building."

"We should probably grab it, just to be sure," Sandstorm said.

"Who were your friends?" Maxum asked, his eyes moving up to Jessa's face.

"A squad of black dragon soldiers on their way to Elmshir," she replied, pointing a finger at Maxum. "They want that egg you're holding on to."

"They want you, too," he shot back.

"Not badly enough," she countered. "They could've captured me shortly after we ran into each other."

"What happened?" Sandstorm asked.

"After we separated, I ran into one of their scouts," she spoke with a wide, triumphant smile. "We exchanged sword blows. He fought like he needed to practice more. I took his sword and smashed him over the head with the hilt. They chased me around for a bit until one of their officers told them," she lowered her voice, "'We have to be in Elmshir to get that egg,' and they moved on."

"*We* need to get to Elmshir," Sandstorm said. "Let's hope one of these armor plates is his."

CHAPTER TWENTY-FOUR

-THE NIGHT ESCAPE-

The rain drummed a steady beat against the wooden roof of the makeshift holding cage sounding like a thousand little hands slapping against a table top. Moira, and Captain Ako huddled miserably close together to try and keep warm. River Rat sat behind them, brooding and keeping to himself. The three were cold and soaking wet. Only metal bars sandwiched between a wood floor and roof stood between them and the elements and whatever else might be out there.

Moira tried to talk to River Rat on more than

one occasion. He would have none of it, he was still too angry with her. It was a highly stressful situation and she was trying to think of any way to break the tensions.

She turned to Captain Ako for conversation. "You've been to Abyssina?"

"Oh, yes," he replied, also seeming eager to break the tension. "Many, many times."

"What's the country like?"

"It's a beautiful place! The people are lovely!"

"HMPH!" grunted River Rat. "That depends on your point-of-view!"

"What are the people like?" she asked, trying to ignore River Rat.

"The abyssins are a tall, cat-like people with several different types and colors of fur," Captain Ako replied.

"Really?"

"Oh, yes, ma'am. The most striking feature about them are their eyes."

"What are they like?"

"Almond-shaped. They have dark colorings from green and blue to brown and gray with a curious black lining around them — beautiful creatures!"

"And heartless!" River Rat shot out.

"What do you mean by that?" Moira asked, shooting River Rat an icy glare.

Captain Ako spoke first; "River Rat's people have had it pretty hard over the last three centuries."

River Rat grunted again. Captain Ako's eyes slid to his sole-surviving crew mate. He looked as though he was trying choose his words carefully. "His people have been forced into nomadic ways by just about everybody in the region — junglewolves, cannidene, hyenids, abyssins and… we dragons."

Moira's gaze at River Rat softened. "I see why they sided with griffons—"

"The griffons are the only ones not to treat us like vermin!" River Rat interrupted.

The conversation came to a tense end. River Rat turned his back to the two dragons and said nothing more.

The rain subsided during the night. The inmates, however, received no relief. The hot, merciless, summer sun beat down on their cage. The humidity was so thick it felt as though they were drinking the air. Cool breezes were few and far between. What else was few and far between was the arrival and quantity of food. Their captors didn't seem too concerned over their well-being. So much so, not even a guard had been placed to watch them. Maybe these soldiers felt they didn't need a guard considering the cage was out in the middle of a pretty open encampment, so every eye could fall on them at any time. That was understandable, the lack of food and water was not.

"How 'bout some food!" Captain Ako shouted at two soldiers as they walked by the cage.

"Eat yer zaltee!" one called back, laughing.

River Rat had been quiet since last night. Moira had made no further attempts to talk to him. She felt sad and somewhat guilty for him and for the plight of his people. Her remorse for not listening to him, back in the woods, was reaching new heights with every passing minute. How was she supposed to know this band of dragons was up to no good? One thing was certain, she will listen to him next time — if there is a next time.

River Rat paced back-and-forth. His eyes bounced around from the wooden floor to the tents pitched near the surrounding trees and shrubs.

"What are you doing?" Moira asked him.

River Rat didn't answer at first. He looked at her for a moment. Not with an angry glare, but a calculating, deep thinking look. "This wood is soft."

"What do you mean?" she asked, a quizzical expression splashed over her face.

He opened his mouth and clicked his teeth together. "I took a sample bite of this floor last night. The heavy rains have made the floor soft and spongy. I could probably chew a hole—"

"You can't chew a hole big enough for all three of us to crawl out of," Moira exclaimed.

River Rat's red eyes twinkled and he flashed a toothy smile. "No. Only big enough for *me* to crawl through."

Moira's brow dropped again, she cast him a confused look. Captain Ako, however, picked up on it.

"Good thinking, lad!"

River Rat stared at Moira.

"I saw where they keep the keys to this cage," he told her, his eyes still twinkled. "They aren't watching us... look around."

She did so.

What were their captors doing here? Security seemed totally lax. Anything could waltz through this camp and these "soldiers" didn't appear to care. They moved about doing a variety of things. The soldiers acted as though the prisoners weren't even here.

"How long do you think it would take to chew through the floor?" Captain Ako asked him.

River Rat's eyes fell to the floor. "An hour, maybe less."

He crouched on his hands and knees.

"You're starting now?" Moira cocked up her eyebrows, her mouth hung open.

"Why not?" River Rat countered, looking up at her. "They haven't fed us much over the last couple of days. To them, it will look like I am trying to feed myself — probably think it's *funny*, too."

He turned to the floor at the northern corner, facing the pitched tents, and the one with the key in it. He drew in a deep breath and slowly let it out as he began to chew. Moira and Captain Ako watched as the chewing sounds spilled out from the cage.

"Thiff floor tafftes terrible," he muttered through a full mouth.

Three soldiers, casually walking by the cage, did stop. They pointed fingers and laughed at River Rat, as he chewed.

Feigning fright, he jumped away from the bars and behind Moira.

"FEED US!" she shouted, launching herself at the bars and shaking them.

The soldiers only laughed harder.

"We'll feed ya," one of them boomed. "We just have to find something to feed you to." The soldiers walked away.

Moira placed her hands on her gurgling belly.

"If they don't feed us something soon," she groaned, her eyes sinking to the floor. "I'll help you chew us out of here."

River Rat and Captain Ako looked at her and grinned.

The sun was sinking behind the forested horizon, dragging much of the day's suffocating heat with it. A soldier finally did bring them some food and drink. They hungrily ripped apart and ate a loaf of bread and gulped down a canteen of water. Soldiers lit torches and posted them around the outer edges of the camp, largely to keep the local wildlife at bay. No torch was placed near the cage. The soldiers, probably felt the inmates did not deserve it.

The darkness was as thick as tar. The shimmering flames of the torches looked like swarms of fireflies for the light didn't seem to extend much further out into the black of night. This suited River Rat just fine. He kept working at his escape hole. After a few minutes, he was out and scurried across the campsite to the tent holding the keys.

He did not come back right away, in fact, he seemed to be gone for ages.

"What's keeping him?" Moira asked.

Captain Ako shrugged his shoulders.

A soldier walked by the cage. Moira and Captain Ako tensed up and exchanged horrified glances. Dragons have good night vision — if he should look and see only *two* prisoners instead of three… Captain Ako swallowed some air and let out a loud burp. Moira glared at him with an 'excuse you' look.

"I didn't want to eat him," he moaned, patting his belly. "But I have to admit, he was tasty."

He winked at her.

"You could've saved me some," she said, in mock protest.

They both watched the soldier, who cracked a smile and then stalked away.

Moira blew out a sigh of relief. "I credit you on your quick thinking."

"Ar me lady," he replied, smiling. "I'm not a captain for nothing."

The cage door creaked open.

Moira and Captain Ako craned their necks to see River Rat standing there.

"C'mon," he said in a loud whisper.

"What took you so long?" Moira asked.

"I left our friends with a little parting gift."

The two dragons crawled out of the cage and followed River Rat into the woods. Moments later, an orange/white flash followed by a loud POP — a tent exploded. Screams and shrieks came from those who had been too close. Tents were flattened. Soldiers ran in every-which direction with terrified and confused expressions. Fire splattered across the camp as though it were attacking the site. The cage was completely engulfed and lay in a twisted, burning pile several feet from where it originally sat.

"What was in that tent?" Moira gasped, looking at River Rat.

"Boxes of black powder and kegs full of some kind of pitch."

Another explosion rocked the fiery campsite.

The three trudged through the woods, the orange glow shimmered on the tree trunks.

"How did you set it off?" Moira asked.

"I managed to pry open a box and spray a small trail of powder to the entrance," River Rat answered. "It took all of the matches I had left. But I figured we needed a diversion. They'll be too busy fighting the flames to be looking for us."

"Or better still," Captain Ako added, "they'll think we were killed in the explosion. Good work, lad!"

They moved throughout the night in a southerly direction. By dawn, the trio emerged from the woods and stood, facing a flat ocean-scape on one side and a grassy plain with a dusty road zig-zagging toward a copse of trees to the South. Captain Ako stopped by the road and drew in a long sniff of the salty air.

"That's more like it!" he crowed, smiling. "I know where we are!"

"Sir?" River Rat said as he and Moira turned to look at him.

"You wanted to see the abyssins, me lady?" he looked at Moira and pointed. "Just yonder, about five miles, behind those trees, is Abyssina and safety."

River Rat's ears cocked up and his pointed nose went into the air.

"You don't need to say it, lad," Captain Ako said, his happy expression slid into one of worry. "We got company."

"What is that?" Moira asked, looking around and feeling a growing vibration from the ground.

"Tyroccs," Captain Ako reported.

"And armor," River Rat added.

Apparently, somebody wasn't convinced they were dead, or that the explosion was an accident.

The three ran across the road and deep into the tall, wavy grass until they could sink down to the ground and not be noticed. Moments later, about twenty black dragon soldiers, all mounted on tyroccs, stopped at the spot where Moira, River Rat and Captain Ako stood only minutes before.

Moira peaked her head above the tallest grass blades and watched the soldiers.

"What are they doing?" River Rat whispered.

"At the moment, they are just having a look around."

Several tense moments ensued...

"They seem to be having a conversation," Moira reported. "A few of them are pointing to the South, toward the border."

"Abyssins would *never* let them cross," Captain Ako growled. "Not without riskin' a war."

"Wait a minute," Moira said, watching the soldiers group together. "One of them is riding to the front of the column with something perched on his arm."

River Rat shuddered, catching Moira's attention. She learned the hard way when he did this, something was wrong.

"Describe it," he demanded.

She peaked over the grass blades, she squinted to try and get a better focus on the creature's features. "It has a small head and a long neck—"

"Does it have a gray, feathered body and a long, puffy tail?" River Rat asked.

"Why... yes."

River Rat's eyes widened and his mouth fell open, his fur bristled. "A myter!"

"A what?" Moira asked.

"A primitive dragon," Captain Ako muttered. "Very acute senses, they have."

"What makes them so dangerous?" Moira asked.

"Fire spitters," River Rat said. "I once watched as two of them, burnt to a crisp, an entire goblin brigade."

Soldiers were now pointing in the same direction where the three were hiding. Moira ducked down, a horrified look galloped across her face. "I think they saw me!"

The three hunkered down and listened for the expected rumbling of feet, the clanking of armor, the gruff demands of surrender.... Nothing happened. Moira, very slowly, lifted her head to the grass tips again.

"They're moving!" she said in a loud whisper.

"Which way?" Captain Ako asked.

"South."

Captain Ako blew out an exasperated sigh.

"That complicates things," he snarled.

"Are they expecting us to be going that way?" she asked.

"So it seems," River Rat replied.

"What do we do?" Moira looked at Captain Ako.

"We can't move," he said. "Not until night fall."

The sun arched across the sky and then slowly sunk in the West, marking the return of the thick blackness of night. Captain Ako stood and looked around. Moira and River Rat were sleeping.

"Come on," Captain Ako roused them awake. "It's time to move."

Moira and River Rat stretched and yawned and stood up. Captain Ako put up a hand to stop them.

"Be warned," he said, a look of the deadliest seriousness on his face. "This beach is full of shallow depressions, mud pits and venomous snakes. It's gonna be a long, slow walk."

It went just as Captain Ako predicted. On more than one occasion, one, or all three, stumbled or fell into a depression. Night, it seemed, slapped a veil over Moira's eyes robbing her of much of her night vision. A pit viper lunged at River Rat, missing him by inches. Moira swung her tail, like a golf club, swatting the snake over a sand dune.

The first rays of silvery, sun light peered over the eastern sea. The border lay about two hundred yards away.

"How many are there, do you think?" Captain Ako whispered as they knelt behind the cover of a sand dune that loomed over five camp fires in the middle of a black dragon encampment.

"I think it's the same group we saw yesterday," River Rat answered.

"Agreed," Moira added. "Their tyroccs are off to the left."

Daylight was upon them, they couldn't stay put any longer.

"We have to go — now," Captain Ako said, standing up and running over the dune.

"Sir, no!" River Rat shouted.

Too late.

Moira and River Rat jumped up and sprinted after him... Tyroccs bellowed in an alarm... Startled soldiers, either lounging around the fires or laying on the sandy ground, half asleep, were jolted awake and raced for their crossbows.

— "Hey!" —
— "Stop!" —
— "Stop them!"—

The trio shot by several dumbstruck soldiers toward a narrow gorge with a shallow, milky, colored stream meandering at the bottom of it. Moira and River Rat jumped over the ledge. Captain Ako, who had fallen behind, ambled over the ledge. A pit viper sprung up from the cliff-face and bit him in the right leg.

Captain Ako let out an anguished cry and ripped the snake away from his leg making two bloody gashes. The soldiers fired their crossbows. A missile hissed over Moira's head, another grazed her left arm. River Rat stopped and turned to his Captain and their pursuers, who now sprinted over the ledge. The zaltee looked on in horror at the confused and unfocused look in Captain Ako's eyes. His mouth hung open and ruby, red blood oozed down his right leg.

"Come on, sir!" River Rat yelled.

"Run!" Moira shouted, terrified.

Captain Ako fell, face first, into the sand,

eight crossbow bolts sticking up from his back and neck.

"NOOO!" River Rat yelled.

Moira grabbed him by the back of his shirt and yanked him over the lazy-flowing stream. River Rat watched, helpless, as black dragon soldiers stood around Captain Ako's lifeless body. Moira and he reached safety. But at a terrible cost.

CHAPTER TWENTY-FIVE

-BETRAYAL-

Robsko had good reason to be concerned. Like Goldeye and Jossic — his two closest allies, he needed no convincing of Zare's treachery. The green dragon leader had become obsessed with the idea Zare was about to do away with him. He had no intentions on just sitting around waiting for the black dragon councilor to walk up to him and kill him. The time for battle had come. He spent many days and nights with his two sons, Garth and El, strategizing.

"If he wants war, that's what he will get!" Robsko told his sons on several occasions.

The three stood in Robsko's office, looking

over a detailed map of Green Dragon Territory, its borders with Black Dragon Territory, due North, and Silver Dragon Territory, due South.

"We've been over this a thousand times," Garth whined.

Robsko's red eyes shot him a cold stare. "We're going over it again!"

"I have the northern defenses and am in command of the wall," Garth droned rolling his eyes.

"That's right!" Robsko said, his gaze slid to El.

"I have the southern defenses and am to supply Garth, if he should need it," El groaned with the same irritation as Garth.

Robsko stepped away from his desk for a moment, his eyes fixed sternly on his sons. "I know this is hard, boys," his voice calm. "Believe me when I say I don't want to do this anymore than you. Councilor Zare is a threat to us. I *firmly* believe he will attack us — or make a move to kill me."

Neither Garth nor El met their father's gaze.

Robsko's mouth lifted into a toothy smile. "I think this is all going to stay a plan."

Both boys now looked at him with their eyebrows cocked up.

"What do you mean?" Garth asked.

Robsko sighed.

"I guess I can say this in good confidence," he replied. "But, Council-Leader Goldeye says he can prove Zare has been negligent with his efforts on the wall. He has also been tampering in the on-going issues between the red and gold dragons. They are no closer to a resolution, now, than they were when this whole mess started during the griffon war."

Garth's brow sunk. El let out a gasp.

"What could that mean?" El asked.

"It means," Garth said, "Councilor Zare could be forced to abdicate his position."

"Hearings are to begin soon," Robsko said, his grin growing wider. "He was notified today. Oh, was he angry!"

Councilor Zare's mansion, Kublisa

"You're wasting time, *councilor!*" Loothar growled, his eyes narrowed and his nostrils flared.

Zare grunted as he paced back-and-forth in the middle of his meeting chamber.

"I told you before," he muttered, "be patient."

"HMPH!" snarled Loothar. "I have other things to do."

The Vordral turned to the darkness.

"The final piece is in place," Zare said quietly. "It is to move — tomorrow."

Loothar chuckled and then vanished into the darkness.

"Fool!" Zare whispered.

Grand Council Chamber, the following day

It had been yet another grueling session. The usual heated debates, accusations and innuendos flew around the chamber, all day, on a wide variety of topics concerning the safety and security of the country. At long last… adjournment was called.

The Grand Council Chamber was now empty except for Goldeye, his assistant, Gisko, Green Councilor Robsko, and one of his aides. They stood over their benches, collecting papers and documents, muttering to each other. Gisko scooped up the last few pages and placed them in a leather-bound case. He took a long key, from under his blue shirt, and slid it in-and-out of a small lock until it clicked. He slid the key out and put it back under his shirt.

"Is there anything else, sir?" Gisko asked Goldeye.

"No, my friend. Tend to your final duties and then you may go home."

Gisko smiled and turned to the chamber entrance, walking side-by-side with the green dragon aide.

Goldeye bent down to pick up a sword he placed behind his bench. Robsko walked to the podium to put the stone gavel away for the day. Goldeye resumed his full height and was about to call on his friend — his eyes slid to the chamber entrance — two dragons in White clan body armor, that didn't seem to fit them very well, raised two repeating crossbows at Robsko. The assassins didn't seem to notice Goldeye standing to their right.

"Robsko!" he shouted, running at the assailants with his sword drawn. "Get down!"

Robsko turned around. The attackers fired off two bolts and slowly re cocked for another shot. He dodged one bolt and swatted the other away with the gavel.

"Come on, you cowards!" he shouted.

Goldeye was nearly on top of the shooters. They dropped the crossbows and drew their swords.

"They want to fight it out," one attacker said. "Let's fight!"

"Don't get cocky!" the other warned.

Goldeye sliced his sword down at one assassin, who parried the blow with his sword. The other ran at Robsko, who was armed only with the stone gavel. The assassin's face lifted into a smile under his visor. He sliced wildly at Robsko's head. The green dragon ducked under the swipe and slammed a shoulder into the attackers middle, causing him to stumble backward. The assassin charged again, he took another wild slice at Robsko's head, missing everything. Robsko slashed the gavel at the attackers head — the impact sent the assassin to the floor. Robsko jumped on him and finished him off with several blows to the head.

Goldeye swung his tail at his opponent's feet, sweeping him to the ground. He slammed his tail repeatedly on the assassin's throat. The attacker lay, spread-eagle on the ground, gurgling and trying to breathe through a crushed trachea. Three more dragons, two in blue dragon armor and one in gold dragon armor (none of the armor fit properly on these three either) rushed into the chamber. The one badly disguised as a gold dragon stopped to face Goldeye. The other two sprinted at Robsko, now holding a sword as well as the gavel.

"Come on, boys!" Robsko shouted, spinning his weapons in his hands. "There's plenty for both of you!"

Robsko's eyes twinkled as a wide, pointed toothed smile stretched around his face. He burst out laughing as he blocked and parried the swipes and strikes the two threw at him. "Is *that* all you've got? And you call yourselves assassins?"

A few feet away, Goldeye and his new opponent squared off. Their eyes locked. The gold armored dragon drew his sword, which was long and arching like a saber. The armor may not have fit him very well, but he swung the sword gracefully, like it was part of his body.

"Who sent you?" Goldeye asked his opponent. "Who do you work for?"

The assassin remained silent. His eyes narrowed, looking as though he were smiling under his visor. He lunged forward, he swung his saber in a series of circular swipes and slices. Goldeye parried the blows, but with difficulty. This dragon was good — and not much into talking. The assassin launched another round of swings and agile swipes. Goldeye deflected and blocked each shot and stab. He swung his tail up toward the attacker's face, who, in turn, blocked it with an armored forearm — he spun around and slapped Goldeye hard across the face, first with his tail, then his fist sending the old dragon to the sandy floor.

The assassin raised the saber over his head. Goldeye stomped a foot into the attacker's left knee, causing a sickening snap. The attacker shrieked and fell into a crumpled heap on the floor. Goldeye finished him off with a sword swipe to his throat. He turned to render assistance to Robsko. It wasn't needed. Robsko had already killed the first attacker. The other swung his sword — Robsko dodged the swing — crushed his opponent's elbow with a forceful swing of the gavel and beheaded him with a swipe of his sword.

Another assassin stepped into the entrance, holding a repeating crossbow. This attacker knew how to use the weapon, he fired, cocked, fired, cocked, and fired again. The bolts hissed by Goldeye and crashed into Robsko's chest. Goldeye pirouetted and heaved his sword at the shooter, who slipped away just before the sword impaled itself into the chamber door. Goldeye caught a look at the shooter's face. "Garth?"

Goldeye ran into the hall, he cranked his head one way, then to the other — nothing. He slowly turned and saw Robsko sprawled on the floor along with the bodies of the assassins. Goldeye rushed to him. Robsko's chest heaved up-and-down, his breathing was labored and blood streamed from his mouth. Goldeye bent down on one knee, he cast a sad look down at his mortally wounded friend.

"You're bleeding," Robsko said, pointing at a trickle of blood from Goldeye's mouth.

"I'm alright."

Robsko's eyes slid to the dead assassins. "Did we...? All of them... Are they all dead?"

"All but one," Goldeye whispered.

"The-the one that... got me," Robsko panted harder, he gurgled as he tried to breathe. "You said... G-Garth."

Goldeye's brows slanted up. "I'm pretty sure it was Garth who shot you."

Robsko chuckled and then coughed up

bloody clots. "Had my... had my suspicions. He-he-he's been acting st-strangely since his meeting with Zare. Do you think he put Garth up to this?"

"Yes! Zare has the most to gain with you and me out of the way."

"Guard yourself well, Goldeye. You are h-his next tar-target."

Robsko's head sunk to the ground. He closed his eyes, drew in one last deep, gurgling breath and let it out — never to breathe another.

CHAPTER TWENTY-SIX

-HANDOE'S TRIAL-

Elmshir

Fras and Fray ordered the trial moved up a day, a calculated move. They knew Handoe's friends were at Cranch Hollow and probably would not be back for some time — if ever. Word had been put out to kill them when they returned. To the brothers, Handoe was going down for something — *anything* they could throw at him.

Leaf anticipated this and prepared himself and Handoe for any, and all, actions that his brothers would resort to trying. Fras and Fray ordered Handoe to he brought into the court chamber in shackles. Leaf objected. Handoe overruled him.

"Let them do it," he told Leaf.

"Why?" Leaf asked, incredulously.

The guard shackled Handoe's hands and feet and the three exited the jail.

"This is a show trial," Handoe said. "They are showing that they will stop at nothing to silence me."

"I don't want the panel to see you like this," Leaf countered. "You don't deserve this humiliation!"

Handoe smiled, his eyes slid sideways to Leaf. "The truth is on our side. Four of us know exactly what happened on the night Cranch Hollow fell."

Leaf nodded.

"Two of them don't want the truth to be made public knowledge," Handoe said.

The three approached a large, five story building with a dome bubbling up in the middle of its roof. Leaf, Handoe and the jail guard pushed through the tall, glass doors and into the cavernous entrance hall and lobby. Rabbits scurried here-and-there on agendas known only to them. Armored guards stood in front of some of the doorways and hall intersections. Their eyes followed the three as they moved to the main court chamber.

"I will warn you now," Leaf said, leaning toward Handoe. "Even though you and I know enough to discredit my brothers over this, it could be dangerous for us. It *will* be dangerous for your friends."

Handoe didn't reply. He kept looking around. Something didn't seem right to him.

"Handoe," Leaf barked, looking at him. "Did you hear me?"

"Why are black dragon troops here?" Handoe asked. "I thought you were autonomous from their rule."

Leaf started looking around with a growing expression of unease sweeping over his face.

What was going on?

"What are *you* doing here?" Walker asked in a haughty tone of voice as he and a squad of eight soldiers walked into General Zmoge and Jinks.

"I don't answer to you, underling," Zmoge hissed as he and Walker stood face-to-face, throwing angry, pompous glares at each other.

Jinks tried to scurry away. Zmoge had placed a leather and metal collar around the lizard's neck that was attached to a chain-link leash.

"Mister General," he whimpered, "Please, this thing hurts my neck. Can't I please take it off?"

Zmoge yanked on the leash, pulling Jinks closer to him. His dead-looking eyes pounced on the cowering lizard, who nervously flicked his long tongue, nearly licking the general's nose. "I'm not yet finished with you, vermin!"

Zmoge's eyes slid to the irate Walker.

"I warn you, general, don't get in my way!"

Zmoge's face split in to a crooked, evil grin. "And I warn *you, underling,* if you get in my way, I'll run you through."

Walker was beside himself with anger; his face flushed, his nostrils flared, his eyes bulged and his breathing quickened.

"I-I have my orders, general!"

"And I have mine."

"Just-just what are your orders, general?"

Zmoge didn't answer.

Walker's attempt at pulling rank was meeting with disastrous failure.

An awkward silence fell over this group.

"I have a trial to attend," Zmoge said, pulling the leash and nearly dragging Jinks behind him. "Get out of my way."

Zmoge brushed the incensed Walker aside

and moved down the hall toward the Main Court Chamber. Walker looked at his troops. Their eyes followed the general. It seemed to be no contest, to them, as to who was really in charge.

"Well, let's go then!" Walker cried, throwing his troops a hurt, scornful look as they all trailed Zmoge.

Getting out of Elmshir was easy enough for Sandstorm, Maxum and Jessa. In fact, it was too easy. Leaf told them as much. He also told them they may have company on the way back. Before reaching Elmshir they separated, entering the rabbit city from either the trees or roof tops.

Maxum watched (from a roof top) a check point that had been set up at the main road entrance into town. Rabbit soldiers moved around and through a growing caravan of travelers. The soldiers were frisking anyone who aroused their suspicions. They poked spears into tarp covered wagons and had some remove their cargoes to see what was hiding in the back. Tensions were building and tempers rising. Maxum cracked a smile and was about to move onto the court house — its dome could be seen easily from where he crouched. He froze as he felt a strange tap and heard a whirring buzz coming from the incubator.

Was the egg hatching? *Now?* This was worst possible time for it to happen. Maxum was probably going to be in a few fights today. He didn't want to be fighting screaming soldiers with one hand while gently rocking a screaming baby dragon with the other.

The tapping stopped and the whirring buzz died down. Maxum breathed a sigh of relief. He jumped from roof top to roof top, like a monkey in the trees, until he was on the roof top adjacent to the Court House. No sign of Sandstorm or Jessa. Had they both been captured? He scanned the tree-lined courtyard and the heavy pedestrian traffic going to-and-from the building. Nothing seemed out of the ordinary.

Regardless of what may, or may not, have happened to Sandstorm and Jessa, he had to get Handoe out of this mess. He and Handoe weren't friends — not yet anyway. He knew Handoe was innocent and he wouldn't stand by as the jackrabbit was being led to his death. The tapping started again along with the whirring buzz. *Not now!*

Main Court Chamber

Handoe's return had generated quite a buzz among the Elmshir residents. A coward coming back to face his accusers? That didn't happen very often here — or anywhere else for that matter. The Main Court Chamber resembled an amphitheater. It was large and cavernous with a long, Judges' bench against the back wall. The bench loomed over two, rectangular tables. One table was for the Prosecution and the other was for the Defense.

Handoe and Leaf took their seats at the Defense table. Jaylem, bespectacled, and in a fancy blue military jacket, with medals and badges all over it, strolled to the Prosecutor's table. He wore a smug expression on his face and shot a contemptuous glare at Handoe as he sat down. Spectators filed into seats around the chamber including Zmoge and Walker. Handoe's eyes toured the court chamber at the rabbit faces peering back at him. Not a familiar face anywhere. No sign of Sandstorm or the others.

A door opened behind the bench. Five rabbits, dressed in red, cassock-like robes, including Fras and Fray, walked single file and took their seats. All stood, the hiss of whispers faded away. Handoe's fur bristled at the sight of Fras and Fray in judges robes, about to pass their twisted judgment down on him.

"Take it easy," Leaf whispered out of the corner of his mouth.

"The sight of them makes my fur crawl!" Handoe whispered back.

"Do you still think something's up?"

"Now more than ever."

"Be seated," spoke an elderly, brown furred rabbit with a white beard sprawling out from under his ears and dripping down from his chin.

This judge sat in the middle of the panel and appeared to be the senior ranking member. Handoe knew who really pulled the strings around here. The middle judge wore the most serious of expressions as he glared down at him. Two, dark furred female judges sat on the right of the elderly judge, while Fras and Fray were perched to his left, and closest to the chamber door. A thick tension had fallen over the court room as had a seeming feeling of hostility toward the accused. Had they already reached a verdict? Were the judges going to verbally torture and toy with him in front of all of these strangers before condemning him to the gallows? Rabbit court proceedings were usually short affairs with the Prosecution going first, to throw out the charges for all to hear. The Defense followed, to offer a rebuttal and try to debunk the charges. Witnesses and evidence were allowed — if any were present. After hearing everything, the five judge panel would huddle and reach a verdict. Then the senior judge would tell the verdict. If guilty, no appeals. Sentences would be carried out immediately.

"Prosecutor Jaylem has the floor," the elderly judge snarled.

Jaylem stood, snorted at Handoe, and faced the judges.

"Good Judges and people of Elmshir," he spoke in a loud and clear voice and slowly circled to face the audience. "No doubt you've read in the news prints about the accused and his... so called... heroics with the Dragonsrod police. Even the Council-Leader, himself, sent a plea to spare the accused and to let him go," whispers and hisses arose from the audience. "Yes. The news stories spill out *flarb* about what kind of a hero he is. He has medals and accolades and praise of his courage *blah, blah blah*! That's not why he is on trial here." The audience was deathly quiet. "The reason the accused is on trial is for what happened *before* he joined the Dragonsrod police and became the *hero,* the presses say he is.

"At Cranch Hollow, the night it fell, he showed *none* of this courage he seemed to have inherited after word. In fact, he RAN — before even the first crossbow bolt had been fired in anger. The accused, in his fright, left his troops to fend for themselves," Jaylem pointed at Handoe as he continued to speak. "His cowardice spread through his ranks like a disease. Soon his entire line gave way leaving the right flank abandoned — the center vulnerable — defeat, definite. His cowardice was so complete, he even left his crest behind, making some horrible story as to how it was lost during the battle," a new wave of mutterings and whispers swept around the court chamber before fading to silence. "When the gallent defenders regrouped, here in Elmshir, his cowardice was sniffed out by our Lordships, Fras and Fray," Jaylem motioned a hand to the two seated closest to the door.

"The accused was ordered, under penalty of death, to never speak of this. The accused was ordered, under penalty of death, to leave Elmshir and all rabbit territory. The accused was ordered, under penalty of death, to never return to Elmshir. Yet, he didn't listen… Because here he is! Apparently, he wants to end his shame and be given the doom that awaits cowards like him. I say we give it to him. He cost us our homes. He cost us our very ways of life! He turned us into refugees," Jaylem pointed his finger again at Handoe and was shouting, " and *that* is why he should be sentenced today — *sentenced to death!"*

Jaylem sat down amid a some calls of "Here-Here," from some of the audience. He laid it on pretty thick. Handoe sat silent, seething with rage. More than once, Leaf had to nudge him in the ribs and give him warning glances to settle down. Jaylem cast a glance at Fras and Fray, who in turn, gave a single nod of approval.

"The floor now belongs to the defense," the elderly judge said...

It wasn't easy trying to sneak into this place. Especially if you're armed with a repeating crossbow, a sword and two daggers. It also doesn't help if you're not a rabbit. Sandstorm had his work cut out for him. He knew the rabbit guards would be all over him like bad smells over garbage if he tried to storm through the main entrance. His grayish eyes coursed the courtyard, the trees and the building itself. He spied an open window on the corner of the third floor with a large chestnut tree growing close to it. He scanned around the courtyard to see if any one was watching him. Rabbits walked in and out of the building, none of them seemed to notice — or care — that he was there.

That chestnut tree was his ticket inside. The branches looked a little too small and thin up top, but he had to chance it. Sandstorm casually walked to the tree, took another look around, flexed his claws, and proceeded to climb.

Jessa took the direct approach by walking through the front doors. She fell under the gaze of a rabbit guard stationed near the lobby entrance.

"You, there!" he called, pointing to Jessa and

the large canvas bag she was carrying. "Stop right there."

She did so and faced the skeptical, salt and pepper furred guard, wearing a shinny breastplate.

"Is there a problem?" she asked looking innocent.

"What's in the pouch?"

His black eyes narrowed as he looked from the bag to Jessa.

She cracked a smile, while opening the pouch. "Let me show you."

She swung the pouch up and slammed the shields against his face, resulting in a loud *clank!* The guard flew back and lay, spread-eagle and unconscious on the floor drawing surprised gasps and startled stares from on-lookers.

"Oh, goodness," she said, doing her best to look as surprised as those around her were. "I was opening the bag. It contains a Logger turtle — very rare — kind of aggressive, as we just saw. This is for a court case," she looked at two stunned rabbits, "If you could just drag this poor soul to that bench over there — that's it, thank you."

She moved through the crowd as it began to disperse.

Maxum watched Jessa approach the court house. He knew she was up to something by the way she was rattling the armor in the sack like something was alive inside it. He followed her from a distance, so not to arouse too much suspicion. He drew the hood of his traveling cloak over his head and walked to the Court House. The incubator tapped twice and the low whirring buzz hummed again.

'The incubator will let you know,' he remembered the mystics telling them.

It chirped out a few mechanical *zip, zot* sounds.

The whirring stopped. He could not lose his focus on what he was doing at the present time. Suddenly, rabbits bunched into the entrance — something happened. Maxum went with the flow into the building. He didn't look at Jessa, but kept his ears on her. "…It contains a Logger turtle — very rare — kind of aggressive — as we just saw…"

Like a shadow, he slid along the back wall and down the corridor…

Leaf stood up and addressed the audience; "Good citizens of Elmshir, the very notion of this trial of my client, Handoe Wextal, is," Leaf's eyes fell hard on his brothers, Fras and Fray. *"laughable!"*

Fras and Fray scowled, but remained silent.

Leaf continued; "Handoe is as much a coward as I am," gasps and whispers ran another lap around the chamber. "I ask you, good people, would a coward return to face his accusers after being banished, especially if he was guilty of being a coward, let alone, a deserter? Knowing full well he will die if he returned? I think not! I was at Cranch Hollow the night it fell. Sure Handoe ran. But so did everyone else. Handoe was *not* the reason for our retreat. We were outnumbered, placed in a hopeless position! We had one objective that *our leaders,"* he threw another sharp look at Fras and Fray, "seemed to forget about."

"What exactly was your mission?" spoke out the female judge sitting next to the elderly, bearded judge.

Leaf turned to face her. "Our mission was to get everybody out of Cranch Hollow as quickly as we could."

"For what reason?" she asked, her dark eyes fixed on Leaf.

"Enemy forces, primarily goblin and zaltee were closing in on the warren from the North and the East. It was a defenseless and an indefensible position."

"Did you succeed?"

"Yes. But only just."

"What do you mean by 'only just'?" scowled the elderly judge.

"By the time we got the last of the civilians into the escape tunnels, the enemy poured in on us." Leaf responded.

The elderly judge cleared his throat. "I have some questions for the accused."

All eyes fell on Handoe.

"What rank did you hold at Cranch Hollow?"

"I was a captain, sir."

"Among the other officers, what was your status ?"

"I held the most junior rank, sir"

The elderly judge paused for a moment, then spoke again; "What became of Captain Rhil?"

"He was killed, sir," Handoe responded. "That night, along with most of his command."

"How many did you lose?"

"Over half, sir. None of the rest of us escaped without injury."

The Main Court Chamber was so quiet, one could almost hear a fly on the wall breathe.

"Where were you injured?" the elderly judge asked, not taking his gaze away from Handoe.

He held up his left arm and pointed to a long, straight scar that ran from his chest to under the arm. "I also suffered two broken ribs where I had been struck by a war hammer."

The judges panel sat silent for a moment.

"Where did you lose your breast plate?" Fras asked, heaving a malicious glare down at Handoe.

"Somewhere at Cranch Hollow," Handoe replied.

"How did you lose it?" Fray asked.

"When I was stabbed," Handoe retorted, glaring at Fray. "The point of the goblin spear cleaved through the shoulder strap, on the left side, rendering the plate practically useless."

"When were you hit by the hammer?" Jaylem asked.

Handoe turned to the prosecutor and spoke with a forced calm, "Minutes before I was stabbed with the spear."

"And just what happened to the goblins, you claim, assaulted you?" Jaylem spat.

Handoe grimaced. "I killed them."

Loud voices and the sounds of a struggle were heard outside the chamber… silence. The audience gasped and gawked as the chamber doors squeaked open. Jessa and Maxum stepped over four unconscious rabbit guards and entered the chamber. The eyes of all in the room fell on the newcomers. Handoe's face lifted into a smile, but quickly faded. Where was Sandstorm?

The startled judges all stood up and glared at the pair. The elderly, bearded judge was livid.

"Who are you?" he shouted. "What is the meaning of this intrusion?"

"We bring evidence for the defense," Jessa said, walking to Leaf's table and dropping the slightly bloodied bag on it.

"What kind of evidence?" asked the female judge sitting furthest away from the elderly judge.

Fras and Fray threw glares at Jaylem, who looked completely nonplussed. Jessa dumped the two rusted and beat up breast plates on the table.

"That's her!" Walker exclaimed, drawing puzzled gazes from those around him.

"What are you blathering about?" General Zmoge hissed.

"That female dragon. We ran into her at Cranch Hollow… She bludgeoned one of my dragons with his own sword!"

Zmoge squinted as he leaned forward to get a better look at Jessa, who at the moment, was getting an earful from the irate, elderly judge.

"Yes," Zmoge said slowly, a crooked, toothy smile ripped across his face. "I know who she is!"

Walker shot Zmoge a sharp stare. "Who is she?"

Zmoge turned to four soldiers standing behind them. "You come with me," he turned to another soldier, who was holding the leash tethering to Jinks. "Release the lizard."

The solder did so.

"Oh, thank you, Mr. General. Thank you." Jinks groveled as he backed away.

Zmoge craned his head back to the scene and studied it for a moment. "Where's the snow leopard?" He looked at three soldiers standing behind Walker. "You three, there's another member of their troop, who isn't present. He's a snow leopard and can't be that hard to find. Get him!"

"Yes, sir," one of them said, all three scooting to the chamber doors.

"Now just a minute!" Walker shouted.

Zmoge ignored him and pointed to the last remaining soldier. "Make sure he stays here!"

"Yes sir," the soldier clamped a hand on Walker's shoulder.

Zmoge stood up and walked toward the chamber floor.

"What is the meaning of all these intrusions?" shouted the elderly judge, his eyes bulged as he quivered with rage.

If this judge's fur could change colors he would be differing shades of puce. Conditions were ripe for all spleck to break loose in his court chamber.

CHAPTER TWENTY-SEVEN

-THE ABYSSINS-

Abyssina/Dragonsrod border

River Rat was devastated. He owed Captain Ako much in the form of gratitude. The Captain, along with Goldeye's help, pulled a lot of strings to get him out of the prison camps and into society. River Rat proved his worth and he quickly became friends with all of his crew mates. Now, seemingly, in the blink of an eye, all were gone. He had to continue, he was exhausted from days of hard travel, spot naps here-and-there, little to nothing to eat. Watching Captain Ako being murdered and not being able to do anything about it, ripped away whatever energy and drive that he had left.

Moira had to carry him until she too, could no longer go on. They needed to rest. They were safe, for now. At least from any more rogue dragon soldiers, who would not dare cross the border to chase after them and risk an international incident with the abyssins — would they? It did not seem so, unless they were being extremely stealthy and could crawl through this thicket without making a sound. That also seemed unlikely.

Moira jolted herself awake. Her eyes shifted to the left then to the right. Nothing to see in this dense, gloomy forest of tall cycad trees except shadows creating things that were not there. Whoops, screeches and squalls resonated through the trees. Her eyes sunk to River Rat, still sleeping, next to her. She didn't know what to say to him. She felt terrible pity for him. She knew how it felt to be yanked away from the ones she loved. She felt confident she would see her husband again and hoped to finally see her child. Once again, a wave of anger swept over her. She still felt as much anger at Goldeye as she did love for him. After all, it was his decision

Warriors of Dragonsrod

to split the family apart.

'I wasn't able to protect our children and I don't think I can protect you,' she remembered Goldeye telling her. *'...I cannot guarantee your safety. As long as you are here, you are a target for my enemies...'*

Her mind kept taking her back to that last night they had together. Her eyes welled with tears. She could not get over that sad, mournful expression on Goldeye's face. She knew he did not want her to leave...

"Are you alright, ma'am?" River Rat croaked.

She slid her eyes back to him, his eyes were irritated and puffy.

"I'll be fine," she said. "I really miss my husband."

"You'll see him again," River Rat replied. "I'm sure your child is safe as well."

Moira's face lifted into a tight lipped grin.

River Rat's fur bristled.

"What?" she asked.

"Listen!" he said, his face dropped and his eyes slowly scanned the woods.

"I don't hear anything."

"Neither do I. Several minutes ago, this forest was alive with sounds."

River Rat's ears perked up. Moira looked around. Their tails twitched in a stiff, nervous way.

"We can't stay here," he warned, fear racing over his face.

The two slowly rose to their feet, their senses on full alert. Tensions mounted, panic levels were about to blast off into the stratosphere. They slowly moved, one foot in front of the other. Something else was here, quite possibly stalking them. River Rat's eyes scoured the ground.

"What are you looking for?" she asked him.

"A big stick, a rock, a bone," he replied calmly. "Something to use as a weapon."

Moira started looking around for something to use.

"Stay calm," River Rat spoke in an even voice. "We don't want to make any sudden moves."

Everything in Moira was screaming at her to run. Yet, she felt if anyone was going to get her out of this predicament, it would be River Rat.

"Find anything yet?" she asked him with a forced calm to her voice.

"No," he answered. "You?"

"No."

Warriors of Dragonsrod

River Rat's eyes darted to the right. He saw a two reptilian shapes streak from tree-to-tree.

"We could be in trouble," he cast a concerned gaze up at Moira.

"Why?"

"I think we are dealing with pack animals."

"Oh, dear!"

They heard what sounded like a deep, guttural grunt from somewhere behind them.

"Get ready to run," River Rat whispered.

"Couldn't that trigger their predatory instincts even more?" she asked, the fear evident in her voice.

"Yes. At least we'll have a chance. We stay put and they will tear us apart."

"I see."

Another grunt was heard to their left — something snapped to their right.

"RUN!" River Rat shouted.

The pair sprinted forward. Whoops, screeches and yells of seeming delight echoed from all around them. One of these creatures bolted out from the rising dust and shadows and lunged at Moira. She dodged to her left as the Dromaesaurus-like creature glided past her. The sickle-clawed beast opened its gaping, tooth filled mouth and screamed at Moira as if it were angry because she dodged its attack.

River Rat slammed a stick across its head and knocked it flat. More shadowy figures charged at them. Moira and River Rat kept running as fast as they could. It seemed to be their only defense. The speedy creatures were rapidly gaining on them. Another one leapt off the ground at Moira, who slapped it away with her tail.

Arrows hissed through the air and stabbed several of the creatures — killing some and wounding others. Moira and River Rat stopped suddenly as though they slammed into an invisible wall. The creatures disappeared back into the gloomy cover of the forest. Out from the cycads emerged ten, tall and slender cat-like beings, all holding bows and arrows, and aimed at the two.

"Abyssins!" hissed River Rat as he rose the stick, and assumed a defensive pose, ready to strike the first one to come at them.

"Be careful, zaltee, at how you address us," growled the largest one of the bunch, he was muscular, gray furred and tall with almost glowing yellow eyes. "Who are you and what...

are you doing here?"

Moira slowly rose her hands, while keeping eye contact with the large, male abyssin. "My name is Moira," her tone of voice was calm but nervous. "I am the wife of Council-Leader Goldeye from the Dragonsrod Republic."

"Yeah, right," the large abyssin barked. "And I'm the griffon emperor."

"You'd never make it," River Rat spat. "You're too stupid!"

The large abyssin snarled, his bow creaked and groaned as he pulled the string back ready to launch a missile at River Rat. Moira stepped in front of him with her hands held out.

"Enough!" shouted a female voice from behind the big abyssin. "Bolten, step down."

A tall female abyssin with an hour glass shape, short, tawny fur and a medium length tail, stepped out from behind Bolten. His eyes slid to her face and gave her a loving look and bowed his head. She apparently held a high rank with these beings. Her black, cone-shaped ears and dark, brown, almond shaped eyes fell on Moira's face.

"Lower your weapons," she ordered.

The abyssins did so.

Moira looked down to River Rat. "Drop it."

With the utmost reluctance, he lowered the stick to the ground.

"I'm Shayara," the female abyssin confirmed, still looking at Moira. "My lead-warrior asks a valid question. Why are you here?"

Moira stepped away from River Rat, who spoke first; "It wasn't by choice."

Shayara's eyes glinted as they fell to the zaltee. "What do you mean?"

Moira answered this time. She told her all about the hasty departure from Dragonsrod. She mentioned the doomed *Mudskipper* and the tragic death of Captain Ako and being chased here by rogue dragon soldiers.

"A nice sob story," Bolten growled.

Shayara shot him a warning look. He, again, bowed his head.

"You must excuse my lead-warrior, Bolten," Shayara spoke, trying to ease the still sky-high tensions. "He's the best at what he does. Yet, he is naturally doubtful of any and all strangers he comes across."

Bolten and Moira exchanged nods.

"If you are who you say," Shayara continued, "that makes you a dignitary of Dragonsrod. I...

should take you to see my mother, Queen Catra."

Bolten's eyes narrowed and his face dropped. He looked as though he wanted to protest, but appeared to think better of it.

Shayara looked into his eyes.

"Come, my love," she cooed. "We are an escort troop now. Let's let my mother deal with them."

"My lady," he muttered, dipping his head.

Aizon, capitol city of Abyssina; Queen Catra's Palace

Aizon was as large and as modern a city as any in Dragonsrod. Many stone and metal buildings sprouted up like monolithic trees in a forest. The citizenry — nearly all the cat-like abyssin race — seemed generally at ease, yet busy.

The royal palace sat on a hill in the middle of the labyrinthine city. The earth and brick walls of the palace were thick enough to withstand any siege. The walls were a good twenty five to thirty feet high cornered by towers and littered with defensive battlements.

It wasn't unusual to see visitors of other

nations and species touring the long and narrow streets of Aizon. It was unusual for a dignitary from another country to drop by unannounced. In fact, it had never happened... until now.

Queen Catra was an older version of Shayara in nearly every description. Except for some graying fur around her muzzle and her ears, and deep blue eyes, they were identical. Catra was the latest in a long line of a highly educated, vigorously trained maternity. She was kind as a ruler, fair but firm. She knew her people well, she loved her people and they loved her and for good reasons. She and her lineage have brought peace and prosperity to Abyssina for the last two-hundred years. That was a streak she had no intentions of breaking. Nor did she intend for her daughters to break it after she passed on.

Queen Catra stood with her Chief-warrior, Kaymo, and a troop of staffers, soldiers, and some members of the abyssin press. They were in the castle's Public Court Room, a large chamber on the ground level with a throne, on a long, rectangular platform, at the far end, opposite the entrance. Any and every one could come in to seek an audience with the Queen, so naturally, security was super tight. One could expect to be frisked at least once before entering the castle. Once inside, one was under the scrutiny of the palace guards, highly trained soldiers with crossbows, swords, knives and various martial arts. As soon as one entered the Public Court Room, they were watched by the Royal Guard at the entrance and in front of the throne. These soldiers carried repeating crossbows and swords and were deadly accurate shots.

Today was like the rest, Queen Catra held audience with her people over a wide variety of matters ranging from personal, and sometimes trivial issues, to serious subjects such as disputes and disagreements. During a break in the action, Queen Catra stepped away from her throne and was conversing with Kaymo, a large, blonde furred, and green eyed male abyssin. Catra's youngest daughter, Serena, a taller, thinner version of Shayara, ran into the chamber and toward her mother and Kaymo.

"Mother," Serena's brown eyes twinkled and an excited look stretched over her face. "Shayara has returned. She is with a female white dragon and a *cute* little rat-like creature."

"A white dragon female?" Catra repeated, casting a glance to Kaymo before returning her gaze to Serena.

"Yes. She is at the entrance to the castle."

Dragons in Abyssina was no big deal. Dragons from every clan came and went from the country every day. But when a female white dragon was being brought to the Queen by a troop of soldiers — a dragon, for whom, could be the missing wife of the Dragonsrod Grand Council-Leader — it might be a good idea to find out about her and who she is.

"Kaymo, I want you to meet with this dragon."

"Yes, my Queen."

"It could be Goldeye's wife, she's been missing for several days now."

"I shall talk to her."

"Take Serena with you. Bring them in and make them comfortable. I will meet with them after this session has concluded."

"At once, my Queen."

Kaymo and Serena bowed, turned and exited the chamber.

Moira and River Rat were questioned at length by Kaymo before he allowed them into the castle. They were showed to neighboring guest rooms and waited while Queen Catra conducted her business.

Moira's room looked comfortable enough. It had a dragon sized bed under cozy looking blankets and two fluffy, white pillows positioned against the front bed board. A bath and a wash room were positioned on the opposite end of the room. She went to the large, rectangular tile bath pool and turned on the two faucets at the front of it. She ran her fingers through the hot water as it flooded into the pool. She let out a delighted squeal and her face lifted, uncontrollably into a wide smile.

This was more like it! A hot bath to look forward to. Moira's eyes fixed on a clothes closet, like a child to sweets, she eagerly went to it. She opened the closet and started rummaging around in it. She found some shirts and dresses that looked like they might fit her. Not everything fit, some of the clothes were just a bit too small. Some of it was much too big, like maybe an elephant stayed here at one time and may have left some of her wardrobe here. No bother. Her eyes sunk to the rags she was wearing. No way she would let Queen Catra see her in *this!*

Moira felt refreshed and renewed after an incredible bath and a nap on such a soft and warm bed. She wanted to forget about the last few days of trying to sleep against cold tree trunks, rough rocks and prickly bushes and waking every time a twig snapped. She wanted to forget it, but knew there was no way she could — too many died for her to get here.

A knock at her door.

Moira opened it. Shayara and Serena, both in white, sleeveless tops with gold belts around their waists, stared back at her.

"Good evening," Shayara said, politely. "Queen Catra will see you now. Please follow us."

"Your friend is welcome to join us if he wishes," Serena added.

Moira stepped out of her room and banged on River Rat's door. Moments later, the drowsy zaltee answered it.

"Queen Catra wants to see us," Moira told him. " Want to come?"

"Sure."

It appeared as if River Rat had taken similar liberties with the contents in his room as Moira did in hers. He looked rested and smelled of bath soap. Yet, he still wore his old sleeveless red shirt and his ragged, brown pants. He seemed to read her facial expression.

"Nothing fit me," he explained. "Some of it was so large, it could've been used as a tent with a sky roof."

The Public Court Chamber was empty except for Queen Catra, Kaymo and Bolten. Shayara and Serena flanked Moira and River Rat as they entered the chamber. The four dropped to one knee and gave a respectful bow.

"Rise, please," Catra said.

She was in a long, brilliant green gown that seemed to make her eyes turn from shades of aqua-marine to turquoise.

The four rose. Shayara and Serena took their places next to their mother and opposite Kaymo and Bolten.

"Welcome, Moira, I am Queen Catra. You've already met my lead-warriors, Kaymo and Bolten."

Moira's eyes slid from Catra to her muscular warriors, exchanged nods, and moved back to the Queen.

Catra continued; "I must say I was surprised

by the unannounced visit. We had no time to prepare for your arrival."

"We do thank you for your hospitality, Highness," Moira said. "Our visit to your country was… well… by accident."

Catra's eyebrows cocked up. "Oh? May I ask where you were going?"

"We were going to the Cannis Republic, but it was not by choice," Moira replied.

"I see. What do you mean, 'it was not by choice?'"

"My husband feared for my safety after the — the destruction of our egg clutch."

"Have you heard anything from your country?"

"No, we've been on the move through the country over the last few days and have not seen, or heard, anything from civilization."

Catra flashed her eyes to Kaymo, who stepped down from the throne platform. His chest and shoulder armor clanked together as he moved and stood face-to-face with Moira.

"We regret to inform you that an assassination occurred there a few days ago," he told her.

Moira's eyes widened, her mouth fell open and whatever color she had in her face drained away. River Rat also looked shocked as he reached for her hand, she grasped it. Her thoughts instantly went to Goldeye.

"It- It wasn't—?" she stammered.

"No, it wasn't your husband," Kaymo told her. "It was Councilor Robsko. Your husband *was* at the sight when it happened."

That was about as bad. She liked Robsko very much. He was like family to her. He was loyal to Goldeye.

"Our deepest condolences on your loss," Queen Catra said.

"We read the news prints from all around the region," Kaymo mentioned. "We follow the events carefully. Your country has become active recently. Problems in the Grand Council Chamber; protests in the streets of several cities nation-wide; talks of disunity and possible civil conflict?"

"I can see why Goldeye would send you away," Catra added.

"Do the prints make any mention of my sole-surviving egg?" Moira asked, desperate for any kind of news from that front.

"Alas," Kaymo said, "nothing other than it is missing."

Queasiness churned up Moira's stomach. Her legs felt like they had turned to jelly. Both River Rat and Kaymo reached a hand to steady her.

"Are you in need of a physician?" asked Catra, looking concerned.

River Rat answered instead; "With respects, Your Highness, it has been a very long last few days. Too much has happened. She's just tired."

Moira hung her head and stared at the floor for a few moments. She had a thousand questions. It appeared there were no answers. She felt completely out of touch and alone. Those conflicting feelings flooded back into her mind, like a recurring bad dream.

She appeared to gain Queen Catra's sympathy. She stood and approached Moira.

"I truly am sorry for all you have gone through," she consoled. "You are a guest here, you may stay as long as necessary."

"Thank you," Moira whispered.

"We have a tele-wire system," Queen Catra said. "Call your husband and tell him you're safe," her face lifted into a smile. "Tell Goldeye I said hello."

CHAPTER TWENTY-EIGHT

-GOLDEYE'S PROOF-

Robsko's death had the feel of an upper-cut to the stomach to Goldeye. He knew Robsko for many years. They had served in the Dragonsrod Army together and were involved in countless battles and scrapes, both on the battlefield and the Grand Council Chamber floor. They were like brothers. Together with Jossic, they were a powerful trio.

Now Robsko was gone. Councilor Zare had catapolted himself to the top of Goldeye's suspect list from the get-go. He was third in line, now number two. Make that would-be. Goldeye would see to it that Zare never, *ever* becomes Number Two. Zare would not tolerate being the next in line, not with his greed and ambition. The black dragon councilor wanted it all and would bowl over anybody to achieve it.

'You were right not to trust Councilor Zare,' he remembered the vordral, Loothar, telling him. *'He's much too ambitious. Watch your back.'*

Good advice.

His mind drifted back to the assassination. Why was he not targeted? Did the assassins not plan on the possibility that he, too, might be there? Or were they operating on orders from Zare? Somehow, it all led back to the black dragon councilor. Yet, the physical proof was still not there. Anyone could have ordered the assassination.

Goldeye stood alone in his home. Alone with his thoughts. Alone with his anger and sadness. His heart ached for Moira. He regretted more with each passing day having to send her away. Now she's missing. He knew Moira could be resourceful when she had to be. He took some comfort in that thought. He knew nothing of his unborn child. Where was it? Where were Handoe, Maxum and Sandstorm? Were they still alive? Too many questions to be running amok inside his head. He had confidence in the many questions to be running amok inside his head. He had confidence in the three to do the task set before them.

Goldeye stood in front of a mirror in his bedroom. He put on his old *Manticore Legion* armor. He was glad to see it still fit. It was in this armor, he met Robsko, who at the time, was a young officer in the Green Dragon *Gortha Legion*. Memories flash-flooded through his mind, many years together through good times and bad, Robsko was always there.

He was going to remove his armor and change into a black tunic. No. Robsko was a warrior. He was one of the best flixing soldiers to ever don armor! He died the way he wanted — fighting. Armor is what Goldeye would wear. Anyone who knew him and Robsko would understand it. Robsko would have loved it! Besides, if the roles were reversed, Robsko would have done the same thing.

Goldeye left from his house in his armor which gleamed in the sunlight. The metal softly clinked and clanked as he walked. He knew the press would have a field day with this. *So what?*

"Councilor Goldeye!" Gisko called from behind him. "Sir, you have a wire message."

Goldeye stopped and faced his loyal aide. Being the leader of a country, Goldeye received hundreds of wire messages every week. What was so important about this one?

"Okay," Goldeye said. "Read it."

"I think you should, sir," Gisko replied, smiling and handing the papers to Goldeye. "It's from Moira."

The old dragon beamed with delight. This was a much needed lift. Moira's words flooded the pages with a detailed explanation of her journey. She spoke of River Rat — The explosion of *The Mudskipper* — Captain Ako — the forced detention by the black dragons in Silver Dragon Territory. Goldeye's joy ebbed away as he read.

"Is everything alright, sir?" Gisko asked, studying the darkening expressions on Goldeye's face.

"She's encountered some trouble on the way to Gane," the old dragon returned.

"This message didn't come from Gane, sir."

"Where did it come from then?"

"Aizon, Abyssina."

Abyssina. Just a little shy of the original destination by about five-hundred miles.

Goldeye continued to read; The black dragons tried to starve them and treated them like prisoners, accusing them of sabotage and murder — the escape — the death of Captain Ako by the black dragon soldiers — the arrival in Abyssina — meeting Queen Catra…

"Ah, Queen Catra!" The smile returned to Goldeye's face.

"Sir?" Gisko asked.

"Queen Catra, the leader of the abyssins, and I go back many years. She even says hello in here"

"Oh."

"It looks as though Moira will be staying in Abyssina for a while. Contact Skit and Zephyr, in Gane, and tell them of the change in plan."

"Yes, sir, at once."

Moira was safe. That was the best news and one less thing to worry about. River Rat did his job well, to the old dragon's great relief. The actions of the black dragon soldiers is what perplexed him. They don't just go rogue. No, Zare would never allow that. He has too much of an iron fisted rule over his people. They were ordered to do it. This also confirmed his suspicion of the black dragons taking over Silver

Dragon Territory. Moira, whether or not she knew it, just added to the fire to cook Zare's goose and oust him once and for all.

Councilor Zare's mansion, Kublisa

If Zare was worried or panicked, he did not show it. He knew Goldeye would figure things out sooner or later. No matter, Goldeye's days were numbered. He will soon be joining Robsko under ground. Dragonsrod will cease to be a republic and become a kingdom or an empire — his. He already controlled Deela's lot. He had Zhangi and Tabric at each other's throats. He had no idea, or care, as to who won that dispute. They will *all* be answering to him pretty soon.

Zare cracked a smile as he entered his large, open, dimly lit meeting room. He wore his battle armor and he drew out his sword. He twirled it over his head and slashed down in a diagonal slice to his left. His armor clanked softly as he spun around and thrust his sword forward as if he were fighting an invisible opponent.

Zare moved around gracefully, as if in a dance, swishing and swinging his sword and tail and kicking his feet. Yet, this was no dance contest he was preparing for. War was coming.

He was supremely confident and rightfully so. Things were going his way. One major obstacle had been removed, one more, of any importance, remained. He would personally take care of that problem. What of his soon to be last remaining enemy, Jossic?

Zare walked to the front door and picked up a circular shield, leaning next to it, against the wall. He silently stepped to the middle of the room and flew into another kata.

What about Jossic…?

Zare crouched behind his shield and rose the sword over his head, making himself look like a tortoise with a scorpion's tail. He rose and thrust the shield forward, while spinning the sword over his head and launching it in a forward attack.

What *about* Jossic?

Zare swished the shield edge in a head-level attack — thrust the sword at neck-level and threw a groin-level right kick.

Jossic will be destroyed, as will his people. Zare did not like the Blues. It wouldn't bother him in the slightest to eradicate the whole pesky lot. The white dragons will suffer the same fate. Once Goldeye is dead, the Whites will be...

stomped flat. Their territory will be incorporated into Black Dragon Territory. That only left Sheema and her orange dragons. Zare side-stepped to the left — pivoted his body to the right, swished his tail, followed by a sword swipe at head-level, ending with a shield thrust at chest-level, before slamming the edge of it to the ground.

Sheema will see which way the wind is blowing and fall into her place, simple enough. Zare stood up and sheathed his sword. That just left his… allies… the vordral. He needed Loothar's people. He was not sure if he respected them or not. He trusted Loothar and his minions about as high as he could lift his mansion.

Zare gripped the shield handle with his left hand. He threw the shield up to head-level then swiped it down at leg-level for a sweep of his invisible foe's feet. He performed a nimble right shoulder roll — his armor clanked as his momentum hurled him forward back to his feet. He swung the shield again at head-level followed by a nasty one-two right inside crescent kick and tail swipe at the same area.

Zare was angry. Graff's intelligence system

had failed again. He heard Moira had reached Abyssina. He also heard that four of the six assassins were black dragons, which Goldeye would probably use as proof of his involvement. Robsko's eldest son and killer, Garth, was on the run, even Zare, himself did not know of his where-abouts. Graff hadn't screwed up completely, but he still had a lot to answer for. Zare did not want anything leading back to him. What part of this did Graff not understand? Thanks to his network's bumbling incompetence, it seemed as though Graff had all but announced it to the rest of Dragonsrod as to who was behind the attacks. Answer for it, he would.

Zare slammed the shield edge hard to the ground, ending his cadence.

CHAPTER TWENTY-NINE

-THE HATCHING-

Elmshir Warren Court House; Main Court Chamber

"I will have order in this court!" shouted the incensed elderly judge.

A gasp erupted from the stunned audience. Fras and Fray swapped nervous glances. Things had spiraled out of control in a hurry.

"Enough of the this non-sense," the elderly judge thundered. "The only way to solve this is for the accused to try on the armor. Do it now!"

Handoe did not need to be told twice.

He glanced at Leaf, who pulled a key out of his coat pocket and removed the shackles from his feet and hands. His eyes landed on the rusted, beat up breast plates. He didn't recognize the smaller plate. His eyes slid to the bigger one — the rusted grooves and scratches and the large dent just under the spot where the crest was supposed to be. Handoe studied the inside of the plate. He looked to the judges panel and smiled in recognition of the object.

"All the straps are gone," he announced, "except for the left strap, which had been cut clean through."

Another wave of whispers hissed around the court chamber as Handoe held up the breast-plate for all to see.

"Silence!" ordered the elderly judge.

The whispers faded away.

Handoe lowered the breast-plate to his body, while Leaf stood and held it to his chest. It looked like a perfect fit. Horrified expressions exploded over Fras and Fray's faces. Jaylem sunk in his chair.

"Lift your left arm," commanded the female judge sitting furthest from Fras and Fray.

Handoe did so.

He slowly turned in a circle so all could see the scar under his arm and where the strap had been cut. Fras and Fray had just lost their case and they knew it. This never happened before. Handoe's story checked out. Proof positive, they wrongfully accused one of their own of cowardice. The two stayed where they were as the other three judges leaned toward each other in a hushed, but deep, conversation.

The buzzing and whirring sound started again in the incubator on Maxum's back. Zmoge's eyes darted to him. "You, with the egg."

Maxum turned to face the general as did Leaf, Jessa and Handoe.

"What is the meaning of those sounds?" Zmoge inquired.

"I don't know," Maxum lied.

"I don't believe you."

"I don't care."

The judges broke their huddle. The elderly judge called for order and gazed down to Handoe, yet his stare was not as fierce as earlier — a good sign.

"Handoe Wextal, we three believe you have been wronged," he pointed to the two female judges. "The evidence coincides with your story," his gaze slid to Fras and Fray, whose expressions were so dark they could have passed as shadows. "Therefore, by a vote of three to two, you are found not guilty of cowardice or treason. I recommend, that the life ban, placed on you, be lifted."

"Agreed," said one female judge.

"Here-here!" the other seconded.

Handoe couldn't help but flash a wide, ear-to-ear smile. All eyes in the court room fell to Fras and Fray, who sat slumped, and deflated in their chairs.

"Fine," Fras snarled, "life ban has been lifted."

"But that doesn't excuse you from the second charge of smuggling," Fray chirped. "The accused, and his band, are moving stolen property!"

"Really, now," the elderly judge glared at the two. "It doesn't seem to us that he is smuggling anything. I see no reason to keep him here."

"But I do," Zmoge interrupted.

A collective gasp floated across the chamber from the audience.

"We do too," Fras yelled, pointing at Maxum. "The puma has the egg!"

"And I am here to claim it," Zmoge hissed, glaring at Maxum. "He *will* hand it to me."

Maxum drew his sword, as did Jessa. Handoe reached to the table and grabbed the shackles. A dragon soldier raised a crossbow and cocked it.

"Stop this!" shouted the elderly judge as he put out his hands. "Put down your weapons or I'll call in security!"

Another soldier rose his crossbow and fired it. The bolt slammed into the elderly judge's left shoulder. He crumpled to the ground, the two female judges threw themselves over him to protect him. Sandstorm stood, from behind a startled Fras and Fray, and shot his repeater, hitting the shooter between the eyes. Handoe swung the shackles like a flail, catching the other cross bower across the face, sending him, unconscious, to the floor.

Rabbits ran every-which-way. They stampeded for the chamber doors. Screams of panic — cries for more security — calls for names, wails and shrieks of fear echoed off of the walls. The other black dragon soldiers tried to get to the scrap, but were nearly trampled by the horde of fleeing spectators.

Leaf bounded from the Defense table to the bench. He pulled folded pieces of paper from a coat pocket and presented it to the three judges.

"What-What is this?" asked a female judge, nearly paralyzed with fear.

"It's the truth about what happened on the night Cranch Hollow fell," Leaf replied.

The three stared fixedly at Leaf, who continued, "My brothers were responsible for the disaster. Since Handoe was the most junior officer, he was made the scapegoat…"

Jaylem stood away from the Prosecutor's table when the melee began. Fras and Fray looked imploringly at him to do something. They couldn't do anything with a repeating crossbow aimed, point-blank at them.

Zmoge approached Maxum. "You will give me that egg!"

"Come and get it," Maxum said, his eyes twinkled and he twirled his sword.

Jessa stepped in front of Zmoge.

"Out of my way, sister of Zare," he hissed as he stepped by her.

Maxum and Zmoge raised their swords. Jessa pivoted to her right and swung her tail like a club at the back of the general's head. The impact sent the him flying over the Defense table. He lay in a heap, unconscious, at the bottom of the bench.

Jaylem's eyes landed on an abandoned crossbow, with the bolt still in the chamber and ready to fire. He lunged for it. Maxum and Handoe also saw it, but were too far away and would not be able to get to in time. Jaylem grabbed the crossbow and aimed it at Leaf. Sandstorm saw him and fired, the bolt sliced through the air into Jaylem's chest. Fras and Fray used this opportunity to escape. They shoved Sandstorm into the wall and ran into the judge's chamber and out through a window.

The court room was a wreck. Tables and chairs were over turned, blood lay in pools on the floor and splattered on the walls and bench. One black dragon soldier was dead, along with Jaylem, with two more dragons knocked unconscious. This incident, which before had only been a local matter, would surly be making the news prints not just here, but Abyssina,

Vulcria, the Griffon Empire, Cannis Republic — anyone and everyone who knew how to read, would be following this story.

Rabbit soldiers had secured the scene. Many were cleaning up the mess. Medics had taken the elderly judge to a hospital. The two female judges looked upon Leaf, Handoe and the others with a mixture of reverence and revulsion at what just happened here.

"Judge Ernu," Leaf nonchalantly said. "Judge Ketti, I do hope you are well."

The two had been shocked speechless.

A few moments passed before Judge Ernu, clutching the confessional in her right hand, her black eyes fixed on Leaf, finally spoke. "This is damning. Fras and Fray will be shamed in the eyes of Elmshir's people once this is made public knowledge. They will, no doubt, go into hiding. An investigation will be launched to see what else those two have been up to."

"What I don't understand is why? Why did they do it?" Judge Ketti asked.

"A power grab," Leaf said. "Plain old greed."

"And sympathy," Handoe added.

"Sympathy?" Judge Ketti looked quizzical at

Handoe.

"Yes," Handoe countered, "they wanted to be looked upon as victims…"

Maxum stood listening to the conversation as to how Fras and Fray swindled, conned and probably murdered to get to the top of Elmshir society. They were the ones who fled before the crossbow bolts started flying at Cranch Hollow, not Handoe.

The buzzing and whirring of the incubator started again. This time it was constant and seemed to get louder. Something else was happening — heat. This had to be another sign. If it was not, Maxum would start to think he had a bomb strapped to his back. His attention shifted back to the conversation.

"…So that must be where Jaylem came into it," Judge Ernu said.

"Yes," Leaf replied. "When questions of the disaster came up, he was given authority by my brothers to change everything so that Handoe took the fall, not them."

"Being the most junior in rank," Judge Ketti added, "he couldn't contest the ruling, so he was forced to flee, making himself look even worse in the eyes of his people."

"Precisely," Leaf replied…

Maxum stepped away, the heat seared against his back. He could smell the leather pouch burning. He yanked off his traveling cloak — the conversation abruptly stopped. All eyes in the court room focused on him as he pulled on the straps holding the pouch against his back. Maxum's fur started to burn, he tore the pouch away and quickly set it on the Prosecutor's table.

"What's up, Max?" Sandstorm asked.

"I think the egg is hatching!" Maxum exclaimed.

He stood back and watched with every one else as the pouch burst into flames and melted to ash. The incubator whirred and whistled like hot water in a tea kettle. Everybody ducked, expecting the red-hot incubator to blow up and shower the room with shrapnel. A loud hissing noise erupted instead — a couple of clicks — a pop — silence. Another pop, the incubator's hatch flew open, a mushroom-like, white smoke cloud floated up and then engulfed the now silent machine.

Everybody gasped….

Council-Leader Goldeye's Office; Grand Council Chamber Building; Kublisa

Goldeye labored at his desk mulling over paperwork and reports concerning a wide variety of issues. They ranged from the on-going drought in the Blue and Red Dragon Territories to a proposal to colonize the Buffer Zone. Pressure was building in his head. It turned to a throb of searing pain. He scrunched up his face, he winced and cupped his hands over his face. His head felt like it was about to explode — his teeth started to ache — his eyes pounded and felt like they would blow out of their sockets. Yet, as soon as it started, it stopped. He had suffered the occasional headache before, but something was different about this one. It felt as though he had just been tapped into a sub-conscious channel, but with what? Who?

"What just happened?" he gasped, slowly removing his hands from his face.

Queen Catra's Palace, Aizon, Abyssina

Moira collapsed in her room. Her head pounded, it felt as if it were on fire and her skin and flesh was being peeled and scraped away with jagged knives. She groaned as she clamped her hands over her face. Her skull felt as if it were about to blow apart. The throbbing stopped almost as fast as it started. She, too, noticed something different was happening.

Mommy. Daddy, a child's voice erupted inside their heads. *I've hatched! I'm okay!*

Moira smiled.

Goldeye smiled.

Skeleton Valley, the Buffer Zone

The griffon Seer was jolted from a deep sleep. He didn't suffer from any blinding head aches, but he knew something was happening.

"The child is born," he said, the corners of his mouth lifted into a smile. "Things are going to be very different now."

Cranch Hollow

The Mystics huddled around their cauldron as it hissed and spewed bluish-white light and steamy vapors. Their eyes were black with white slits for pupils.

"The deliverer has come," all seven chanted. "The war will now begin."

Eastern wastelands

Loothar looked as though he were feeling the effects of a bad headache. He groaned and winced. He sat in a thatched hut with a orange, glowing fire burning in the middle of the floor. The elderly dragon on Zare's staff sat across from him.

"Highness, are you alright?" he asked.

Loothar nodded.

He opened his eyes and fixed them on the old black dragon. "The egg of Goldeye has hatched. Inform Councilor Zare we are attacking Dragonsrod whether-or-not he is ready."

Main Court Chamber, Elmshir

A tiny hand with four long, skinny digits grasped one corner of the still smoking incubator. Moments later, a second hand grabbed another corner. Its skin practically glowed, it was so white. No one moved. A small, alligator-like head on a skinny neck slowly rose between its hands. Its cobalt blue eyes blinked several times as it surveyed its surroundings.

Maxum rose and walked to the baby. Its eyes locked on him, giving him a fond, affectionate look. Maxum's eyes twinkled as he looked down at the new-born chick. His face lifted into a smile. He thought about his wife and children. They were taken from him far too soon.

"GAK!" the baby coughed, flashing a gummy smile at Maxum.

Yes, his family was gone, but their memories will live in him as long as he lives.

A wave of fatherly pride swept over Maxum. He threw on his traveling cloak. The sudden motions and the ruffling sounds, made by the cloak, scared the baby. It squeaked and darted back into the incubator.

"Sorry about that, kiddo," Maxum said, holding back a laugh. "This is a traveling cloak. It won't hurt you."

The baby cautiously rose its head from the incubator and eyed the fabric. It reached for the course, thick material and pawed at it. The fright seemed to fade into a look of fascination.

"Goo. Nook," cooed the baby.

"Come on out of there," Maxum said, holding out his left arm for the baby to crawl on.

The baby was long and thin with slender arms and legs — glowing white, scaly skin and two bat-like wings, which drew a wave of gasps and whispers from those in the court chamber.

"That *is* unusual," Jessa gawked, staring at the child. "No dragon has been born with wings in centuries."

"What does this mean?" Judge Ketti wondered.

"The proverbial *chosen one*," Handoe replied, awestruck.

A sense of urgency flooded over the guardians, but none as much as Maxum.

The baby was no longer an object hidden away in a protective metal case. It had evolved into a living, breathing being, who seemed blissfully unaware of what was going on around it.

This also made the child much harder to defend. Before, it had been curled up inside the incubator, pretty much impervious to outside attacks. Not now. Only Maxum and his traveling cloak stood between itself and danger. They had to get this child to the Cannis Republic — soon.

CHAPTER THIRTY

-DUEL AT DUSK-

Kublisa

Councilor Robsko had been laid to rest. His funeral had all the pomp and pageantry suitable for someone of his status. Flags were unfurled and flew at half mast. Dragons from every clan paid their respects as did beings from other races, who Robsko had worked with over the years. Goldeye delivered a stirring eulogy and preached unity and fellowship in the face of the imposing dangers looming over Dragonsrod. El would be sworn in tomorrow as the new Green Dragon Councilor, he will serve out the rest of his father's term.

Goldeye excused himself from any further funeral related activities. He claimed he wanted to mourn in private. Mourning, however, was the last thing on his mind. It was time to settle a score. Time to seek revenge on the one who has caused so much trouble over the last couple of months. Time to end a war before it starts.

Goldeye walked through the city park, near the spot where he encountered Loothar some time back. His armor clanked as he walked down the stone path. He stopped. His ears picked up the sounds of armor somewhere in the darkness, just ahead of him. He thought maybe Loothar was paying him another visit. No. He squinted his eyes a little and saw a shadowy shape in the form of a dragon approaching him.

The other dragon pulled out his sword. Goldeye drew his. He recognized the other dragon's walk — Zare.

"No one left to do your dirty work?" Goldeye spat.

"If anyone is going to kill you, it will be me," Zare growled.

"Enough talk," Goldeye yelled. "Defend yourself!"

The two rushed at each other, the metallic clank of swords and armor smashing together shattered the stillness of the darkened park. They slashed their swords at each other in a series of attacks and parries. Goldeye swung his sword at Zare's head. He blocked the slice and thrust his shield into Goldeye's face, making a dull, thudding noise, causing the old dragon to tumble to the ground.

Zare launched his sword at Goldeye's neck in an attempt to finish him off. Goldeye, still on the ground, pivoted his lower body and swung his right leg — throwing an inside crescent kick — deflecting the thrust. Zare tried to jump on top of Goldeye and finish him with a guillotine-like slam of his shield edge to the other's neck. The old dragon lifted himself up in time and kicked Zare away from him.

Zare attacked again. He sliced downward — Goldeye blocked the attack with a right parry — threw a round-house punch and a tail swipe — both landing in a one-two succession across Zare's face, sending him staggering backward. Zare quickly recovered and slashed his sword at

Goldeye's head once again. The old dragon blocked it away just in time to be slammed in the chest by another shield thrust. Goldeye stumbled back, he bounced against an oak tree with a very thick trunk. Zare took another swing at Goldeye's head. The old dragon ducked as Zare's blade sliced into the tree trunk and was stuck there, showering the two with a volley of acorns. Goldeye rolled under Zare's right arm, thus missing another shield punch, which slammed into the tree.

Goldeye tumbled forward, slashed his sword at Zare's tail and sliced it open. Zare yelped as he slammed his shield into the hilt of his sword, yanking it free from the tree. He picked up the sword and cussed under his breath. He inspected the gash on his tail, it was a deep, oozing, ruby red blood. Another battle scar. His pale yellow eyes scanned the darkness, expecting another sword swipe to his head at any moment... nothing. Goldeye had vanished. Zare heard twigs breaking and branches scrape against armor somewhere in front of him. Time to end this — kill this old *son-of-a-berk* and take control of this country.

Goldeye ambled in the darkness between the

trees. He was stunned and hurt by the shield kiss to the right side of his face, which was puffy and bruising with a red trickle of blood from the corner of his mouth. Zare was much faster and better than he anticipated. The old dragon felt fortunate to still be alive. He started to feel a debt of gratitude to that old oak tree. It seemed to hold Zare's sword just long enough for Goldeye to make his move and get away while he still could.

He knew the injury to Zare wouldn't hold him back for long. Zare could still run, he could still use his arms and swing those cursed weapons. No doubt Zare was moving now, creeping in the darkness like a tora cat stalking a grou mouse. Perhaps, if he survived all of this, he would, one day, pay some kind of homage to that tree. Goldeye's armor clanked as he walked — it masked any sounds Zare might be making. The darkness provided little cover for him. Dragons have good night vision, so he may as well have been carrying a torch and shooting off flares.

Zare flew out from behind a large maple tree — swinging his sword in a downward slice toward Goldeye's neck and shoulder. The old dragon barely deflected the blow with his sword. Zare shield-punched Goldeye again in the chest. The old dragon tumbled down a gently slopping hill that was over grown with small shrubs and tree shoots. He had to keep rolling for Zare was right behind him. Goldeye managed to hang on to his sword as he stopped rolling. Zare charged at him again. Goldeye pivoted his body, swinging his tail and his legs up and deflected another shield thrust. He got up and slashed his sword, again, at Zare's head — Zare rose his shield causing the sword to glance off of the edge. Zare launched his sword under the shield — Goldeye dodged to his right, pivoted to his left, slammed his tail against the back of Zare's head causing him to stumble forward. Goldeye thrust his sword at Zare, who tried to kick it away — the blade passed through his left leg, grazing his femur.

"AAARRRGGHHH!"

Zare tried to get back to his feet, but couldn't. He crumpled to the ground and let out another piercing scream.

Goldeye wanted to finish him off. His arms felt like they weighed a thousand pounds each. He had nothing left. He dropped to his knees and then sunk to the ground.

He and Zare kept eye contact.

"Do you," Zare gasped, clutching his wounded left leg, "do you think that by killing me... you're going to stop what has been put into motion?"

Goldeye didn't answer at first. He just stared at Zare, seething with hatred.

"No," he finally said. "But, at least, you would be out of the way."

"The black dragons have officially seceded from Dragonsrod," Zare spat. "So have the Silvers and the Reds!"

Goldeye was shocked at this last bit of information. He kept the angry expression on his face. He was not about to let Zare see the surprise he felt. He knew Zare had manipulated some one other than Deela. But Tabric? What do the Reds have to gain by joining Zare and the vordral?

"A letter," wheezed Zare, "has been sent to your office with all the grievances—"

"Concocted by you entirely!"

"What does it matter now?"

"It matters a great deal! You orchestrated the tensions between Zhangi and Tabric's peoples.

You kept their wounds fresh, you—"

He stopped talking, something happened. He was suddenly alone. An owl hooted in the darkness. A tyrocc brayed from somewhere. Street sounds wafted into the park once again. But no Zare. Did Loothar swing down from nowhere and whisk him away? Did he just crawl away? At the moment, it didn't matter. Goldeye was hurt, but alive.

He was angry with himself. He had committed a cardinal sin in the warrior code. He underestimated his opponent and it nearly got him killed. He rose to his full height and slowly started walking again. Even though his body moved at a snail's pace, his mind sprinted at full speed. Time had come to organize his forces — find out who his friends are and rally them. The time for fighting would soon begin. For now… it was time to go home.

CHAPTER THIRTY-ONE

-MYTERS-

South of Elmshir

If Handoe, Sandstorm, Maxum and Jessa thought things would improve once they left Elmshir — rude surprises were in store for them. The baby, which they called "Gak," because it was a sound he liked to make, was crying, screaming and making a royal fuss. The four had no way to know that the baby could sense the fear and uncertainty surging through his father as he prepared to fight Zare.

"What's the matter with him?" Sandstorm asked, his voice had a mixture of concern and irritation in it.

"I don't know," Maxum admitted. "He pushed away the food I gave him. He doesn't need a change, because I just did that."

Gak wailed and kicked his stubby legs into Maxum's chest. In Elmshir, Maxum made a carrier out of leather straps and canvas cloth for Gak to sit in. He extended the neck-hole of his traveling cloak so that if Gak wanted to peek out and look around, he could. Today, however, the little dragon kept hidden. Maxum ignored the subdued grunts and sighs coming from the other three as Gak continued to cry. *That's okay, they've never been parents — they don't know.*

It might have been the heat. The landscape south of Elmshir was hilly, arid and dusty. A hot wind sprayed a gritty dust in their faces and eyes. Maxum lifted the hood over his head several times. The cantankerous wind kept ripping it back around his shoulders.

A tyrocc brayed from somewhere in the distance. Everyone froze.

"Where did that come from?" Jessa craned her long neck over her left shoulder.

"Could be anywhere," Handoe spoke, from ahead of her, his long ears twitched. "Sounds can bounce off these hills and canyons."

"I'm for getting out of here as soon as possible," Maxum voted.

"Here-here," Sandstorm seconded.

Zmoge was still seething with anger over the "battle" in Elmshir. No one humiliated him like that and lived to tell about it — no one! His mercenary army had assembled just to the east of the rabbit city. His force consisted of about twenty dragons (of various clans,) including Walker and his surviving escorts. The five myter handlers agreed to tag along as did four lions and about a dozen pig-like javilines. It was not much of an army. No matter, he had no plans on storming and capturing Elmshir, that was not his mission.

Zmoge hated mercenaries — untrustworthy, undisciplined, no loyalty. He had seen it many times before. Mercenaries would be hired for a job and then turned on their employers as fast as the winds shift in speed and direction, like in these parts, because the other side offered them a higher bounty.

The myters, perched on the arms of their cannidene handlers, squawked and chirped in an exited way. Their hood-covered heads pointed to the southwest. One myter squealed loudly causing an already skittish tyrocc to bellow out a loud protest. The caravan, which was already moving at a snail's pace, halted.

"General Zmoge," called the lead handler, named Massox, mounted on a tyrocc just ahead of him.

"What is it?" Zmoge snarled.

"The myters have detected the quarry."

"And...?"

"Shall we release them?"

"Of course!"

Massox said something in his native tongue to the myter before lifting the hood from the beast's head. Zmoge didn't catch what he said to it, probably an activation word or phrase like *Go get 'em!* The other handlers removed the hoods from their myters, which lifted from the handlers' arms and flocked together, flying to the southwest.

"Do we follow?" Massox asked, looking at Zmoge, who watched the myters fly away.

"No," he replied calmly. "We move due South. Your monsters will, hopefully, chase them right to us," he turned to the rest of the caravan. "MOVE OUT!"

The baby went deathly silent — this could be a bad sign. Moments ago, he was throwing a real tantrum. Now, not a peep. Maybe he just drifted off to sleep. Maybe he could sense something was wrong. Jessa seemed to sense something was wrong, she cranked her head over her left shoulder to the northeast. Her eyes widened in a look of terror.

"Oh *flix!*" she cussed.

"What?" Handoe asked, his ears turned back toward her, while keeping his eyes fixed ahead.

"Myters!" she gasped. "Approaching from the northeast — *fast!*"

"RUN!" Handoe shouted.

The four sprinted for the opening to a nearby gorge. The myters were closing the gap. The five fire-spitters flew in a tight V-formation, zeroing in on their quarry like sharks to a dying whale.

"Split up when you reach the gorge!" Handoe yelled.

The myters squeaked and squealed in a delighted way. Handoe, Maxum, Sandstorm and Jessa rushed through the gorge-mouth as if they were storming a fortress. The four split up and ran down twisting, winding, labyrinthine corridors that emptied into tree strewn gullies and gulches. The myters flew over the gorge-mouth and zoomed into the maze in pursuit.

Maxum nearly tripped and fell three different times due to the uneven, depression pocked, terrain he was running down. The last thing he wanted to do was squash baby Gak because of an accidental fall with a mean tempered fire-breathing creature, literally hot on his tail. He had to do something, real fast, before the myters fell on him and the baby and turned them into piles of ash. He crouched down at the base of a tall blood-wood tree. His eyes sunk into the neck-hole of his traveling cloak at the baby, who was looking quizzically back at him.

"Come here, kiddo," he said, his face lifted into a warm smile, he padded his left shoulder with that hand.

The baby giggled and crawled up Maxum's arm to his shoulder. The little dragon gently stretched his arms around the other's neck. "Stay under there." Maxum cooed.

A myter squawked from somewhere close by. Maxum's ears shifted and bent as he tried to guess where the shrill chirp came from. His eyes again shifted to the bump under his traveling cloak. "Hang on tight, kiddo, this could get a little rough."

The baby made a babbling sound and then went silent.

Maxum drew his sword and a dagger. He banged the flat-side of his sword against the blood-wood tree, the clanking sound resonated around the gully. Myters were vicious at worst — unpredictable at best. He had heard stories as to how a myter would, every-now-and-then, turn on its handler and reduce him to a flaming crisp. He knew enough about them to realize that when they are pursuing you, you have only one choice — kill them, before they kill you.

Maxum continued to bang his sword on the tree trunk. The baby seemed to realize what he was doing and tightened his grip around Maxum's neck. Maxum looked up into the canape — another squawk, the myter spotted him. The fire-breather swooped down, its mouth frothing flame. Maxum swung his sword with his left hand, to distract the creature, while tossing his dagger with his right hand, up at it. The blade cleaved through the fire-breather's right shoulder. The creature let out an anguished scream as it erupted into a ball of flame and crashed to the ground like a comet hitting the planet's surface.

Maxum sprinted away as the trunk of the blood-wood tree and all around it splashed into flames. As Maxum ran, the baby poked his head over the hood of the traveling cloak and stared fixedly at the inferno.

"Let's go, Gak," Maxum said. "There's four more where that one came from."

Handoe was in serious trouble. Two myters followed him while he sprinted down a particularly twisty and narrow corridor. Twice, he dodged and rolled just in time as a myter spit fireballs that splattered flame on the canyon wall, mere inches away from him. He didn't have time to stop and shoot his repeater — the myters would have fried him. It seemed running, rolling and dodging were his only defenses. He was exhausted, he moved as though his legs were about to give out at any second. He sucked in air in even, short breaths. Instinct, momentum and an extreme will to survive kept him going.

A myter swooped over his head and spit another fireball, which singed the fur on his back and tail. Handoe dove over a large rock and tumbled down a small ravine before rolling into a rock outcropping, a cloud of dust settled over him. A myter zipped over the large rock and swooped down straight for him. Handoe couldn't move. The little fire-breather glided over him, flapped its wings and darted over a near-by hill.

Handoe couldn't believe his luck. He slowly rose to his feet. His eyes fell on a small grove of stunted pine trees at the bottom of a gully. With supreme effort, he ran to them.

Handoe slid under the low hanging branches of the pines at the same time as a myter flew over a rocky outcropping on top of a neighboring hill. The creature zoomed down the slope, straight for the thicket Handoe now hid under. He expected, for a second time, to be roasted into oblivion. His eyes followed the myter's shadow as it zipped closer with surprising speed — it flapped its wings and darted over the tree-tops and out of sight. Handoe could breathe easy for the moment. He figured the myters couldn't see him if he didn't move. As long as he didn't do anything stupid, make any loud noises, or have a myter fly under the canape and hit him in the face, this grove will be a haven, not a funeral pyre.

Sandstorm and Jessa did not split up. The myters relentlessly pursued them, torching a small grove of wild junipers after Jessa tripped and fell, exposing their hiding spot. They dove into the mouth of a nearby cave.

"I'm tired of this!" Jessa spat, drawing her sword.

Sandstorm scowled as he cocked his repeater. His face lifted into a smile as if noticing he had just found hidden treasure. "I have an idea!"

"What?" she asked, casting him a hard gaze.

"I need you to draw their attention."

"What?"

"Draw them to you, so I can shoot them down."

Jessa glared at him. "You're serious?"

Sandstorm patted his crossbow. "I won't miss."

"You better not!" she snapped. "If they spit on me, I'm a goner."

He smiled again. "They have to get close enough. This crossbow shoots further than they can spit."

Jessa pointed her sword at him. "You better not miss!"

"Trust me."

She stepped out of the cave entrance and glanced up at the rocky, sloping canyon walls toward the blue sky.

"Come on, you little *zoofs!*" she shouted. "Here I am!"

She slapped her tail to the ground, causing a small dust cloud, and raked her sword into an arch in the dirt in front of her.

A myter squawked from somewhere close.

Jessa broke into what looked like a dance. Sandstorm squatted down behind her. She wasn't much of a dancer — her "moves" were stiff, rigid and awkward. Sandstorm had to force back a laugh. She scooted to the left, shimmied to the right and did some kind of a heavy-footed pirouette.

"Here it comes," she said, watching a myter fly over a hill-top and swoop toward her.

Sandstorm said nothing.

The little fire-spitter squealed and seemed to increase its speed toward her.

"Do you see it?" she squawked, not hiding the worry in her voice.

"Keep going," he demanded.

She strutted and shuffled.

The myter was getting bigger, very fast. Flame danced in its mouth, between its short, pointed teeth.

"It's getting closer!" she threw him a panicky look.

She kicked her right leg out and swished her tail.

The myter squealed again, drooling out orange flames, it was within one-hundred yards and rapidly closing. Jessa lifted her tail toward her head and did a flat-footed twirl. Sandstorm pulled the trigger and cocked in a new bolt. The projectile hissed between her head and tail, missing both by inches, it sliced through the air and impaled the little beast between the neck and right shoulder. The myter let out an anguished scream before erupting into flames. The fireball bounced off the ground twice before skidding into a large rock and exploding.

"You were a little close with that last shot," Jessa huffed.

"You're still alive, aren't you?" Sandstorm countered.

Another squawk.

The myter folded its wings back and dropped into a dive. Both could see it.

"It probably saw its buddy blow apart," Sandstorm speculated. "It's mad. We got it where we want it."

Jessa looked like she was winding down, she stopped her odd dance and started jumping up-and-down, throwing out her arms. "Come on. Come and get some!"

The myter blew two wads of flaming saliva — Jessa shoulder rolled to the right. Sandstorm jumped out from the cave-mouth, pointed his repeater up and pulled the trigger before running back inside the cave just as the fireballs splattered around the entrance. The myter folded around the bolt as it slammed into its body. The creature smoldered and then burst into fireball before plummeting to the ground.

Moments later, Sandstorm emerged from the smoke drenched cave. Fire danced and raged near the entrance. His eyes fell to Jessa, who was covered in dust and slowly rising to her feet, her chest rose and fell as she sucked in one deep breath after another.

"You alright?" he asked.

She nodded.

"Let's go find the others," he said.

A short pause followed.

He looked up at her and grinned. "You're a lousy dancer."

"Shut up!" she huffed.

Handoe had been betrayed — by a simple body function, he sneezed. A myter heard it, squawked, and zeroed in on the trees he was hiding under. Handoe scrambled out from the grove just before the myter proceeded to incinerate it. Handoe fired his repeater — the bolt sailed harmlessly by the myter, which swooped down for another attack.

Another myter squealed in front of him. Great! Caught between two fire-breathers. He cocked another bolt into the chamber. He could get one — but he'd be cooked before he could cock in another round. What a way to go.

Perhaps sensing a kill, the myters swooped down on him from opposite directions. Handoe pivoted to his right, aimed and pulled the trigger. He heard a loud pop from behind him, followed by a shower of smoldering myter remains. His bolt had found its mark as a fireball smashed to the ground in front of him. Who killed the other myter?

He heard a mechanical click, he turned around and saw Jinks standing in front of him with a small, hand-held crossbow pointed at his face.

"I suppose I owe you for that one," Handoe said.

The fat monitor lizard wore the most deranged of looks on his face. Handoe and Jinks went back a few years, but their relationship was mostly adversarial, there was no love-loss here.

"For that," Jinks yowled, "and *so much more!*"

"What do you mean?" Handoe asked with a growing degree of caution in his voice.

He made no sudden movements. He knew Jinks would not think twice about shooting him.

Jinks ran a clawed finger along the length of the scar on his nose, while grimacing at Handoe. His tongue flicked faster, his whip-like tail swished in a hard, aggressive way.

"For this!" he screamed, a maniacal glare in his marble-like eyes. "For the humiliations at the cantinas. You did this to me!"

"No Jinxy," Handoe said calmly. "Your own greed and actions is what got you into trouble. You did this to yourself."

"No!" Jinks shouted, he tightened his grip on his crossbow, his eyes bulged and he started to shake. "I will not be humiliated any more!"

Maxum emerged from a nearby rock outcropping. Jinks turned to Maxum and pointed his weapon at him. Handoe cocked his repeater — Jinks turned back to him. The two stood poised and ready to shoot each other.

"We don't have to do this, Jinxy," Handoe said.

"DON'T CALL ME THAT!"

Maxum drew his sword.

Jinks jerked his body toward the puma. Handoe's finger tightened around the trigger.

"You have the egg," Jinks's eyes glinted and a wide, ugly smile split open his face. "Give it to me!"

Maxum shook his head. "Not possible."

The smile vanished from Jinks's face. "What do you mean, 'not possible'?"

The lizard looked as though he were about to blow several blood vessels. He seemed to have gone out of his mind.

"Jinks," Handoe said, a warning tone to his voice.

The baby poked his head out of the neck hole

just under Maxum's chin. Jinks gasped, his eyes bulged out even wider and his jaw hung open.

"It hatched!" he murmured to himself.

His eyes darted back-and-forth, he looked to be deep in thought. Words spilled out of his mouth. "Oh, Zare will reward me handsomely for this! I will be rich beyond my wildest dreams!"

"You'll have to get by me first," Maxum snarled, his face scrunched in to a toothy sneer, his ears lowered behind his head. He drew out his other dagger.

"Then you'll have to get by me," Handoe growled, his eyes narrowed.

He and Maxum glanced at each other and grinned slightly.

Jinks was completely out-matched — he had to know it. He kept turning his head from Handoe to Maxum. It seemed as though the fat monitor lizard was having an internal battle between his common sense and his greed. His greed won out. "YOU WILL GIVE ME THAT BABY!"

Jinks pulled his trigger. The bolt sailed toward Maxum's head. Maxum swished his sword in an outward, clockwise motion — he flicked his dagger with his left hand at Jinks. Handoe fired his crossbow — Maxum's sword deflected Jinks's bolt with a loud *clank!* The dagger stuck deep into Jinks's chest — Handoe's crossbow bolt sliced through the lizard's neck. Jinks dropped to the ground in a bloody heap — dead.

"Sorry, Jinxy," Handoe lowered his crossbow. "I know you deserved better."

Zmoge's mounted caravan inched forward. He smirked at the dejected looks on Massox and other handlers' faces. They could easily see the many inky black smoke plumes snaking up into the hazy, graying, afternoon sky. None of the myters returned, no bother. The handlers can always get new ones. Time to move on. His eyes fell on a black dragon, sentry mounted on a tyrocc behind two dark furred rabbits, one with a monocle over his left eye. The two scampered for the caravan.

"ALL STOP!" Zmoge yelled as loud as his damaged vocal chords would allow.

"Stop you two," ordered the sentry, trotting his tyrocc after the pair.

Zmoge's eyes twinkled and his face lifted into

a delighted, twisted, evil smile.

"Fras and Fray," he snarled, almost laughing at their dirty, tattered long tailed coats.

"We surrendered to your scout," Fras sniveled, "in hopes of seeking your audience."

"We wish to add our services as humble citizens of Black Dragon Territory," Fray added, desperation wringing out of his voice.

"Do you now?" Zmoge's crooked, pointy toothed smile parted his cheeks even further from his chin.

"We know these lands very well," Fras croaked.

"As do I," Zmoge countered.

Fras and Fray let out exasperated gasps.

"I know what you *really* want," he said keeping his gaze firmly on them. "You want revenge."

Fras and Fray's faces perked up into hopeful looking smiles, their ears lifted up from their backs.

"Yes we want revenge!" Fras screamed.

"We want our city back!" Fray yelled.

"I'll be the one to decide what you get," Zmoge growled.

Fras and Fray's smiles faded. They knew

Zmoge was one not to be toyed with.

"I, too, know what happened the night Cranch Hollow fell," he snarled. "I know all about your cowardice and treachery! If you do anything that dissatisfies me, I will kill you and leave your carcasses to rot where they fall."

Zmoge's eyes lifted to the sentry, he pointed at the other. "Take them — they are to ride with you."

"Yes, sir."

The sentry dismounted, grabbed the now droopy eared and crestfallen Fras and Fray by the scruffs of their necks and threw them on the tyrocc's back.

"We have to make a quick trip to the border and I want nothing to slow us down. MOVE OUT!" Zmogge yelled, holding a hand over his throat.

CHAPTER THIRTY-TWO

-DRAGONSROD DISSOLVED-

Grand Council Chamber, Kublisa

Goldeye didn't bother to change from his armor. His battle with Zare left him bruised and sore. He ignored the whispers and muffled talking from many of the remaining delegations. He stood at the podium, clutching some paper in his right hand. His mismatched eyes floated over the reptilian, mammalian and bird-like faces of the loyal councilors and their entourages; his Whites, El's Greens, Sheema's Oranges, Jossic's Blues and Zhangi's Golds. His eyes stuck on the swath of empty seats between the green and white dragon delegations, where Tabric's red dragons once sat.

"Councilors and staffs," Goldeye said in a sad, almost defeated voice. "As you can see… three delegations chose to leave us," his eyes moved over the Gold, Blue and Orange entourages before briefly resting on the empty seats of the Silver and Black clans, on the far right. "Councilor Zare has manipulated Councilor Deela and Councilor Tabric into secession. Dragonsrod has been effectively — split in two."

The delegations exchanged mutterings with one another. Goldeye held up the thirty page manifesto/secession notice/declaration of war. The whispers faded and all attention was once more on him. He spoke again; "Councilor Zare has listed over one-hundred grievances with me, with various councilors, here today, with Dragonsrod itself. I will not read these accusations aloud — there are too many and they are baseless!"

Gisko and Bard handed out copies of this treasonous blather to the councilors and their staffs to read.

Goldeye continued; "Zare feels this style of government is antiquated. None of us are capable of leading a garbage detail in his eyes, let alone our territories. So he feels he can do it with us... or without us."

Zhangi stood up, a baffled look on his face. "This does not make sense!"

"None of it does!" Sheema squealed, shooting him a sharp look.

"What does *he* have to gain by turning us against each other?" Zhangi boomed.

El stood, his red, snake-like eyes flicked to Zhangi. "Divide and conquer! He manipulated my brother in to killing my father!"

"Just as he managed to get Deela to lower her defenses so he could walk through her territory and take it over," Goldeye added.

A silence fell hard on the chamber and its stunned occupants. Zhangi, Sheema and El returned to their seats. Jossic stood up, a look of worry filled his indigo eyes. "Does this mean we are going to war… against our own people and the vordral?"

Goldeye's brow slanted up and he dipped his head toward the lectern. He could not bring himself to say it — he could only nod.

"I have five regiments in Green Dragon Territory," Jossic said. "Now that Tabric has joined Zare, that leaves only the Orzolla Pass as a lifeline between Green Dragon Territory and the rest of Dragonsrod. If that falls… so could Dragonsrod itself."

Another wave of mutterings swept around the chamber.

Goldeye had thought of this too. The Orzolla Pass was a fossilized river bed, that used to be a drainage region for the Sandrega River until it turned its flow northward, turning it in to a sandy scar that separated the Northern Grash mountains from the southern half of the chain. The Pass was squished between four territories. The whites owned it; the blacks disputed the claim, their territory was directly to the North; the reds were immediately due South; while the Pass emptied into Green Dragon Territory.

"The Pass must remain open at all costs," Goldeye said, his eyes moving across the chamber. "Jossic is right. It is too important for our survival. It must-not-fall!"

"What do you want us to do?" Sheema asked.

"Prepare your peoples," Goldeye countered. "War isn't coming — it's here! It will stay here until either this group, or Zare's group falls. The first battle will be at the wall in Green Dragon Territory. I don't think that Zare has any control over his vordral allies. I'm going to be there, until further notice… session is adjourned!"

He pounded the cracked and blood stained gavel on the podium. No one left. Everyone stood up, all eyes fixed on Goldeye.

"We stand with you," Sheema proclaimed.

"What are your orders?" Jossic asked.

An uncontrollable smile stretched around Goldeye's face. He was touched by this show of unity. His smile would soon fade.

"This will not be an easy, or a quick operation," he warned. "Zare will be a worthy opponent, he has a good military mind and is unlikely to make too many mistakes. We *must* stick together in this. I am confident that if we stay united, we will keep this country together and in peace, as it should be. I want to end this by swaying as many black, red and silver dragons away from his grasp and back into our fold as soon and as bloodless as possible," the old dragon's eyes glinted and a savage look crossed his age-lined face.

"Dragonsrod will *never* recognize Zare's regime!"

"And what of Zare, Deela and Tabric?" Zhangi inquired.

Goldeye paused for a moment. His jaw muscles tightened.

"Deela and Tabric will be welcomed back, if they come to their senses," he spoke. "Zare has too much to answer for. It is my guess that he does not speak for all of his people and we must use that against him."

A brief pause.

Jossic stood. "What of the vordral?"

"The griffons are at war with them," Goldeye replied. "We will need the griffons' assistance in dealing with the vordral. They have offered their talons in friendship… I suggest we take them up on it."

A few short months ago this sort of thing may have been unthinkable to him. Sure the griffons were a powerful enemy, one that very nearly defeated and conquered Dragonsrod. That, however was in the past. The griffons could be even more powerful friends. Friends that could keep this region in safety and security. Goldeye's options were limited. He faced war on two fronts — he needed any and all help that was offered and it didn't matter now from who.

El stood up. "I suggest we do it."

Jossic also stood. "I concur!"

Sheema and Zhangi exchanged glances and then stood up. "We agree!"

Goldeye met with his councilors later that evening. He wanted Sheema to establish the proper communications with the griffons to make this alliance official. Next, she was to travel to Abyssina to aid Moira in gaining support for their cause in the vordral issue. He sent a wire to Queen Catra asking her to host a series of talks to gain support from her people. He sent wires to the junglewolves, the Nelvainians, Vulcrians and any other race that lived in these lands to attend the conference, if Catra gave her okay. He wanted Moira to be the lead speaker for Dragonsrod. He knew she had some experience in diplomacy. He knew Sheema was much more experienced at it and would make an invaluable tool to help her. Questions were sure to rise about Dragonsrod's internal troubles. He wanted Moira and Sheema to down-play the uprising as nothing more than that.

He wanted Zhangi to take charge of Dragonsrod should he not return. The gold dragon councilor was smart and aggressive and was nearly equal in rank to Jossic, who was going with Goldeye and El to Green Dragon Territory.

Goldeye snoozed in his office. Midnight had come and gone. A little desk lantern provided a weak, pale yellow glow that captured a few of the room's highlights against the dark. He sat behind his desk, his eyes were closed and he snored softly. His snout pressed against his chest and his hands were clasped on his belly. It had been three days since he last slept.

His office door opened with a squeak. He lifted his sleepy eyes to Gisko, standing in the doorway.

"Yes, Gisko?"

He studied the troubled look on his subordinate's face. "Come in please, pull up a seat." He perked up, laced his fingers together and rested them on the desktop.

Gisko pulled a chair away from the wall and sat down across the desk from Goldeye.

"I want to speak with you, sir."

"Of course, what's on your mind?"

"Is it a good idea for you to be going to the border, especially now?"

Goldeye sensed this had been coming ever since he mentioned it earlier in the day. He met Gisko's concern with reassurance and calm. "I feel I have to. All this happened on my watch. The news of Zare's secession is flooding all the newsprints, fear is gripping the country. Uncertainty, rumors of war are everywhere. Many are telling me to right this wrong. Others want me to resign. Still others want my head on a sliver platter. I have to go. It's the only thing I can do."

"I wish to go in your place," Gisko said, defiance in his voice.

Goldeye let out a chuckle. "Sorry, m'boy, I need you here. Besides, I've already made up my mind."

That settled that.

Gisko dipped his head, he stared dejectedly at the floor.

Goldeye understood exactly how his young aide felt. He was there once — young — book-smart — eager to prove himself…

"You must stay here and work with Zhangi and Sheema," he said calmly. "You are in charge of White Dragon Territory until I get back."

"Yes, sir," Gisko whispered, still looking

crestfallen.

Goldeye kept his gaze on Gisko's sad looking face.

"Don't be too anxious for war, my friend," he warned. "As leader of a country, it's the *last* thing you want."

Goldeye rose from his chair, flashed a tired, sad grin to Gisko, who also stood. "It's time for us to go to our homes, have a good meal, get some sleep. The gods know when that will happen again."

Good advice.

Goldeye hoped Gisko understood what was in store for him. He knew the young dragon would likely be cooped up in Kublisa for a long time to come.

Queen Catra's Palace, Aizon, Abyssina

Moira had been summoned to the Public Court Chamber. It was empty other than for Queen Catra, seated on her throne. Shayara and Serena knelt on either side of her. The blond furred Kaymo stood beside Shayara. River Rat accompanied Moira, Bolten was their escort.

Moira was under considerable strain. The baby was flooding her head with its own thoughts and fears, thus re-igniting her maternal protective instincts. She read a Dragonsrod news print telling about the withdrawal of the Black, Red and Silver clans from her country.

Catra rose from her throne, her silky, red gown shimmered and gleamed as she moved. Her eyes fixed on Moira's stressed face. She clutched a paper in her right hand.

"It appears Goldeye wants a council," Catra said calmly. "He wants a conference, and he wants you to be Dragonsrod's lead representative. He wants the junglewolves, the Nelvanians and anyone else in the region to come here. He's afraid your war could spill across our borders and swallow us. He also seems to think the dragon rebels will send a faction to gain sympathy for them. We seem to be very important to you all of a sudden. He's asking for my permission to have the conference here."

Shayara and Serena exchanged glances, before fixing their stares back to their mother and Moira.

Moira couldn't read Catra's facial expression. Her tone of voice echoed a combination of concern, irritation and intrigue.

"What do you think, Highness?" Moira asked in a hushed voice.

"I don't know. Abyssina has not been at war in two centuries. We aren't being attacked. My people won't see the danger and may not wish to get involved in what they would see as being someone else's problem."

That sickly feeling had slugged Moira in the stomach again. She didn't know what to say. She felt nervous and was not sure what Goldeye was asking her to do.

"With respects, Highness," River Rat requested.

Catra's eyes slid down to him. "Yes?"

"He wouldn't bother you with this if he didn't think it of utmost importance. There is a danger — however unlikely — that this conflict could spread over the border into Abyssina and beyond. Will you, at least, listen to what they have to say?"

"Of course," her eyes slid to Moira. "As I said earlier, we watch the events in neighboring countries with much interest. We will hear what *all* parties have to say, including the dragon rebels."

River Rat's face dropped.

Catra continued; "I don't know what other issues are going to be brought up and I don't even know who, if anyone, will show up. It will be heard and dealt with fairly. So be warned, you may not get what you want, you may leave here disappointed."

Such was the politics of diplomacy.

Catra slid a look to Kaymo. "Send word to all the countries in the region about this conference — meet here for an urgent summit in say… two weeks time?"

Moira nodded.

"At once," Kaymo bowed low and exited.

Zare's mansion, Gronoz, Black Dragon Territorial capital city.

Gronoz was the third largest city in Dragonsrod, named for a black dragon council-leader, who succeeded Gortha The Great. Only Kublisa and Drallics were larger and as modern. It was a good city to be the capital of a fledgling country. Two rivers, the Big Black and the Zoopour flowed around the city, providing natural defenses. Shipping ports littered the banks of these rivers bringing commerce, big business and wealth to this city. Mounds of wealth.

Zare's finger prints were all over much of these operations, both legit and illegal. He was enjoying life right now. Deela and Tabric seemed to be falling in line with his views. He had succeeded in ripping Dragonsrod apart. Goldeye was, again, with his back to the wall and in some trouble. Yes, life was good and getting better with each passing minute.

Zare lit a long green cigar, drew in and blew out a heavy, swirling fog-bank of milky, gray, peppery-sweet smoke. He grasped a cane and hobbled into a war-room where Tabric and Deela stood on opposite sides of a long, rectangular table with a detailed map of eastern Dragonsrod draped over it. Zare puffed on his cigar and stopped next to Deela. He pointed a finger at the little strip of land (the only piece of White Dragon Territory on the map.)

"The Orzolla Pass?" Tabric croaked.

"Yes," Zare said, a gleam in his eyes. "It's the only life-line to Green Dragon Territory from inland. If we take it, we could can starve the Greens out and force them to surrender."

"Goldeye would have thought of that already," Tabric snapped.

"Maybe not," Zare countered. "I was down there about two days ago — completely undefended!"

"Goldeye *does* have the Pass defended," Loothar said, seemingly from out of nowhere. He clomped into the room and stood at the head of the table. "The Orzolla Pass is of little importance at this time and is a secondary target."

Zare turned sharply to Loothar. "What do you mean it's of little importance? We take the Pass and we could cut them off and bring about their defeat. Cause them to sue for peace!"

"No," Loothar countered. "We will attack Goldeye's Army behind their defenses and annihilate them there. It will become a mere mop-up operation after that."

Tabric now turned to Loothar, his eyes glinting. "A mop-up operation? In case you have forgotten, the standing armies of the Blues, Whites and Golds will fight you every step of the way!"

Loothar's red eyes narrowed. His black face lifted into a tight-lipped grin. "We will destroy them all. Either one at a time, or all at once."

Deela looked to Loothar. "You sound confident."

His eyes slid to hers. "I am, my lady," his gaze fell to Zare and Tabric. "Concentrate on the border. The rest will fall in due time."

Zare and Tabric grunted. Deela remained silent.

CHAPTER THIRTY-THREE

-THE VORDRAL ATTACK-

Eastern Green Dragon Territorial border
Goldeye, Jossic and El toured the defensive wall with the watch commander (a gold dragon named Florus.) He showed them the camouflaged trenches in front of the wall that concealed long, pointy wooden spikes. Abates and booby-traps were set behind the trenches. After the tour, the trio walked through the maze of tents and huts that made up the dragon camp, to a large, multi-chambered tent located near the middle of the encampment. A flurry of smells flooded their senses — various foods mingled with the bitter smells of coffee and wood smoke.

The slight sour stench of body odor from the thousands of dragons cooped up in such a small area and once in a while the stink of the sewer lagoons would waft into camp and cause a few complaints. But for most, the prolonged exposure made them numb to the mixture of these aromas and odors.

The three entered the tent and stood in front of a large table with a detailed map of Green Dragon Territory spread on top of it. A red dragon dressed in dull gray chest and shoulder armor over a chain mail shirt stood at the other end of the table.

"Councilors," Goldeye said, his eyes moving from Jossic and El to the red dragon. "This is General Goza, overall commander of the eastern defenses."

Jossic and El nodded to the general, who returned the gesture. The councilors tensed up at the sight of a red dragon pouring over their plans. Goldeye sensed the brewing hostility and decided to put an end to the tensions before it got any worse.

"General Goza is loyal to Dragonsrod," Goldeye explained, his eyes darted to his fellow councilors. "He had been interviewed at length and *not* found to be suspicious in any way."

"I do not agree with my province's reasons for leaving Dragonsrod," Goza spoke in a croaky voice that reminded Goldeye of Bard. "I've never liked Zare and I wish to see his head impaled on a pole. Now, shall we focus on the job at hand?"

That sounded convincing enough.

"Proceed," Goldeye looked to Goza. "Give us the status report."

"The defenses along the this boundary are complete," Goza reported. "The line of works running the length of the Sandrega River Valley are the problem."

Goldeye lowered his gaze to the map. Several solid green lines, indicating Dragonsrod positions, were stacked together behind jagged scribbles for the wall. In front of that, in a large red circle, represented the last known vordral position. Not much room for the enemy to maneuver with in front of the wall. If all goes to plan, it would be the ideal bottleneck.

"The problems are going to be with the forts," General Goza continued. "They are too widely dispersed and the gaps between them are too large."

Every one's attention fell to the tiny green dots and broken, squiggly lines stretched across the south banks of the Sandrega River.

Goza spoke; "There is no way we can hold the entire valley against a well coordinated attack. If Zare overruns even one fort along this line, he could drive through the center of this territory and cut us off."

"My father was preparing us for such an event," El said, his snake-like eyes coursing around the table. "He was convinced Zare was about attack. The plan was to have Garth," El paused after saying his brother's name. "Garth was to command the northern border, while I command the southern defenses. I was to aid him if he needed it."

"If it were necessary," Jossic inquired, "how long would it take to move your support troops to the northern defenses?"

"From where they are now," El replied, "two days."

General Goza opened his mouth to speak, but instead, slid a gaze in deferral to Goldeye. The old dragon kept his eyes fixed on El. "Bring half of your secondary force up here to re-enforce the forts. Make sure they are positioned where they can lend help to any fort that may need them."

Goldeye looked sideways to General Goza. "Is that satisfactory, general?"

"It will have to do," he sighed, but didn't sound too confident it would be enough.

"That brings us back to the vordral," Jossic said.

"I don't understand," El piped out. "Why don't we just attack them?"

Just like his father.

Goldeye grinned and fixed his eyes on the youthful green dragon. "We can't. To the world, we need to be the victims."

El cast a bewildered gaze at Goldeye. The youngster does not understand. But he soon will.

"We need to unite as many dragons under our banners as possible," Goldeye continued; "An attack by an outside force, such as the vordral, will do just that. Many of Zare's legions do not trust Loothar's people and will view them as a possible threat. One that represents just as great a threat to *them* as they do us."

"And such an assault will galvanize dragons against the vordral," Jossic added. "Without his allies, Zare's cause is doomed."

"The vordral seem all too eager to be the aggressors," General Goza put in.

After a brief pause, Goldeye determined this meeting to be about over. "Councilor El, begin the movements of your troops to the forts as soon as possible. See to it, personally that they get in position in the next two days."

"Yes, sir," El saluted and exited the tent.

Goldeye blew out a sigh and glanced to Jossic and then to Goza.

"Let's make the final preparations," he said. "I think they are going to attack in the next few days."

Goldeye stood on the wall. He stared into inky blackness of night. His eyes coursed from the many sentries, lining the earthworks, to the rolling grasslands. He half expected to see thousands of vordral charging at them. Nothing, not even a bat chasing a moth. Only the cool night breeze caressing his face. This was good, it meant that no battle would be happening tonight. It was deeply disturbing at the same time for no enemy activity could be seen. No campfires, no smoke trails, no sounds other than the wind whispering warnings over the tall grass — *The vordral are out there, take heed!* They may be hunkering down in the ravines or hiding behind nearby copses of trees. For all he knew, the vordral may even be able to spring up from the very ground itself and tear out his heart and lungs before he even knew what was going on.

Little to nothing was known of the vordral. Goldeye was definitely curious about these beings. What did they eat? What were their habits? What was their culture like? What have they been doing over the last three hundred years? Goldeye knew he would not be getting these questions answered anytime soon.

"Are you alright, sir?" came Bard's croaky voice.

Goldeye faced his massive body guard and grinned. "Yes, I'm fine."

The two faced the grasslands.

"It's been a week," Bard said. "Do you still think the vordral are going to attack?"

"This is the hardest part of it," Goldeye returned. "I hate the waiting. Part of me wants them to attack — get it over with, we all know it's coming. Part of me wants them to turn east and keep going, live their lives and leave us to ours. *All* of me wants Dragonsrod back as a single, united country again. I will do practically anything to get it back. General Goza is right about Loothar, he craves the taste of blood."

Bard blew out a sigh.

"What do you think?" Goldeye asked.

"I don't believe we will survive this," he replied. "I remember all those dead at the griffon outposts…"

Goldeye cocked up an eyebrow. He had thought of this too.

Bard continued; "I think they will attack us until they overwhelm us. I'm sorry, sir, but you did ask."

Goldeye nodded. He felt the same way, yet he could not openly say it.

"Well, my friend," he said patting Bard on the shoulder again. "I hope you are wrong."

"As do I, sir."

Goldeye was asleep in his tent when Bard entered and gently shook him awake. "Sir!"

"Huh-wah?"

"Sir, they're coming!"

Goldeye sat up and rubbed his eyes. "Is everything ready?"

"Yes, sir," Bard said, a hint of excitement mixed with fear in his voice. "Councilor Jossic and General Goza are already at the wall."

The faint booming of what sounded like wardrums could be heard and seemed to be getting closer. Goldeye grabbed his sword and helmet. "Get me to General Goza!"

"Yes, sir. Follow me."

Soldiers scurried to their posts and ducked down behind the ramparts setting their shields and crossbows against the wall. The booming of drums grew louder and more rhythmic bouncing over the defenses sounding as though the vordral were just outside and about to pour over at any moment. Goldeye made his way to General Goza.

"Report."

"Moments ago, scouts noticed dark masses emerging from behind those trees," Goza slowly swept his left hand over a shadowy grove of wax leaf trees, about two miles away. "They signaled the alert and we ran to our posts."

Goldeye leaned his hands on the parapet, he could feel the booming and rumblings of the enemy as if he were taking their pulse. He stared at the vordral army as it moved like a black mist over the rolling hills and contrasted with the paling morning sky. Their spears and banners stabbed at the air. The enemy drums thudded and pounded a more ominous beat the closer they encroached.

The old dragon's gaze slid behind him to the encampment. He saw torch-bearers standing in front of a row of archers, poised and ready. His attention shifted even further back to trebuchet and catapult batteries and could make out the shadowy figures loading projectiles into the weapons' baskets.

"RISE!" Goldeye ordered.

"READY CROSSBOWS!" General Goza called.

Armor clanged and tinked as soldiers rose to their feet. With machine-like precision, they lifted their crossbows and cocked them in unison. The vordral tramped closer. Their individual features could be seen now. Some appeared to be wearing armor or chain mail. Some looked to not be wearing anything at all. Some carried shields of various shapes and sizes. All carried hand weapons.

Goldeye lifted his eyes over the hordes and

saw clouds of arrows coming at them.

"SHIELDS!"

The soldiers ducked and lifted their shields over their heads.

A swarm of arrows bounced and glanced away from the shields — stuck in the ramparts with a loud series of thumps, thuds, clanks and tings. Some arrows managed to find their marks, a few dragons gasped, yelled, or let out anguished groans. Some made no sound at all, they just sunk to the ground, never to rise again.

Loud crashes followed by blood-curdling screams and cries came from the other side of the wall.

"They've just discovered the first of the traps," General Goza boasted, smiling.

Goldeye's attention again shifted to the archers and torch-bearers. The archers rose their bows, aiming at the sky.

"FIRE!" he called.

Dozens of fireballs hissed over the wall toward the charging enemy. The trebuchets creaked and groaned to life hurling huge boulders through the morning sky followed by dark, blossoming plumes of dust and dirt accompanied by loud, slightly vibrating thumps from the impacts. The vordral kept coming...

"Crossbowers, prepare to fire!" General Goza yelled.

The vordral fell through the shallowly covered pike-pits releasing a new cacophany of shrieks and screams. Yet, they still charged on. The survivors of the first two waves scampered to the top of the earthworks.

"FIRE!" Goldeye shouted.

The cross bowers fired, cocked and fired again. The first two waves of vordral infantry had been sent to whatever god of the afterlife they believed in. Goldeye stared over the carnage to see a third and a fourth wave of enemy running, yelling and looking just as maniacal and demonic as the first two waves did. Vordral archers loosed another volley of arrows at the defenders.

"SHIELDS!" Goza shouted.

"RED ARROWS!" Goldeye yelled.

Torch bearers lit the tips of four arrows before the archers launched them into the morning sky. The flaming balls turned from a dull yellow-orange to a brilliant red; the signal for the trebuchet and catapult operators to release their projectiles at short, medium and long ranges.

Vordral arrows again bounced and glanced away from the shields and stabbing deep into the ramparts.

General Goza groaned. Goldeye turned to him.

"I'm alright," Goza said, pulling an arrow out from his chain mail shirt. "It's just a scratch."

The vordral ran over and through the pits — impaling and ensnaring still more of them. As if programmed to a specific function, they charged up the hill — seeming to ignore the dead and dying under their hooves.

"FIRE!" Goldeye shouted.

All that was necessary was to aim, shoot and cock and shoot again.

Black Dragon encampment number 7; Zare's Headquarters; North banks of the Sandrega River.

Zare fumed as he sat alone in his tent. He was perched behind a desk with a map of Green Dragon Territory sprawled over it. His eyes glided over the lima bean shaped circles that indicated the last known green dragon positions. He looked to the solid black lines showing his troops poised to cross the river at his command. He shifted his attention to the tiny Orzolla Pass.

His face scrunched into an angry sneer. Loothar didn't want him to attack the Pass. *Loothar.* Zare balled his hands into fists. Just who did that mammalian fool think he was anyway? He hijacked meetings — showed up whenever he wanted — gave orders and forced his opinion, whether-or-not it was asked for!

Loothar did not do anything! After all, it was he, *Zare,* who orchestrated the secessions. It was not Loothar, who divided the Dragonsrod council turning them on each other like starved hyenids to an overturned meat wagon. All that vordral did was stand back and watch while he, *Zare,* did all the work.

Dragonsrod was *his* for the taking — *not* Loothar's! Leave him to tend to his own matters. Zare had more than enough soldiers to cross the river when *he* gave the order — not Loothar! His eyes fell to the Orzolla Pass again. The Pass is where this war will end. He will take that miserable strip of land and trap Goldeye — surround him — destroy him. *Zoof* on Loothar! The Pass is, probably, lightly defended and will be easy to take. *That* is what he will do, a two pronged attack! A feint across the river, while thrusting his troops, and Tabric's forces, at the

Pass, crush Goldeye, then march into White Dragon Territory and to Kublisa.

Eastern defenses, Green Dragon Territory.
Four waves of vordral lay dead or dying in front of the earthworks. Hundreds, thousands probably, compared to relatively few dragon casualties. Goldeye had never seen this much deliberate sacrifice. Jossic stood beside him and General Goza at the top of the wall.

"I don't see how they can keep this up," Jossic gawked, gazing out at the heaps of enemy dead.

"We don't know how many vordral there are," Goza countered. "They may be trying to wear us down."

Goldeye looked out at the carnage. "There seem to be both males and females in the ranks."

Bard stepped up behind the leaders. He appeared unharmed, but wore a worried expression on his face. "Begging your pardon, sirs."

"What is it?" Goldeye asked.

"Soldiers, up-and-down the line, are reporting their ammunition is nearly exhausted."

—"Here they come!"—

What looked like three long and rectangular forms of living, breathing beings charged through the dust and smoke toward the wall. The traps and pits were filled with dead and dying vordral — no longer effective as a defensive barrier.

Goldeye turned to the other three; his eyes coursing over their faces. "Tell all cross bowers and archers to fire everything they have left. Everybody is to prepare for hand-to-hand fighting — Go!"

Jossic and General Goza went in opposite directions.

"Bard, wait," Goldeye said, "tell the artillerists the same order. Get every one, who can carry a weapon up here... Go now!"

"At once!"

The vordral charged up the hill again.

"FIRE, AT WILL!" Goldeye heard Jossic call.

Dragon cross bowers and archers launched their rounds until none were left. Rank upon rank of the vordral threw themselves over the defenses like a tidal wave hitting the beach. Foot-to-hoof, body-to-body, dragon-to-vordral they fought. Dull bangs and clangs of swords, axes, maces and shields intermingled with the sickening crunch of bones, anguished cries, bloodcurdling screams and shrieks and the gurgling gasps from the living and the dying filled the air. Death's whirlwind had again swept over the field, taking with it yet another rich bounty.

   Goldeye slashed his sword through the shoulder and neck of a vordral warrior carrying a metal, knobby-headed mace, virtually cleaving the creature in half. The old dragon threw his eyes to a young looking vordral grasping a double-bladed ax. The youngster charged. Goldeye stepped backward, and on the mace, he fell backward as the vordral swung his ax at Goldeye's head. He felt the whoosh of the blade pass over him. He picked up the mace with his right hand and rose to his full height, he locked eyes with the young vordral. Goldeye bedecked in his bloody, dented battle armor, held his sword in his left hand and the mace in his right — holding them like they were extensions of his hands. The vordral had scraggly hair on his head, barely concealing two small, goat-like horns. Short, course fur covered his head, upper body and arms, while shaggy, long, thick fur covered him from the waist down to his hooves. The vordral clutched the handles of his ax so tight, it seemed as though he was choking the life out of it.

This youngster was no match for Goldeye, who knew it. He considered trying to talk to the creature. The vordral narrowed his red eyes to slits and scrunched up his face, releasing an ear-splitting shriek. He threw his ax over his head and charged. The old dragon thrust his sword through the vordral's torso. He swung the mace at the youngster's head, crushing it. He saw it coming, the youngster's body language all but announced to Goldeye that he was going to charge. He took no joy in the killing. He could not think about it. Instead, he threw his sword out to deflect a swipe coming from behind him by yet another attacker.

Loothar stepped over the wall carrying a large, anvil-shaped war hammer in his muscular hands. He had already crushed a white dragon's skull and caved in the rib cages of two orange dragons before he had taken five steps. Now Bard stood in his way. The large white dragon swung his sword up at Loothar's face. The vordral stepped away from the swipe. Bard chopped his sword in a diagonal, downward slice — Loothar again stepped away. Bard lunged his sword at Loothar's chest. The vordral swatted his thrust away with the handle of his hammer. He kicked Bard just under the body armor and slammed his hammer into his right arm, shattering it. The large dragon swung his sword skillfully with his left hand using one attack and thrust after another. Loothar blocked and parried each and every attack with various parts of his hammer, from the handle to the head. Bard swung wildly at Loothar's head again. The vordral ducked inward, toward Bard, and slammed his hammer behind the dragon's legs, sweeping him off of his feet. Loothar swung his hammer at Bard's head — finishing the fight.

Goldeye watched in horror as Loothar dealt the killing blow to Bard. His eyes locked onto Loothar's from across the battlefield. Loothar smiled. They ran at each other — weapons raised. Loothar swung his hammer in a wide circle — Goldeye hurtled over the hammer swing — shoulder rolled, behind Loothar, and slammed his mace into the other's back resulting in a thick, meaty, cracking sound.

Loothar arched forward and let out loud yelp. He quickly recovered, pivoted and swung his hammer at the spot Goldeye was a moment earlier. Goldeye swung his sword at Loothar's head — he crouched under the swing and shoved his hammer into Goldeye's chest, sending the dragon stumbling backward. Loothar stomped toward Goldeye. He slammed his hammer at the dragon's head. Goldeye rolled out of the way. Another hammer strike, then another — Goldeye blocked one hammer attack with the mace, which flew out of his hand, causing stinging vibrations all up-and-down his arm.

"Surrender now," Loothar demanded. "You and your surviving troops can leave here with your lives."

Goldeye didn't answer. He glanced around at the dead and wounded dragons and vordral. He looked at those still fighting. His eyes fell on the broken body of his friend, Bard, laying a few feet away. A wave of anger swept over him. Surrender now and Bard would have died in vain, as would Goldeye's unborn children, as would Dragonsrod itself.

"I'd rather be roasted alive until I'm no more than a pile of ashes," Goldeye countered an angry twinkle in his eyes.

"That can be arranged," Loothar chuckled.

"Why?" Goldeye asked. "Why do this?"

Loothar's eyes narrowed. "As I said, revenge. I was on that battlefield three-hundred years ago against Gortha the Great. That fool, Zare, thinks he is in charge. He thinks he manipulated the other two dragon clans to leave you," he let out a loud, contemptuous laugh," I manipulated *him!* His ambition did most of the work. I hate dragons. You're such an arrogant, self centered race. It wouldn't bother me to destroy every one of you."

Goldeye stepped forward and swung his sword up to Loothar's face.

The vordral stepped to his right, deflected the attack with a upward crescent swing of his hammer. Goldeye backed up and out of the hammer's range.

"Three-hundred years is a long time to sit around and brood after a defeat," Goldeye stated. "You seem to have magical qualities about you."

Warriors of Dragonsrod

"My people call on me when they need me," Loothar smiled.

"You mean, you call upon them when you're bored!"

The smile dissolved from Loothar's face.

"Don't toy with me, dragon! Enough talk! I will destroy you, like I did your children."

Goldeye's eyes narrowed, he tightened his grip on his sword. "Then give it your best shot!"

"As you wish."

The two charged at each other again. Goldeye fought with a renewed vigor, with renewed energy, with controlled fury. He threw everything he had at the Vordral leader. He sliced, chopped, swung and hacked with his sword. He slapped with his tail, he punched and kicked Loothar, who deflected, parried and dodged nearly every shot.

Goldeye slashed his sword, in yet another swing at Loothar's head, that would have cleaved it in two had it have connected. Instead, the vordral stepped back — Goldeye's sword slammed to the ground. Loothar stomped on the blade yanking it out of Goldeye's hands. Loothar threw a round-house kick with his left hoof — it connected across Goldeye's face, sending him flopping to the ground, next to Bard's sword. Loothar swished and twirled his hammer, his eyes fell on to Goldeye, lying spread-eagle on the ground. Loothar lifted his hammer over his head. Goldeye grabbed Bard's sword and heaved it spearing Loothar through the left side of his torso.

Loothar shrieked as he sunk to the ground next to Goldeye. Many vordral stopped fighting and looked to their imperiled leader. A fatal mistake as several were cut down. Many others ran to Loothar, who was on his hands and knees, blood streaming from his stab wounds. The two locked eyes again.

"You are a worthy opponent, Goldeye, Council-Leader of Dragonsrod."

Goldeye remained silent. He sat up. He and Loothar were now surrounded by vordral warriors, who reached down and gently picked Loothar up off the ground. Goldeye fully expected to have his head crushed at any moment by an angry enemy soldier.

"I look forward to meeting you again," Loothar said, being carried away. "We *will* meet again!"

The surviving vordral scurried over the wall leaving the dragons in control of the field.

CHAPTER THIRTY-FOUR

-MOIRA'S MOMENT-

Queen Catra's Palace, Aizon, Abyssina.

Moira sat, upright, in her bed in a stunned silence. Her eyes slid down the front page of the *Drallics Gazette*. She soaked in as much information as she could about the battles fought yesterday in Green Dragon Territory. The dragons who wrote these stories did not seem to leave too many details out as far as the carnage that happened up there. Her country was safe, for now. Moira had been in bed since yesterday due to a series of blinding headaches. She felt better today, the headaches were not as bad. River Rat sat with her throughout the ordeal.

He would get her an icepack if she asked for one, or a blanket, or a pillow, or whatever she wanted. Mostly, all he could do was sit and watch her writhe and groan and wince.

The baby picked up on the extremely intense emotions Goldeye was experiencing and pipe-lined them, telepathically, to her. Moira was still having a hard time understanding how the baby was able to do this. She had made a few attempts, though feeble, to open a link with her child. No luck. Maybe it will happen in time. For now, it seemed the baby possessed the only link.

She wondered how, or if, Goldeye was dealing with the baby's rather intrusive thoughts. Were they invading his mind as easily as they did hers? Did they all have a psychic connection with each other? If so, could she, some day, establish a link with Goldeye?

"I would bet the Reds and Silvers are rethinking their reasoning for leaving Dragonsrod now," River Rat said, slurping coffee from a small cup and reading the front page to *The Kublisa Times*.

"That would be nice," Moira muttered.

A knock at the door. River Rat answered it.

Shayara and Serena, both wearing black, sleeveless tops and gold belts around their middles, looked down at River Rat, who ushered them into the room. They walked to the foot of Moira's bed. She greeted them with a somewhat strained smile.

"Are you feeling better?" Shayara inquired.

"Yes," Moira responded. "My headaches are not as bad today."

"The Queen wishes to see you this afternoon at three o'clock," Shayara said. "Most of the other delegates are arriving today. She would like for you to be there when they do."

"I look forward to it," Moira returned.

Serena's gaze slid down her nose to River Rat, who had retaken his seat at the foot of Moira's bed.

"You're going to need new clothes," she told him.

"Nothing in my closet fits me," he countered.

"I think they can find you something to wear," Moira said, her eyes now fixed on him.

"Well—" he started.

"If you are going to sit in on these talks," Moira interrupted, "you will need to have something other than those rags you've been wearing."

"I wasn't going to argue," he returned, looking taken aback.

"Serena will take you to get new clothes," Shayara said to him.

"Let's go," he grinned and looked to Serena

Three o'clock. Moira and River Rat, who donned a gray, short sleeved shirt and black trousers, accompanied Serena to the Public Court Chamber. Queen Catra, resplendent in a shimmering, silky, purple gown, sat at her throne. She looked tired to Moira. She appeared to have had a long day. The Queen perked up when Moira, Serena and River Rat entered the chamber. Catra and Moira exchanged smiles.

"Ah, you are just in time," Queen Catra said.

"Highness?" Moira asked.

Just behind them, walked Shayara and Councilor Sheema. The two dragons embraced and exchanged pleasantries.

"Welcome Councilor Sheema," Catra invited, her eyes twinkled as her face lifted into a smile.

"Highness," Sheema said bowing.

Bolten entered the chamber standing in front of two gold-furred wolves. They were tall and wore brown jackets. The lead wolf had coal-black eyes and very short, gray, stubbly fur spreading around his muzzle. His adjutant had hazel eyes and stood about two inches shorter and appeared to be younger than the first one.

"Your Majesty," Bolten called, "The Jungle-wolf delegation," Bolten motioned to the lead wolf. "Captain Skit," the dark-eyed wolf gave a military bow. Bolten motioned to the second wolf. "Lieutenant Zephyr," the hazel eyed junglewolf also dipped in a military bow.

Queen Catra nodded to each as they were introduced.

Kaymo entered the chamber with an aging griffon with brown and white tipped head feathers, amber eyes and a brown, hooking beak. He wore a blue tunic with a star shaped badge, with the imperial crest on it, just over his heart.

Kaymo motioned to the griffon. "Your Majesty. From the Griffon Empire, Ambassador Marco."

Queen Catra and Ambassador Marco exchanged polite nods.

After a short pause, the delegates grouped together and exchanged pleasantries. Queen Catra stood from her throne. The chatter faded

Warriors of Dragonsrod

and all eyes lifted to her.

"Ambassadors, diplomats," Catra said, her glittering eyes moving over their faces. "Welcome to Abyssina. We are currently waiting for representatives from the Nelvainians and the *Dragon Triumvirate*..."

Moira dipped her head to Sheema, who wore a neutral, statue-like expression.

"The Dragon Triumvirate?"

"Councilor Zare's lot."

"Oh."

Queen Catra talked, apparently not noticing them. "...The Vulcrians were contacted, but will not attend this conference. They have declared neutrality and have closed their ports to any, and all, potential combatants."

No one said much. Moira studied the others' faces. Stoic, expressionless. Of course she was not expecting an out-pouring of emotions of grief and anger. Yet, she seemed to be the only one surprised by this news.

Moira was in uncharted territory. She had almost no diplomatic experience. Sure she accompanied Goldeye to official government functions in the past, but it was nothing like this. Sheema had the experience in diplomacy. Moira considered giving the responsibility to her. No. Goldeye, for whatever the reason, wanted her to do it. He wouldn't hand this responsibility to just anyone. He had good reason for bestowing her with the representation of her beloved Dragonsrod, didn't he?

Sleep eluded Moira. Her nerves were a jumble and her mind was too active. Doubts plagued her thoughts with fears over what was coming. She was not stupid. She knew these talks would not be over in a day, or a month, maybe not even in a year. What was the problem then? She saw two problems. One, she had not the foggiest of ideas as to what to expect from the other ambassadors. Two, *failure.* She could be Dragonsrod's only shot at securing help from the neighbors. She could be the only one to keep this fight between the dragons as just that. But if she made a mistake, or exposed her hand too soon, the other ambassadors might round on her and tear her to pieces, thus leaving Dragonsrod on its own to face not only the rebel dragons, but the vordral as well.

She needed to relax. She was probably the only one who was having problems sleeping.

She could not let that show — it would look like a weakness. What could she do? She needed sleep but she needed to rid her mind of these nagging, pesky, doubts. She thought of Goldeye and whenever he couldn't sleep, he would let the cool night air wrap itself around him like a blanket.

She liked to take a bath when she needed to relax. A nice, hot, steaming, soothing bath. She walked to the tub and turned the faucets on full and the hot water flooded over the tub's basin.

Yes, that's the ticket! She sat and soaked in the water for seemingly hours. The steam swirled up and caressed her face and shoulders. Her mind was clear and her eyelids grew heavy. She had to give sleep another try. She crawled out of the tub, toweled off, put on a clean night gown, and slid under the blankets feeling much better.

Moira was awakened by a loud knock at her door.

"One moment."

She threw on a bath robe and answered the door. Sheema, looking rested and alert, stared back at her.

"Good morning, ma'am," Sheema said. "Did you sleep well?"

"Yes, fine, thank you," Moira mumbled.

Sheema smiled. The long face and baggy, bloodshot eyes and the wide, gaping yawns Moira was letting out, suggested otherwise.

"Actually," Moira sighed, "I didn't. I'm too nervous. I don't know what to expect."

"I know how you feel, ma'am," Sheema returned. "I don't think I slept at all during my first conference I had to attend. I've slept through most of them since, however."

Sheema grinned.

Moira chuckled.

"Seriously, ma'am," Sheema cast a mentor-like look to Moira. "Just listen at first to what is being said. Get a feel for the conversation and be prepared to sit through a lot of small talk and tyrocc zoof. Most importantly, follow your instincts."

Follow your instincts.

Moira was learning about that, and often, the lessons came the hard way.

The conference room was as large as the Public Throne Room. A long, rectangular, marble table, with one dozen chairs parked around it, sat in the very center of the chamber. A high-backed chair was placed at the head of the table for Queen Catra. Moira, Sheema and River Rat were the first to arrive at the conference room. They took their seats near the front of the table. Moira tensed up as she sat down. Her nerves were becoming a jumbled mess again. Sheema and River Rat sat on either side of her.

The griffon, Ambassador Marco, entered the chamber. His eagle-eyes coursed the Dragonsrod delegation. He nodded his head but remained stone faced. "Ambassadors."

Moira opened her mouth to speak, but nothing came out.

"Good morning, ambassador," Sheema said, nodding her head, seeming to pick up on Moira's attack of nerves.

If Ambassador Marco picked up on it, he didn't, or wouldn't, show it. River Rat smiled and nodded politely at the griffon. Skit and Zephyr entered the room followed closely by Queen Catra, Kaymo and Shayara. All stood as Catra, in a metallic blue gown that closely matched her eyes, glided by them to the high-backed chair.

"Delegates," she began, "the Nelvanians are sending an emissary to hear what will be said regarding the vordral," her eyes shifted to Moira. "A delegation from the Dragon Triumvirate will be here tomorrow. The purpose of their visit is to seek sympathy from an international audience and to gain recognition and independence from Dragonsrod."

No pressure.

The conference officially began the following day with the arrival of the horse-like nelvainians, three in total. The lead emissary sat near the back of the table with his aides sitting behind him. The beings were tall and seemingly muscular. They had somewhat bulging black, or dark, eyes with a long hairy mane sprouting up from their heads and traveling down their necks. They had three stubby fingers and an opposable thumb on each hand. All three wore what looked like capes or cloaks over white, high collar shirts.

They seemed, to Moira, stiff and rigid. It appeared that if the lead nelvainaian were to sneeze, the aides were to follow suit. She knew absolutely nothing about these beings. Yet, the dragons sitting across from the nelvainains she knew all too well. Four black dragons, a silver and a red, all trying to look important in their gray military jackets with long, squiggly insignias on their shoulders. Moira refused to acknowledge the other dragon delegation. The nerves she once felt were replaced by anger and hatred. She could not forget what happened to her and River Rat at the hands of black dragon soldiers. Talks about the vordral threat and — gods forbid — the right of the Dragon Triumvirate to exist as its own nation began in earnest. Moira was ready to get things going and take care of these matters once and for all and waste as little time as possible while doing it. Instead, chit-chat. Idle talk. Dancing around each other, a lot of verbal probing. No wonder why diplomatic affairs take so long for anything to come of them.

"What were you expecting to happen?" Sheema asked.

Moira, Sheema and River Rat were the last three still in the chamber after the meeting.

"I don't know," Moira grumbled, not hiding her disappointment.

If this was how diplomacy was done, she was in for the longest, most boring time of her life.

"I don't know if I can do this," Moira confessed. "This seemed to be such a total waste of time!"

Sheema's eyes darted around the room and the doorway, looking to see if anyone else was around.

"Be careful, ma'am," she warned. "It's okay to be unsure in private. But never, *never* show it at the table. The other delegates will *eat - you - alive.*"

"What do I do?" Moira asked, her eyes locked on to Sheema's

"There are clues."

"Clues?"

Sheema nodded. "Watch their body language. Watch their eyes, see if they narrow, or twinkle, or glint in an unnatural way. Watch for a tightening of the jaw muscles — a sudden twitch or motion. Pay particular attention to their facial expressions. Most of the time you won't see much there."

"Then why watch for it?"

"Because sometimes, even the best diplomat will let his true feelings show on his face. And if you're good enough, you can read his face like a book. They give themselves away. That's when you *pounce!*"

"I see."

Sheema's eyes bore into Moira's face. "I can tell you're not sure. You are confused and afraid. You must learn to conceal your own body language. Put on a false face and keep it on throughout the meetings. The other delegates are studying you and are waiting for you to stumble. You will see that sometimes diplomacy can be just as bloody and deadly as armies fighting on the battlefield."

"Show me what to look for," Moira said.

Sheema smiled. "Of course. It won't be easy and it will take time."

Moira nodded.

The following day was much the same. Moira did watch as the delegates talked... and talked... and talked.... After the meeting, Moira met with Sheema and River Rat in her quarters.

"Tell me," Sheema instructed. "What did you see?"

Moira sat on her bed. She scrunched up her face in thought. "Well, the nelvainian seemed to be really impatient. He kept moving around in his chair like he was sitting on nails."

"Good!" Sheema clucked.

River Rat grinned.

"What else did you see?" Sheema pressed on.

Moira sat silent, running the events of the day's conference through her mind. She shrugged her shoulders and cocked up her eyebrows. "I don't know."

River Rat's smile faded.

"What should I have seen?" Moira had a disappointed tone to her voice.

"The black dragon, Graff, was talking... a lot," Sheema revealed.

"Everybody was talking," River Rat added, looking as confused as Moira.

"Yes," Sheema countered, her eyes moving from River Rat to Moira. "They talked mainly with the junglewolves and Catra."

"They said nothing to the griffon," River Rat gasped, looking as if a bright idea had just come to him.

"Yes!" Sheema cried, giving him an approving look.

"I don't see it," Moira sighed, giving her a quizzical stare, feeling completely stupid. "The black dragons have nothing to gain from the griffons," Sheema observed.

"Okay?" Moira's face was blank as a clean sheet of paper.

Sheema sighed. "The griffons are at war with the vordral, who are allied to Zare's lot."

"It's a start," Sheema groaned after a short silence. "It's also late."

Moira glanced out the windows into the indigo blue sky. She then looked at the shadows that flickered and danced around the room from the torch light.

Moira was tired and frustrated. Her brain felt like it had melted to goo. This verbal dance contest was not for her. This was definitely Sheema's game to be playing. Follow your instincts, she kept telling herself. Her instincts were telling her to do something extremely undiplomatic.

Captain Skit began the next day's talks with a comment about an article from the *Drallics Gazette.* "I have read this news print," his eyes set on Moira. "It says that Triumvirate forces have crossed the Sandrega River and appear to have overrun several Dragonsrod outposts and scattered its defenders."

Graff couldn't help himself, his face split into a wide, pointed toothed smile.

"Did the vordral attack Dragonsrod's eastern defenses again?" Catra asked Skit.

"No," came the deep voice of Ambassador Marco.

Graff's smile faded, a look of complete contempt now spread over his face.

"What do you know?" Skit asked Marco.

All eyes shifted to the griffon.

"We — the griffons — have launched a two pronged offensive."

"Against who?" Moira spoke to Marco.

Marco's face lifted into a big smile and his eyes twinkled like stars. "We have driven the vordral back into the wastes. We have also destroyed several goblin villages and towns."

"Goblins?" River Rat blurted out, his fore head and ears lifted.

Marco's eyes slid to River Rat. "Yes, my zaltee friend. We never really trusted those little trolls — too shifty. They destroyed bridges, food stores, supply depots, transports in aid of the vordral. They are paying for their treachery."

"I have seen enough," the Nelvainian

Warriors of Dragonsrod

emissary announced, standing up, his aides also stood and seemed all too ready to follow him out of the room. All eyes shifted to the horse-like beings.

"This sounds as though they are internal matters between the dragons and the griffons," the Nelvainian emissary continued. "Therefore, of no interest to us."

"May I remind everybody that the vordral are at the core of the resent events involving the dragons and the griffons," Zephyr spoke up. "These events are important to all in the region, including the Nelvainians."

The Nelvainain emissary cast Zephyr a dark, scathing look. "So?"

Captain Skit spoke first; "Lieutenant Zephyr is an expert on the vordral. He has spent much time in the Haxokrin Mountains, which run the through *all* of our countries."

"There is a sizable population of vordral in that mountain range," Zephyr said, some urgency could be heard in his voice. "They have made raids in Dragonsrod, the Griffon Empire, and two days ago, they raided a small town on the slopes of the Haxokrins in the Cannis Republic."

The equine ambassador sneered at Zephyr. "I shall alert my government. Otherwise I don't see any real gains to be made here—"

"My country was attacked *without* provocation," Moira spat, glaring daggers at the Nelvainian. "It's only a matter of time before the vordral attack Abyssina or Nelvainia!" She stood and pointed at the Nelvainains "Go on, run and hide! Pretend nothing is going on. But mark my words, you will be attacked! Once the vordral have the taste of blood in their mouths and are too intoxicated by victories over defenseless villages elsewhere, they will spill over your borders and you *will* be right back here begging us to help you! Your choice... Mr. Ambassador!"

A stunned silence fell over the chamber. All gazed at Moira with wide eyes and open mouths. She didn't care, it was about time these talks got going on what was important. If Moira's eyes could have blasted out of their sockets and strangled the Nelvainians... The Nelvainian Emissary stared at Moira for a moment. She still stood, chest puffing out and in, her fists tightly clenched together.

"Ambassadors, please," Queen Catra said calmly, shock sliding from her face.

The Nelvainians sat back down, as did Moira.

"Please, Lieutenant Zephyr, continue," the Nelvainian emissary said, still looking at Moira.

Moira felt a sudden onrush of pain surge through her temples.

Mommy, came a voice from the baby, inside her head. *We're coming. We are being followed. We are in danger!*

CHAPTER THIRTY-FIVE

-BATTLE AT THE BORDER-

Silver Dragon Territory, near Abyssina border

General Zmoge deliberately held the caravan behind the egg-bearers. He knew where they were going. He wanted to lull them into a false sense of safety. That's when he would strike — surround the egg's guardians and destroy them. Then Zare could use the egg for whatever bargaining chip he wanted.

Zmoge was using his cannidene mercenaries, with their superb sense of smell, as scouts. Whether-or-not the egg bearers knew it, they left behind a trail of skin cells and fur particles that all but announced *'Here we are! Come and get us!'*

"General Zmoge," called Massox as he and another cannidene rode to the lead of the now stopped caravan.

"What is it?" Zmoge answered in a lazy voice.

"The egg bearers are approximately two miles ahead of us and moving due South."

"Go on."

"We've picked up a new scent."

Zmoge cocked up an eyebrow. "What do you mean?"

"It's a new-born dragon."

"That explains why they have not stopped much over the last few days," Zmoge said, his eyes twinkling. "They must *not* be allowed to cross into Abyssina."

Zmoge shifted on his saddle and craned his neck over his right shoulder.

"WALKER!" he yelled, while gently messaging his throat.

The dejected looking young dragon sat uncomfortably on a thin tyrocc. The beast gave the impression that it was ready to collapse and die from underneath his rider at any moment as it lumbered up to Zmoge.

"Congratulations, underling," Zmoge wheezed, his face twisted into a crooked smile. "I'm promoting you to your first combat command!"

Walker straightened up and gawked at Zmoge. "What?"

"You will take half the squad and ride south to the abyssin border. Mass up whatever help you can and take charge of it until I get there. Massox will ride with you."

"Alright," Walker muttered, the corners of his mouth curled up in a slight grin.

"Give you a chance to put some medals on that black saddle cover of a jacket you're wearing," Zmoge said as he burst out laughing.

Walker's grin plummeted into a deep set frown.

"Take those two rabbits with you," Zmoge hissed, throwing a contemptuous glare at Fras and Fray. "I'm tired of their sniveling. Get moving, you have no time to waste!"

Walker perked up and snapped out of whatever depression he seemed to be in since that fiasco at Elmshir. He swung his tyrocc around, yelling out orders at the soldiers and mercenaries. Their eyes slid to Zmoge. When they saw he was not over-ruling the orders, the troops split up and half rode out with Walker and Massox.

Queen Catra's Palace, Aizon, Abyssina.
The Public Court Room was empty except for Queen Catra, Kaymo and Moira.

"I wish to accompany a patrol to the border," Moira requested.

Catra and Kaymo cocked up their eyebrows.

"The night patrol has already left," Catra said. "Why?"

Moira hesitated.

Catra gave Moira an intense, searching look.

"This may sound hard to believe," Moira kept eye contact with Catra. "But, my child is no longer in an embryonic state. He hatched some days ago."

"I see," Catra replied. "And…?"

Moira hesitated again. "He — uh — told me."

"Told you?" Catra looked nonplussed.

"He told me, last night, that he and his caretakers are coming, they are being followed, and they are in danger."

"I see," Catra said. "And you want my permission to let you go to the border."

"Well?" Moira countered. "Yes."

Catra leaned forward, her blue eyes twinkled and seemed to high-light against the black gown she wore.

"Very well," she said. "Shayara and Bolten are leading the dawn patrol. But know this, The dawn patrol is *not* to engage in battle unless provoked. You are not to put yourself or the patrol in any kind of danger — is that understood?"

"Yes, Highness," Moira forced back a smile.

She felt a wave of relief sweep over her — instantly followed by a wave of uncertainty and terror.

"Shayara and Bolten are in charge of the patrol," Catra reminded her. "Keep up with them and above all, listen to them."

Moira's face lifted into a smile. "I will, Highness, thank you."

Silver Dragon Territory/Abyssina border.
Handoe, Maxum, Sandstorm and Jessa crouched behind a sand dune, overlooking a black dragon camp.

"How many are they?" Jessa whispered.

"Thirty, so far," Handoe replied in a hushed voice.

"Mostly black dragon soldiers," Maxum muttered. "I did see two lions and some javilines."

"Mercenaries," Sandstorm snarled.

Handoe's fur bristled. "Fras and Fray."

His eyes followed the two dark furred rabbits as they trailed behind a black dragon in a solid black, medal free, jacket with a very irritated expression on his face.

The four surveyed the camp. Several tyroccs walked or stood around in a circular pen. Saddles were piled in a heap next to the makeshift corral's gate. Campfires shimmered and danced, tents were pitched, crossbows lay on the ground or hung at the soldier's sides.

"They don't suspect anything," Sandstorm said.

"Any ideas?" Handoe asked to all.

"The way I see it," Maxum answered, "we have about... two to three hundred yards, through the camp and down over that ravine," he looked to Handoe. "You and Sandstorm have the fire-power, Jessa and I have the cutlery. *We* have the element of surprise. Split up if things get too rough. I have to get Gak, here, to Abyssina, and hopefully safety."

The others traded looks and nodded.

Sandstorm's eyes sunk to squiggle marks along the dunes and through the grass. "Pit vipers."

The others looked at him.

"Poisonous snakes are all over the place," he warned. "Be certain they won't be taking sides when the crossbow bolts fly."

"Duly noted," Handoe replied.

"When do we go?" Jessa asked.

"No time like the present," Maxum drew his sword. "Hang on Gak!"

He charged over the dune with Jessa right behind him.

Handoe and Sandstorm cocked their repeaters.

"Let's do it," Handoe said.

— "Oh, flix!"—
— "Zoof! Not again!"—
— "Get to your repeaters!"—

Soldiers and mercenaries raced for their weapons. Others craned their necks trying to see what the shouting was all about. Others just stood dumbstruck not really knowing what to do.

Jessa cross-checked a javiline mercenary to ground and stepped on his pig-like face as she ran. A black dragon soldier swung his sword at Maxum, who hurled over the swipe, did a perfect two foot landing, and kept running. A javiline, carrying a large, wooden club with two spikes at the top of it, charged at Handoe. It belched out squeals of pain as Handoe shot a bolt into its left shoulder and right leg. A black dragon soldier charged out of a tent carrying a cross bow, his head cranked to the right then to the left. Sandstorm picked up a coiled pit viper by the head and tossed it at the soldier's face as he raced by. The soldier let out a terrified yelp and fell backward over the tent.

General Zmoge and four others sat on their tyroccs and watched the chaos. Dragons, javilines and cannidenes scurried here-and-there, most with confused expressions on their faces. A black rabbit with a repeating crossbow shot down a mercenary — A puma, in a traveling cloak and with the most determined look on his face zipped from tree-to-tree and tent-to-tent and moving in a southerly direction. The sneaky snow leopard and the female dragon were nowhere to be seen. No bother, they will be flushed out soon enough. The quarry has just run in to the trap — time to spring it.

Zmoge drew his sword and thrust it forward. "CHARGE!"

Complete pandemonium. Crossbow bolts hissed, whizzed and zinged through the air — perforated tents — smacked into tree trunks — tangled in bushes like flies in a spider web. Yells and screams permeated the dusty, gritty air. Adding to the confusion, five rider-mounted tyroccs charged from the western flank, while five more came in from the eastern flank.

Jessa ran to the undefended tyrocc pen. The big beasts were skittish already, all this excitement had driven them into a near panic. She studied the rickety gate and the pen. The soldiers must have been drunk when they built this enclosure. All one these creatures had to do to get out, it seemed, was to sneeze at it, pass gas toward it or burp at it and half of the crude structure would come crashing down. Jessa glanced around to see if anyone else was near. She lifted her sword over her head and sliced it down on the gate handle, which was a mere rope wrapped around the gate and a fence post, causing it to swing open. She threw her arms up in the air and yelled at the tyroccs. Some reared up and bellowed. Others punched through the make-shift pen and in to the camp with Jessa right behind them.

Maxum and Gak's road to safety had run into a huge roadblock in the form a lion with a flowing brown mane. He stood a head and shoulders taller than Maxum and much more muscular. He wore a black sleeveless shirt and brown trousers with scuffed black boots. His amber eyes fixed on Maxum with the utmost malice.

"You have something I want," he growled in a low voice.

"Sorry," Maxum said, gripping his sword tighter. "I don't know what you're talking about."

The lion's eyes narrowed and he flashed a pointy-toothed sneer. "Don't insult my intelligence. You have the baby. Hand him to me or I will crush you where you stand."

Maxum side-stepped to his right. The lion stayed in front of him. Maxum sheathed his sword. The lion balled his hands into large, furry fists.

"This is your last chance," the lion snarled, he had a 'please try something' look in his eyes.

Maxum did not respond.

Instead, he tried to run by the lion, who anticipated such a maneuver. He grabbed Maxum by the traveling cloak and tossed him backward. Maxum shifted his body to keep from squishing Gak. He did a shoulder roll before standing up-right. The lion did not follow.

"Please, try that again," the lion flashed a smile, his eyes glinted. "Draw your sword — I can fight you with it, or without it."

Maxum's eyes sunk to the baby, hiding under the cloak. The child was worried and he sensed it. He lifted his gaze to the lion. Sure he was large. Sure he looked ready to fight — he definitely seemed to like fighting. But how smart was he? It appeared that sprinting by him was no longer an option. The things he could do seemed limited, stand there and get killed, or try and outwit him. Maxum took off his traveling cloak and set Gak down.

"It's alright," he said to the baby.

The lion flexed his claws and glared maliciously down at Maxum. "Come on! Quit delaying the inevitable."

The baby stared at Maxum with a pleading gaze.

Maxum stepped away from him and faced the lion, who lunged, his arms straight in front of him. Maxum grabbed the lion's left arm (around the wrist and triceps) pivoted his body, and threw the lion over his shoulder. The lion tumbled to the ground and quickly got back to his feet.

The large cat smiled, his eyes twinkled even more maliciously than before. "Good! I didn't want this to be too easy."

He balled his massive hands in to fists and assumed a boxing stance. Maxum didn't move.

Things were settling down. The tyroccs were calming, soldiers started to move in on the places where Maxum and Handoe were last seen. The dash for freedom was in jeopardy. Sandstorm, who had taken to hiding in the trees and bushes, crawled out from behind a string of abandoned tents. It appeared another diversion was needed. A small, unattended campfire burned and crackled in front of two tents. He glanced around, no one was close. He drew his sword and sliced off a dried branch with many, finger-like, skeletal looking shoots on it and set it in the flames.

The flames hungrily devoured the tents and quickly spread to neighboring trees and bushes — embers floated and drifted in the smoky air setting smaller spot fires here and there. Sandstorm's ears perked up when he heard someone shout out "FIRE!" He couldn't stay here any longer. His eyes landed on a trio of tyroccs huddling close by. His face lifted into a smile and he slowly walked over to them.

Handoe literally ran into Fras and Fray. For a brief moment they exchanged surprised gasps and gazes. Handoe lifted his repeater at them. "Give me one reason why I shouldn't kill you both right now!"

His eyes glinted and narrowed, his finger tightened around the trigger.

Fras stood rooted to the spot, his eyes wide and his mouth agape, seemingly paralyzed with fear.

"Go ahead," Fray snarled, a glint in his eyes and a dark expression clouding his face. "Kill us!"

Fras shot him a sharp look. "Us?"

Fray ignored him, he seemed not to care what happened anymore. Fras, was a different story.

"Speak for yourself!" he shouted in his brother's face.

Fray shoved him away.

A frightened tyrocc ran between the three, nearly trampling Handoe. Fray drew a small, pistol-like crossbow and pointed it at Handoe and pulled the trigger. The little dart sliced through Handoe's right ear. He squealed in pain — lifted his repeater and returned fire. The bolt ripped through Fray's chest. He fell to the ground dead. Fras chose not to go the way of his brother, instead he vanished into the thick scrub. Handoe did not chase him, it was time to make good on *his* escape.

The lion threw a right round-house punch followed by a left. Maxum dodged both swings. He stepped away from another shot aimed at his head. The lion was getting angry, his punches were faster, wider and had more force behind them. Maxum dodged here, moved there — blocked a punch or two — but remained calm. The lion stepped closer, threw a right roundhouse punch in combination with a left uppercut, which connected, lifting Maxum off of his feet. Maxum crumpled to the ground. The lion kicked him in the ribs, knocking the wind out of him.

The lion walked over to the baby and picked him up under the arms. He held Gak up to his face level.

"Wow," he growled," you're an ugly one."

His eyes bore into Gak's eyes. "If you weren't so valuable, I would rip you apart right here and save Zare the trouble."

The lion laughed and was about to set Gak down — but couldn't. The lion was unable let him go and he seemed unable take his eyes away from Gak's. The baby's cobalt blue eyes had turned jet-black. The lion seemed completely transfixed, his arms started to tremble and his knees quaked together.

Maxum sat up and watched the lion as his body tightened up and shook in an uncontrollable way. The lion's eyes widened, his mouth fell open and he let out an exasperated squeak. He sunk to his knees, his arms dropped to his sides, letting Gak fall to the sandy ground.

Maxum threw a side kick to the lion's head, violently slamming him to the ground.

Sandstorm emerged from behind them, riding a tyrocc, and holding up his crossbow. "You alright, Max?"

"Other than a sore jaw, yes."

"How's Gak?"

Maxum's eyes fell to the baby, whose eyes were their normal blue again. The baby looked to Maxum and smiled in a sweet and innocent way.

"Fine, I guess," he said, though not really sure about what he had just witnessed. "I don't know what happened between him and the lion."

Sandstorm held out his hand. "C'mon, grab Gak, let's get you two across the border."

The baby flashed another gummy smile at Maxum as he bent down to pick him up. "Let's go, kiddo. Time to get you out of here."

CHAPTER THIRTY-SIX

-THE DASH TO FREEDOM-

Abyssina/Dragonsrod border

Moira collapsed to the ground, blinding, searing pain tore through her head. The dawn patrol was forced to stop. They were in the cycad forest, not the safest of places to be.

"Ma'am?" River Rat asked, a concerned expression splashed over his face.

"I'm alright," she gasped, she cupped her left hand over her eyes and leaned against a cycad tree.

Shayara and Bolten walked to her.

"I told you something like this would happen," Bolten snarled. "She has slowed us down enough. We should leave her here."

"No," Shayara countered, her eyes sliding up to meet Bolten's face. "We can't leave her here, it's too dangerous," her eyes shifted to Moira. "We must continue, Councilor."

Bolten's eyes narrowed, but he remained silent.

"I'm alright," Moira assured them, standing rather feebly away from the cycad. "My son exuded extreme anger. I've never felt anything like this before. My son's protectors are in a fight for their lives just over the border. I'm ready, let's go."

Shayara and Bolten exchanged sideways glances.

"Keep moving," Bolten called to the patrol. They did so.

Silver Dragon Territory/Abyssina border

Fires blazed all around the campsite. Thick, black plumes of smoke blossomed into the air accompanied by an eerie silence. No cries or voices, or even a tyrocc bellow, just the rumble and hiss and crackle of the flames were heard.

Sandstorm single handedly destroyed the camp. After lighting the tents ablaze, he walked to the tyroccs, climbed on to one and ran the others over the rest of the site. The beasts smashed tents, knocked over food spits, crushed crossbows and chased off any frightened mercenaries that were unlucky enough to run into them. He let the other two tyroccs run off and fend for themselves and he picked up Maxum and Gak and brought them over the milky stream across the border in to Abyssina.

Maxum dismounted from the tyrocc. His and Sandstorm's attentions were fixed on the smoky northern banks of the stream. Handoe and Jessa were nowhere to be seen.

Maxum paced back-and-forth. Sandstorm rode back across the stream searching for Handoe and Jessa. Sandstorm swung his crossbow at a black dragon, in a dirt covered black jacket, as he emerged from some bushes with his arms up and Handoe behind him, holding his repeater to the dragon's back. Sandstorm's face lifted into a smile, which soon faded at the sight of the bloody hole in Handoe's right ear.

"Who do you have?" Sandstorm asked Handoe.

"He says his name is Walker, and he is a member of Councilor Zare's staff."

"Do we take him with us?"

"I don't see that we have much of a choice."

"Take me where?" Walker yelped, with an expression mixed of confusion and fear.

Handoe did not answer.

"We could use him as a bargaining chip," Jessa said, crawling out of some bushes behind Sandstorm.

Maxum pointed behind Handoe. "Black dragon rider — his sword is drawn!"

"MOVE!" Handoe shouted at Walker, who practically leapt over the embankment toward the stream.

Sandstorm drew his sword and turned the tyrocc at the oncoming dragon rider.

General Zmoge kicked his tyrocc into a gallop after he heard the puma sound the alarm. He jumped his tyrocc over the embankment and onto the sandy bank. His eyes twinkled and his face twisted into a crooked smile as he watched the snow leopard move his tyrocc at him.

"No!" shouted the female dragon. "Get them over the stream!"

Zmoge's smile faded a bit when the snow leopard turned his tyrocc to escort the black rabbit and the underling across the water. That just left the female black dragon on this side of the stream. His smile returned — wider and evil.

"Well, sister of Zare, we meet again," he hissed as he dismounted from his tyrocc and stalked toward her.

"I swore I'd kill you if our paths crossed again," Jessa snarled, her face scrunched with the look of the deepest hatred in her eyes. "You hurt and killed a lot of innocent dragons. You sent more to prison, where many would die!"

"Too bad," Zmoge brushed the charge away. "You'll be joining them soon enough."

Jessa let out a wild, blood-curdling scream and ran at him.

She sliced in a left, downward angle toward Zmoge's shoulder and neck. He side-stepped — she missed. He launched a side-kick that impacted against her ribs. She staggered back and nearly fell in to the silty water.

"Come on," Zmoge snarled. "You can do better than this."

Jessa charged again, slicing up at a right angle — Zmoge parried the blow. He pivoted his body

Warriors of Dragonsrod   463.

and slapped Jessa hard across the face with his tail, knocking her to the ground.

"Run, Jessa," Handoe shouted. "Leave him!"

"Yes, run," Zmoge said, the malevolent grin returned to his face. "I'll just hunt you down and kill you another time."

Jessa's eyes glinted as they stuck on Zmoge. Her hands gripped tighter around her sword. "No, this ends, today. You won't hurt anyone else!"

She swung her sword again and again — Zmoge parried and blocked each and every attack. He slammed a fist across her face and kicked her hard in the belly. She dropped to the loamy soil on her hands and knees.

Handoe drew his sword and charged over the stream. Zmoge's attention shifted to him. Their swords smashed together with a loud clank. Zmoge swung his sword at Handoe's head, the rabbit ducked and kicked him under his chest armor. Zmoge stepped away — Handoe kept after him. Zmoge swished his tail at Handoe's head and missed.

Zmoge kicked sand in Handoe's face, he swung his tail again, catching the rabbit across the mouth, sending him in a violent twirl to the ground. Handoe quickly recovered, his eyes flashed and he grinned as he rose to his feet. "You've got to do better than that."

Zmoge chuckled, then attacked. He thrust his sword at Handoe's neck — the blow was deflected by the other's counter swing. Handoe went on the offensive now by thrusting and slicing at the little dragon, who started to back-peddle. Handoe swung at Zmoge's neck and shoulder level — the dragon blocked the shot. The duel intensified, they crashed their swords together with loud, metallic clanks accompanied by the occasional swoosh of a missed attack. The two swung at the same time, their swords resonated with a loud *bang* and seemed to lock together. Handoe and Zmoge pressed and jockeyed in a circle, sneering and glaring toward the other. Handoe launched a series of snap-kicks at Zmoge's gut, just under the armor, impacting each time.

Jessa stood and watched as Zmoge retreated a few paces, out of Handoe's kicking range. The general's attention shifted back to her. He moved a little further away as Handoe and Jessa both lowered their blades at him. The general's dead looking eyes darted to Walker, standing on the other side of the stream. "Give me some assistance, underling!"

Sandstorm, still on his tyrocc, pointed his repeater at Walker's head. Walker's eyes were glued to the very pointy bolt tip aimed so ominously close to his head. He remained perfectly still.

"Coward!" Zmoge spat.

"You want another shot at him?" Handoe asked Jessa.

"You seem to be doing pretty good with him."

"I'm starting to think that he isn't really much competition anymore."

Zmoge launched into yet another furious attack slicing, swinging and chopping at Handoe, who slapped and deflected each blow away. Zmoge slashed down — Handoe swung up, their swords locked together again. Zmoge reached under his chest armor and pulled out a dagger and slashed at Handoe's unprotected belly and legs.

"AAAAARRRGGGGHHHH!" Zmoge screamed as he arched toward Handoe.

Jessa sliced her sword in to an unprotected gap in the general's armor, between his back and tail. He dropped his sword and dagger. She thrust her sword through his neck, virtually decapitating him. Zmoge sunk to the ground in a dead, bloody heap. Handoe and Jessa exchanged looks.

"Let's go," he panted, giving her a 'thank you' look. "We need to cross the border before his friends come to see what became of him."

She nodded.

They wasted little time crossing into Abyssina.

CHAPTER THIRTY-SEVEN

-AFTERMATH-

Grand Council Chamber, Kublisa

War was not what Goldeye wanted. But it is what he had. Sheema wired him, telling him the delegates were leaning toward dismissing the dragon insurrection as nothing more than an internal matter of the Dragonsrod. This was due to the defeats handed to Zare's rebels, including a brilliantly executed ambush on Triumvirate troops just to the North of the Orzolla Pass. Zhangi's gold dragons moved around and surrounded a force of mostly silver and red dragons and wiped them out. The lifeline into Green Dragon Territory was secure— for now.

So far — so good.

Goldeye received an empathic communication from his son earlier in the day, telling him they were safe. It was all he needed to hear. In his house, he laughed, he danced and twirled around before he collapsed to a couch and cried. A reprieve. A needed release of all the walled up emotions, the fear, the anger, the uncertainty of it all. He was paroled. His chains and shackles were broken, he felt free.

He had similar difficulties, as Moira, in trying to stop, or control, the invasive wave of emotions and feelings and thoughts the baby regularly fired at him. He, too, suffered headaches, sometimes bad ones, like the last one just a few hours ago. Goldeye's pain tolerance was high. He had mastered keeping a neutral face in public no matter what the magnitude of the headache may be.

He needn't bother today, he was elated! Romar was here. The Grand Council Chamber was packed to beyond capacity with dragon councilors and entourages, the press and representatives from other races to witness this very historic event. All eyes were set on a polished, dark wood table with two chairs behind it. Goldeye, in his body armor that was cleaned and shined in the light, and Romar, in his medal and decoration heavy jacket, walked side-by-side, with Gisko and a young looking griffon aide trailing behind them, to the table.

Goldeye and Romar faced each other and shook hands before turning to the audience.

"Councilors," Goldeye called, " entourages, representatives, distinguished guests, members of the press. Today is a very important day. Important because we have gathered here to end a painful chapter in our history. One filled with mutual anger, hatred and misunderstandings. We are here, now, to begin a new chapter. One filled with mutual hope, understanding and friendship.

"We have common enemies… We have common friends… We have common goals. This alliance will forge these goals toward a better future for the next generations — not only for dragons and griffons — but for *all* who live in these lands. Without further ado, Ambassador Romar and I will now sign our new partnership into affect."

Goldeye and Romar sat down.

Gisko and the griffon aide opened two

rectangular folders, which contained copies of the treaty, and set them in front of the two ambassadors. Each aide quickly opened a small bottle of ink and placed a quill next to the documents and stepped back. Artists and writers scribbled and etched on paper pads what they were witnessing. Goldeye and Romar signed their names to each document. The two stood and smiled widely and shook hands amid a thunderous applause from all in the chamber. The new alliance was official.

South banks of the Sandrega River, Green Dragon Territory

Zare was not a happy dragon. Several disturbing dispatches have fell under his angry glare. He had learned of the vordral defeat. Although disappointed, he wasn't surprised by the results. Repeated attacks against such a well defended position could not have ended any other way. He felt Loothar to be idiotic for underestimating Goldeye.

News of the disaster at Orzolla Pass angered him even more. Zhangi laid out a beautiful trap. What angered him most was the shameful conduct of many of his troops. The stinging, embarrassing reports he read about entire regiments, either deserting as soon as they crossed the river, or surrendered as soon as they encountered any enemy forces. The tip off that these reports were true, were in the casualty lists. A few killed and wounded, either by accident or by enemy fire. Hundreds — maybe a couple of thousand — missing and presumed defected.

Zare flew into a towering rage after reading this. He ordered *"No quarter"* for any black dragons taken in enemy armor or colors. He issued harsh warnings to his soldiers that any further attempts to defect would be dealt with, with the utmost severity. He blamed resistance infiltrators, cowards and poorly motivated officers for these debacles. No more! He needed Zmoge up here. He received the notice of Zmoge's death two days ago. Such was war.

Zare took personal command of this operation. Today he sat on the back of a tyrocc. His left leg and tail throbbed. He winced and groaned when his mount would shuck and jerk about, being spooked by the loud sounds of soldiers in double quick march. Two thousand, five-hundred infantry troops, mostly black and silver dragons, clad in the charcoal black chest armor and chain mail shirts. The soldiers held crossbows, carried swords at their sides, and their shields hung over their backs as they formed up in four lines of five hundred troops each. On the other side of these soldiers sat a battery of five trebuchets and then three hundred tyrocc mounted cavalry and the last line of infantry to cover the artillery, should it come under attack.

A young dragon, in black body armor, stopped his tyrocc next to Zare's.

"Garth," Zare said, grinning. "So nice to see you again."

"Graff's intelligence network did a good job keeping me hidden," Garth replied.

"I suppose I should keep Graff around a little longer," Zare muttered.

A short pause followed as their eyes fell on their target. A small, wood, earth and stone fortress stood defiantly before them about three hundred yards away on seemingly level ground. They could see the enemy, or only their heads and shoulders, skirting to-and-from, behind the ramparts.

"What are the defenses like here?" Zare asked, sliding his eyes to Garth.

"The defenses are standard of Dragonsrod," Garth reported. "Two-hundred and fifty troops with standard issue crossbows. The fort is equipped with two short range catapults."

"The walls?"

"Again, standard. The walls are built to withstand some punishment, but not for a prolonged siege."

Zare's face scrunched up, his eyes narrowed. His mind raced. He slid another cold, skeptical gaze to Garth. "How old is your information?"

"I had an agent pose as a member of a supply crew in there two days ago," Garth replied, his face splitting into a tight-lipped grin. "He says little to nothing has been done to improve the fort's defenses."

"Hmm."

"What are your orders, sir?"

"I'm giving you command of this operation, general," Zare said, keeping his eyes on Garth. "Don't fail me!"

The young green dragon could not contain a wide smile. He reached under his chest armor and pulled out a red cloth. He drew his sword and tied the cloth to the tip of the blade. He hoisted it high in the air. "ARTILLERY!"

Zare turned his head to two batteries of trebuchets — the crews stood ready at their posts — projectiles in the baskets — hands on the levers…

Garth slashed down with his sword. "FIRE!"

Trebuchets groaned and creaked in to action. Stone balls hissed through the air. The fort's north wall vibrated violently as rock-after-rock slammed into it.

"ARTILLERY, FIRE AT WILL!" Garth shouted.

Zare cracked a smile. *This kid has promise.*

A loud crack — then a fissure was seen stretching out over the north wall. A well aimed rock hit the middle of the fissure at its center. The wall crumbled into a dusty, chocolate colored cloud.

"INFANTRY — CHARGE!" Garth shouted.

Two thousand soldiers shouted and rushed forward. Shadowy figures from the fort staggered from the wreckage, dazed and confused. Many others ran for their lives.

Zare looked past the trebuchets to his cavalry. The commander's eyes fixed on him. Zare

swung out his sword and swished it forward —
the cavalry charged. The fort was doomed.

Cycad forest, northern Abyssina.

The walk was slow. The cycads were tall and bunched together, blocking out a lot of the sunlight and throwing long shadows. Walker grumbled and complained as he staggered over the dark and rocky, slightly up-sloping ground.

"Quit complaining!" Sandstorm shouted at him. "Whining about it is only going to make it worse!"

"I am a representative of the Dragon Triumvirate!" Walker yelled. "I demand to be—"

"You are in no position to be making demands!" Handoe snapped at him. "Now keep quiet!"

"The Dragon Triumvirate?" Maxum asked.

"That sounds like my brother," Jessa said, her tone of voice swollen with loathing.

"Don't you know anything?" Walker asked incredulously. "The Dragonsrod that you know, doesn't exist anymore!"

Handoe, Maxum, Sandstorm and Jessa exchanged glances.

"Zare has pulled Dragonsrod apart," Walker bragged. "He has taken the Reds and Silvers with him. He has allied himself to the vordral. He will send someone after me!"

"I doubt it," Jessa growled, slapping Walker's face with a hateful gaze.

"What do you mean?" Walker huffed, puffing out his chest and glaring at her.

"You don't have any medals on your jacket — you don't mean a thing to Zare!" Jessa countered sharply.

"Shut up, all of you!" Handoe yelled. "Listen."

Silence…

Handoe and Sandstorm cocked their repeaters.

"We have to keep moving," Maxum said as he walked on.

Suddenly, an abyssin female stepped out from behind a tall, cylindrical cycad. More abyssins, including a large, gray furred male with piercing yellow eyes, emerged from the shadows. All of them were armed with bows and had a full quiver of arrows strapped to their backs. The abyssins and the travelers stared at each other for a moment. The female abyssin held her bow above her head.

"We know who you are," she called. "We know who you have."

Walker pompously puffed out his chest again.

"Not you, idiot," Jessa snarled at him. "They are talking about the child."

Walker slid her a venomous glare, his shoulders sunk and his chest deflated.

"Who are you?" Handoe asked the female abyssin.

"My name is Shayara," she said, "and you are in Abyssina. You're safe."

Moira and River Rat emerged from behind a cycad tree. Her tired eyes were fixed on the travelers. "Which of you has my son?"

"I do," Maxum announced, lifting up his sword.

"I want him!" Moira demanded, running to Maxum.

"Ma'am, wait!" River Rat yelled, trying to keep up.

"Let her go," Shayara said, calmly to him.

Maxum's eyes sunk in to the neck hole. "Hey, Gak, Mommy's here!"

The baby's head shot up from the cloak. His cobalt colored eyes locked on to her.

Moira burst into tears as the baby let out a

welcoming cackle.

Moira and Maxum stopped in front of each other. He pulled the baby out from under his cloak. Moira, overcome by the excitement of the moment and her maternal instincts, practically ripped the baby out of his hands. Maxum stepped back and watched as she wrapped the child tightly in her arms, the baby returned the embrace. Maxum's eyes were fixed on Gak. He detected no treachery, nothing seemed wrong or out-of-place, yet, he had to fight back his own protective instincts. Maxum smiled, though it was a sad one. He was likely not to see Gak again. His mission was complete. Privately, he was grateful now to that strange griffon Seer for whatever it was he did to him. Before, he was tired and wanted rest and wanted to just disappear. Now, it was time to move on. He had a chance to start over — to relive ten years with a clean slate. He stood and watched Moira and Gak for another moment, and then turned to walk away. Handoe, Sandstorm and Jessa were about to follow.

"Where are you going?" Moira croaked, tear streams glistened down her cheeks.

The four stopped and faced her.

"Well," Maxum said, his eyes moved from Handoe, Sandstorm and Jessa to Moira. "Our mission's over."

"No," Moira said, as she repositioned the baby in her arms.

The four all perked up their ears and gazed at Moira.

"You all must help in training my son," Moira implored. "Dragonsrod is at war and he could be the one to end it. There is something very special about him."

"Yes," Maxum responded, "there is!"

"This is all very touching and all," Shayara announced, her eyes set on Maxum. "We are exposing ourselves by staying in this one spot. This forest holds many dangers, we must move on."

"Good!" Walker bellowed. "I am a representative of the Dragon Triumvirate. I demand an audience with my consulate. I was brought here against my will!"

"You are not a prisoner here," Shayara spoke, sliding her eyes to him before moving back to Maxum again.

Handoe fixed his gaze at River Rat with an icy, murderous stare.

Bolten scowled at Shayara and Maxum. He seemed to sense some kind of connection between them and did not appear comfortable with it.

"Let's move," Shayara demanded. "It will be dark before we reach Aizon and a lot could happen between here and there."

The abyssin patrol turned and moved through the forest with their guests straggling behind.

Moira made sure to walk next to Maxum. "Thank you seems… somehow… inappropriate. I am in your debt, to you and your friends."

The baby looked at him and flashed another gummy smile at him.

"I will gladly stay and help your son," he said, grinning.

"Come on," Handoe called, looking back at them. "I don't think that big gray one is too keen on waiting for you."

"I don't either," Maxum said.

For some strange reason, to him, it really didn't matter much at the moment when they reached the abyssin city.

THE END.

The adventure continues with book two in the Dragonsrod Chronicles Series.

SIEGE OF DRAGONSROD

One year has past and war has spread itself like a disease across Dragonsrod. Goldeye's army is reeling toward the Green Dragon capital city of Rampoor with vordral and Triumvirate legions gnashing at his heels.

Zare makes a power grab and crowns himself King, while Loothar charges his hordes into western Dragonsrod, Abyssina and the Cannis Republic for something of great value to him and his people.

The pressures of the job are getting to Moira who changes her son, Gak's name to Alexander. Her responsibilities as representative to Dragonsrod and role as Alexander's mother clash.

Alexander is plagued by nightmares and growing pains and becomes angry and frustrated at the attempts of his elders to prepare him to be something he doesn't want to be.

Jessa embarks on a mission of her own — find her brother, Zare, and assassinate him. She gets Handoe and Sandstorm to accompany her. Before they get too far, they have another mission to accomplish. The trio must stop a possible invasion of Abyssina by a band of elite Silver Dragon cavaliers and help lift a siege of a city called Drallics in Green Dragon Territory.

Queen Catra enlists Maxum and Shayara to build a strike team to rescue her son from behind enemy lines at a city called Qualis. Once they get there, the team realizes they are in over their heads as the rescue mission for one, becomes an operation to save thousands from death and slavery.

ABOUT THE AUTHOR

Fantasy is just one genre that I write in. I also write general fiction, historical, middle grade and Young Adult fiction and have dabbled in non-fiction.

Robert lives in Kalispell, in the northwestern part of Montana, with his wife and daughter.

Made in the USA
Charleston, SC
09 May 2016